THE DAME ON THE DOCK

LOUISE GORDAY

Henry —

Enjoy!

Louise Gorday

2021,

Book Cover Design by Damonza.com
Formatting by Polgarus Studio

Printed in the United States of America
ISBN: 978-0-9885765-3-7

To Mom
One of the brightest, most caring people I've ever met

Also by Louise Gorday

The Pickle Boat House

Bayside Blues

The Clockwise Carousel

The Church at Parkers Wharf

Spirit of the Law

Edgar and the Flyboys

Contents

Chapter One
Down in the Dumps

December 16, 1922

Tate "Shoe" Shoemaker stopped at the corner of Pennsylvania Avenue and Eleventh Street, smoothed his hair in the reflection of the pool hall window, and studied the figure behind him lingering in the afternoon shadows across the street. He recognized a tail when he saw one; he had spent the last six months perfecting the art. Smartly dressed and of dignified bearing, the gentleman was definitely not one of the local crooks who still trolled this area of Washington, D.C., looking for an easy mark. Shoe didn't fear for his own safety, of course. He lived under the generous protection of Keith Henry, the informal king of the thugs, whom he had helped out of a legal jam. Given the current state of Shoe's financial affairs, the stalker had to be a bill collector.

Shoe continued his walk at a brisk pace. He wasn't going to get excited. This section was controlled by Henry's underling Lucky Lewis, and his hoodlums regularly handed out muggings on the next block. And Shoe didn't feel guilty about the man's fate. The bill collector should consider himself lucky. There were scores of other nameless individuals who would gladly shake him down, cut him ear-to-ear, and dump his carcass in the Washington City Canal.

1

Shoe turned at the next block onto Tenth Street, right around the corner from the *Washington Evening Star* newspaper building on Eleventh and Pennsylvania, where he'd broken his acclaimed story about corruption in a small bayside community in Maryland. They'd offered him a decent-sized office and pretty good pay, but he'd turned them down. Competition at the newspaper was fierce, the staff packed with old saws vying for stories. Just like his stint at the *Evening Star* in Nevis, he would be at the end of the receiving line when it came to the handing out of assignments. That wouldn't do. He'd almost won a Pulitzer, for heaven's sake. So, he went freelance—freedom to choose projects, flexible hours, and a chance to be his own boss. If he kept up that mantra, the negatives sort of fell away.

Dead ahead sat the storefront that housed his investigative services—Shoemaker & Shoemaker—the name stenciled in fancy script across the storefront glass. There was no other partner, but two names always seemed more successful than one. He nodded to the group of usual suspects hanging out in the usual places. Poorly dressed and reeking of alcohol, cigarettes, or both, the men looked like common unemployed bums as they leaned against lampposts, lounged in doorways, and shot the breeze in small groups. In fact, they were all self-employed and, at the moment, deep in thought as to whom they could hustle or beat up to earn their dough. Shoe steered courteously through and left them be, as did the other residents and shop owners. During daylight hours they all played nicely. At night, even with Keith Henry's assurances, it was no holds barred.

Shoe unlocked his office. Inside was an efficient, barebones affair: a desk for his assistant, and two gray file cabinets butted up back-to back, creating a cubbyhole for his desk in the corner. It wasn't the Willard Hotel, but there was plenty of potential space if one wanted to hang things on the walls. The only extravagance in the room was a comfortable upholstered rocking chair Shoe used when he needed to cogitate. He threw his hat on his desk and went straight to the window to check on the tail. There was no sign of pursuit. Evidently Lucky Lewis had defended his territory well.

Shoe eased into the rocking chair and unfolded last night's copy of the *Washington Evening Star*. If no one came knocking with work, he'd be forced to drum up potential business from the newspaper. Begging for work was not his preferred method, but his girl, Fannie Byrne, and her thirteen-year-old brother, Jack, depended on his financial support and right now the cupboard was pretty bare.

His research lasted almost all of a peaceful minute. That was when a willowy brunette got up from the assistant's desk and sailed a folded sheet of paper over the top of his newspaper. "Let's see you abracadabra this one, Mr. Shoemaker."

It might be *Mister Shoemaker* this morning, but by afternoon she would be in a better mood and back to calling him *Shoe* like the rest of his acquaintances. "Good morning to you too, Fannie." He gave the official-looking document a cursory review and then handed it back. "Put it in Pending."

Fannie threw the invoice into a box with the other past-due notices. "Boss, filing systems work best if they have at least two files. *Pending* and *Paid* would be a good start."

"Not necessary. I have a good feeling about today. Several good leads right out of the gate." He pointed to a published list of overnight assaults and murders along the Thirteenth and Fourteenth Street corridor—the part of the District of Columbia historically known as Murder Bay. "We've had a nice uptick in the temperature recently and a corresponding increase in petty crime and delinquency in the city.

And over here," he said, sliding his finger across the page to a two-column article above the fold, "it seems your hometown, Nevis, has something to natter about—a rather gruesome murder on the waterfront which is gaining notoriety. No," he said, shaking his head solemnly, "violence is on the uptick. Unfortunate for others, but definitely good for us. I can feel it in my bones. Someone's going to come striding through that door with business that'll fill our coffers."

Fannie pulled a cardigan off the back of her chair and slipped it on. "You think it's warm? Get the heat turned back on in here, that's warm." As she fastened the bottom button, a knock came at the door.

Shoe threw her a smug look. "I'd best get that. They say opportunity only knocks once." He opened the door to a boy wearing a dark suit and a stiff cap with a Western Union Telegram band encircling the brim. He had a telegram in one hand as he balanced his bicycle with the other.

"Telegram for Tatum Bartholomew Shoemaker," the messenger said in a high-pitched voice that had not yet experienced the embarrassing cracking of adolescence. He handed Shoe the message and hung about for a moment. When it became apparent there would be no tip forthcoming, he mumbled something and left with his two-wheeler.

Shoe threw more gloating Fannie's way. The only other time he'd received a telegram was when they nominated him for the Pulitzer Prize. This little piece of paper was sending happy vibrations all through him. He borrowed Fannie's letter opener and sliced it open with a flourish.

"Please tell me you've inherited from a long-lost aunt," she said.

Shoe read the letter silently several times before giving its message voice. "'Representing a client who has urgent need of your services. Stop.

Substantial retainer. Stop. Arriving Union Station 9:30 train. Stop. Please arrange to meet. Stop. Respectfully Douglas Emerson. Stop.'"

"What'd I tell you?" Shoe said, waving the communication in front of her as he sat down on the edge of her desk. "A most interesting case has just fallen into our lap. Where's your brother?"

"School. And I do hope you're not going to pull Jack out for some loco scheme of yours. The agreement with Mother was that he could stay in Washington as long as you were a good influence and could keep him in school. Otherwise, she wanted him back in Nevis."

The trio hadn't been back in Maryland since the night they hopped a midnight mail express out of Nevis and fled to Washington with a news scoop that brought Shoe recognition but little jingle in his pocket. He didn't anticipate any problems with *Mother*.

"*Loco?*" Shoe raised an eyebrow. "Sweetheart, by the sound of this missive, I think you can stamp all those invoices *paid*. It costs a bit of change to send a telegram. The sender says it's an urgent matter, the retainer will be substantial, and that our investigative office"—he consulted the telegram one more time— "has outstanding credentials speaking directly to the matter at hand. Someone seems to think I'm the fox's socks."

She stared a moment and then went back to her filing. "Yeah, you're a duck's quack."

Shoe looked at Fannie, the sting of her testiness lingering. He loved this woman and had proposed often. She politely declined every single time. No longer the naïve young woman who had followed him blindly into the night, Fannie had become an independent, modern woman who wanted a career and a good highball more than she wanted to keep house and have a boatload of kids. He didn't get it.

He slid the letter back into its envelope and handed it to her. "I need you to meet this Emerson at Union Station this morning. Nine fifteen."

Fannie consulted the watch dangling from a chain around her neck. "You want me down at Union Station by half an hour ago?" She snatched her purse out of a desk drawer and pulled a navy felt cloche down over her bob. "Okay, boss, but it won't come cheap. There's a nice pair of shoes in the window down at Hahn's . . ."

"Just get him," Shoe called after her. He watched her pick her way through the local crowd, past the loungers on the front stoop and the other vagrants. She turned a few heads, but for the most part, they ignored her. He didn't fret about Fannie's safety. As long as she didn't take any side trips, Miss Byrne walked freely under the same protect he did. No, it was more the view that concerned him at present. This morning's new fish tugging on the line, what would he think of it? The vacant lot across the street was littered with bricks, empty wooden barrels, a broken cabinet, and the tumbled-down remains of an outhouse. He'd lost a few big ones recently because of office locale, but he'd always managed to find something to keep them afloat. Even though he would never share his concern with Fannie, the ever-growing pile of bills on her desk weighed heavily on him. He wasn't sure how much more personal rejection he could stomach. Without any heat in the office, they'd be good until January, but if the phone service was cut off . . .

"Jiminy." Lucky Lewis was falling down on the job. Shoe watched the rapid approach of the stranger he had managed to dodge earlier. As the man wended his way around the local workers, Shoe gave him the duck test—he looked like a heartless son of a gun, and he moved like someone who wouldn't take no for an answer . . . Yep, a definite collection agent. Shoe dropped below the window sill and cast about for a place to hide—a challenging prospect in the sparsely furnished room. He scrambled under Fannie's desk and made a mental note to install a bolt-hole and back door in his next office.

For the second time this morning, there was a polite knock at the door. Shoe's stomach muscles tightened as knuckles assailed the door.

"Mr. Tatum Shoemaker? Tatum Shoemaker!"

The voice was insistent but rattled, which wasn't surprising given the gauntlet the gentleman had probably just run. Shoe was impressed but not moved enough to offer sanctuary. Everybody in D.C. knew you took your chances when you ventured out alone around here.

The knocking changed into loud hammering. "Mr. Shoemaker, I know you're in there. I sent word earlier today that I'd be arriving by train. Please let me inside. I'm a little over my head out here, I'm afraid."

Shoe poked his head out of the kneehole. "Mr. Emerson?"

"Yes, Douglas Emerson. The dialogue is good, sir, but could I speak inside where it's, er, safer? I assure you, I come unarmed."

Shoe crawled out on all fours and let Emerson in. The poor man's suit coat was a bit rumpled and his bowler misshapen, but he appeared physically unharmed. "Oh, dear," Shoe whispered. He took Emerson's hat and hung it on the hook near the door.

"Yes, then," Mr. Emerson said, adjusting his suit coat. "As we've already established, I'm Douglas Emerson." He thrust out a soft hand that had never seen a day of manual labor. "Apparently my letter failed to arrive ahead of me. I have a business proposition for you, Mr. Shoemaker, that won't wait."

"I'm so sorry. Unfortunately, your telegram just arrived. I dispatched my secretary right away, but obviously you missed each other."

"She's gone out there *alone*?" Emerson asked, the inflection in his voice rising as he glanced toward the window.

"Oh, it's all right, we have an understanding with—" He dismissed the rest of his discourse with a hand gesture. "It's really not important. This a downtown case?"

"Oh, no," Emerson said, shaking his head. "Nevis. Nevis, Maryland."

"Nevis? Now, that's a real shame. You see, I'm not too popular there." *Hated* might be more accurate. He had antagonized a huge chunk of the population, mainly men, by publishing a blistering exposé about the local government being in cahoots with booze runners out of the Delaware Valley. The town's liquor had dried up pretty quickly after that. He offered Emerson his hat back. "I'm sorry you've wasted your time, coming all this way. I'll be more than happy to escort you back to Union Station."

Emerson ignored the hat and stepped further into the office. "At the present, not for love nor money." He gave the office a once-over. "The size of the retainer I'm prepared to offer is enough to cure a whole lot of woes, Mr. Shoemaker. I believe it would be in both our interests to entertain me. I promise not to keep you from, erm, other things."

Shoe gave a quick thought to all his woes sitting in Fannie's box. "Perhaps I was a bit hasty. And after all it took to find your way here, it would be rude of me not to hear you out. You can call me *Shoe*, by the way." He ushered his guest toward his upholstered chair and gave him a glass of water. "Sorry about the chairs. Cases mostly keep me out of the office." He rolled Fannie's desk chair over, studying his visitor as he did.

Emerson's suit was richly cut, his bearing aristocratic. Shoe posited his employer as monied and their working relationship long-term and trusted. He didn't recognize him, even though it had been only a few months since he'd fled Nevis in the wee hours of the morning with a man of questionable intent hunting him down. "I suspect the temperance ladies are the only people in Nevis who wouldn't want to see me drawn and quartered," he said. "So, who sent you all the way from Nevis to retain my services? And what's this all about?"

"At the moment, I'm not at liberty to speak on the first." Emerson gestured toward the rumpled newspaper Shoe had tossed onto Fannie's desk. "You've read this morning's?"

"The atrocious killing in Nevis?" Shoe pulled the paper over and began scanning the account. "Quite sensational, but they aren't giving much out, are they? A woman butchered on the town dock, and a second victim—young, male—found likewise murdered in an alley nearby. I'm guessing you know the vic. Got a name?"

"I'm not at liber—"

"Mysterious markings on the boardwalk body. Are they hinting at occult?" he asked, putting down the paper. "Spiritualism does seem to be all the rage these days."

"A little misinformation thrown into the mix to keep the true murderer on his toes. Police Chief McCall—you must remember him? Hardnosed, all about business? I don't think he gives anything away for free, and I doubt he takes much stock in spiritualism."

Shoe nodded. "Our paths crossed," he said, remembering the anonymous beatdown the copper had given him in a Nevis alleyway when Shoe had begun asking too many questions about illicit liquor. He was as crooked as a Chesapeake Bay Retriever's hind quarter. "I don't think he'd appreciate my involvement in his case."

"Unfortunately, they do not appear to want anyone's involvement. Little has been forthcoming, even in exchange for a little extra cash. We suspect—" Emerson interrupted his suspicions with a drink of water and a gentle patting of his lips with his pocket square. "My client, whom for convenience's sake I will refer to as Mr. X, doesn't need their help. The family wants quick resolution no matter who may be implicated. That's why I'm here."

For the first time, Shoe noticed Emerson's dirty and scuffed-up cap-toe boots. When they were pristine, he bet they'd been real lookers. He'd probably had a nice watch, too— before the local crowd gave him a literal run for his money. Emerson must have been reading his mind. He tucked his feet further back under the chair.

"You're not giving me much to work with here, Mr. Emerson, sir. Given the threat to my safety—which your client, I am certain, is in no position to guarantee; and which the Nevis police force would be disinclined to insure—your fee would have to be a substantial one to entice me to return."

"Would the sum of three thousand dollars entice you?"

"Come again?" Shoe asked, trying to relax his death grip on the arms of his chair. A year's income being thrown at him from one client?

Emerson repeated the same sum. "Probably more than you're used to seeing," he said as he removed his arm from the upholstered chair and brushed off the underside of his sleeve. "You come highly recommended. But if you can't commit this morning, I must move on to the next name on my list."

"I'm in," Shoe said without hesitation, "but I must have half up front . . .so I can tie up loose ends."

"One third down in good faith, another third when you begin work, and the balance when you've provided the specifics of the crime, including the identity of the perpetrator."

Shoe thrust out a hand as his heart danced a lively foxtrot. "Done. But do we have anything else to go on besides the few morsels the *Star* published?"

"There are these, which will not be published." Emerson drew a tan portfolio from an inside coat pocket, unwound the string from the button tab, and withdrew several photos.

"Dear God," Shoe whispered, and promptly heaved his lunch into the nearby wastebasket. "What *was* that?" He heard the creak of Emerson's chair. Hopefully he would provide distance and allow a moment for Shoe to restore his dignity.

"I can't assure you that this is the worst of it, Mr. Shoemaker," Emerson said, his voice now coming from across the room. "This case is going to test your mettle. Still firm in your answer?"

"Uh huh," Shoe said, his reply muffled by the trashcan. He wiped his face with a handkerchief, carried the can out into the hallway, and left it. Someone would swipe it by end of day. Problem solved. He rejoined Emerson, who now stood at the window. The local boys were dispersing under the watchful eye of a beat cop who made a showing about once a week. They'd be back by the time he hit the next block.

"It's settled then," Emerson said. "Now I'm off to see Ru—to other business while this nice policeman can offer me free passage out of here." He put his misshapen hat back on, and as he passed Fannie's desk, he paused a moment and placed a plain white envelope there. "Time is of the essence, Mr. Shoemaker. Ask for me at the Bayside Hotel tomorrow, eleven o'clock, and we'll discuss further."

"Yes, sir. You can expect me."

"Excellent. And these photographs," he said, stooping to pick up the envelope and pictures from the floor where Shoe had left them. "It goes against my better judgment to leave them. If they should somehow find their way into the press . . ." He locked eyes with the detective. "That would be most unfortunate for all parties involved."

Shoe felt queasy again. He closed his eyes. "No, I don't think I will be

needing them. And rest assured that anything between us is confidential."
He hesitated a moment. "Sir. Before you go . . . if I may ask one question?"

Emerson raised an eyebrow. "Certainly. Within reason."

"What happened to the face?"

"We have no idea. It takes a lot of effort and uncontrollable rage to do that to a body, Mr. Shoemaker. We're relying on you to see that something so hideous never happens again."

Chapter Two
Incentives

Shoe sat down in his thinking chair, but not to contemplate the gruesome pictures he had just seen. He had seen enough. Cows in slaughterhouses were treated with more respect than the poor unfortunate souls in those pictures; the killer was depraved. He distracted himself by counting the money in Emerson's envelope. A thousand smackers. That could take him places. But back to Nevis?

Maybe he'd been a little quick to sell his services. Returning there was one of the last things he wanted to do; it was a step down, a step back. He'd worked hard, risked much to snag his Pulitzer nomination. And now he was risking his stature in the nation's capital to investigate a murder—sensational though it might be—in the same two-bit town he'd bolted from?

He took a good, hard look around him. Who was he kidding? He was in desperate financial straits, and other than Emerson, he hadn't had a customer of note in weeks. His notoriety was fleeting . . . Ha! It had already fleeted out the door to frolic with the no-names on the sidewalk outside his window.

He closed his eyes and let out a long, troubled sigh. *Choose, Shoe.* Stay here and slowly sink into a morass he couldn't get out of, or buck up and show the exceptional newshound he was no matter what life tossed in his path. Conquer Nevis once again, and then hightail it back with enough smack to get him out of this dump and Uptown, where his clients didn't have to run a gauntlet.

The fretting was academic. To survive, he had to swallow some pride and go. Hopefully, everything would turn out jake.

And then there was Emerson. He certainly didn't seem the type to back losers, but Shoe couldn't shake the feeling that something wasn't right in all of this. Why would Emerson advance him so great a sum without so much as a contract? It was the gesture of a fool, but Emerson struck him as nothing of the sort. And there were any number of first-rate investigators between Nevis and here. Why venture into one of the most dangerous areas of D.C. to procure Shoe's services? Sure, he knew Nevis well, but any PI worth his salt could quickly bring himself up to speed on the small bayside town. Why him? He tapped the envelope against his open palm. He would proceed cautiously, options-open on this one, ready to back out if things didn't add up. And he would need to spend his newfound wealth sparingly in case he had to repay money for nonperformance of the agreement, in spite of it being a verbal one.

He pocketed the envelope and put his feet up on an old packing crate to await Fannie's return. She would be livid about the fruitless errand he had sent her on, threaten to quit *again*, and then stick it to him at the first opportunity. After all, theirs was a loving relationship. He just needed to watch the eyes. Unlike those of his first heart's desire—the always-perfect Lillian Gish—Fannie's brown peepers could rage like a thunderhead or pull you into a world so peaceful and intoxicating that you willingly gave in to their siren song.

To his relief, Fannie returned singing the latest ditty by Fanny Brice. She swung a Hahn's shoe-store bag up onto her desk.

"Fannie, I'm sorry. Mr. Emerson show—"

"Ut-tuh-tuh," she said, wagging a finger. She walked over and handed him a Hahn's receipt billed to the office account. "Wait until you see these." She kicked off her simple brown oxfords and slid on a pair of fancy red pumps with silver filigree buckles. "You know, you're right. It's going to be a good day." She strutted to-and-fro, admiring.

"Ouch," Shoe said, looking at the $18.50 price tag. Actually, with Emerson's retainer, he could spare the dough. But if Fannie thought she had stuck it to him good, she wouldn't hunt for another way to put him in his place. "Emerson showed up right after you left. A little the worse for running the hoodlum gauntlet outside, but determined to see his mission out." He waved the envelope. "He left a most generous retainer."

"Work?" She snatched it from him. "We should celebrate," she said, executing a graceful twirl before pulling him from the chair.

"The job is in Nevis," he said, eye-watching again.

The waltzing ceased. "No." She dropped his hands and stepped away. "That wouldn't be smart at all."

"Towns change, people change. It's a big town. Mr. Emerson, for example. If he lived in Nevis when we were there, I never met the man. Anybody seeking revenge is eating three squares in the federal pokey. I'm probably old news by now. It's been months."

"Nevis? A big town?" She laughed. "You took on the political machine, honey. Ever hear of institutional memory? Pease don't tell me you're taking on political corruption again."

"Nope." He handed her the newspaper story. "Next to the bootlegging scheme coming out of the mayor's office, it's the most sensational crime to hit Nevis in recent memory." He shook his head. "Nah, it'll be fine. Besides, I think there will be other targets if people's feathers get ruffled. When he left here, Emerson was headed over to the

Star—to see someone else. Rudy Becker, I think. Rudy and I go way back in Philly. Ran neck-and-neck with stories. There's no way I'm going to let him crack this case and publish the riveting story." Competition wasn't always a bad thing, but with the amount of money at stake . . . It suddenly struck him that should Rudy get an early jump on him, Emerson might even kick Shoe to the curb.

Fannie smacked the envelope into his midsection and turned away. "My mother always says it's a mistake to compare your life to someone else's. You should just try to be the best—"

"If your mother was here, she'd say, 'Fannie, put away your dancing shoes, pull out that wonderful, Drexel-educated brain of yours, and support your man.' And I, in turn, would promise to take you on a nice long vacation afterwards. You can even pick the place."

She took off the shoes and swaddled them in their tissue paper as she considered what he'd said. "Yeah, just like you promised to take me down to the Ellipse on Christmas Eve. President Coolidge is bringing a Christmas tree all the way from Vermont and it's going to be decorated." When she looked over at him, her eyes were flashing, a bit like a yellow caution signal at a railroad crossing.

Shoe walked over and rubbed her back. "We can still do that."

"Oh, Shoe," she said, her shoulders beginning to droop. "Don't you understand? It's just like keeping soldiers down on the farm. We've seen *Paree*. I don't want to go back home. Washington has everything I'd ever want."

"Please don't throw Sophie Tucker songs at me. Consider this a nice little vacation with a bigger vacation afterwards."

As he had seen so often before, Fannie let him dangle a moment. Shoe was never sure whether this was a tactical move on her part, or whether she was actually taking time to consider the merits of his ideas.

At last, she threw her arms around his neck and pecked his cheek. "Yes, then. But only if you're positive someone won't hurt you. And I want to stay at the Bayside Hotel, not with Mom."

That had been too easy. For the second time today, he felt as if he'd been outfoxed. But Fannie was happy with him for the moment, and he had money, and exciting work to sink his teeth into, so he'd go with it.

Before he could nuzzle her neck, the door opened and in strode a fast-moving young boy with a head of unruly curly hair. He bolted the door behind him and went directly to the glass candy dish on Fannie's desk, where he fished out two foil-wrapped Hershey's Kisses. "If you're going to hold my sister like that, you should at least marry her."

Shoe reluctantly let her slip out of his grasp. It wasn't that he hadn't tried, but apparently Fannie thought bare pockets were never a good start to a marriage.

Fannie took one piece of chocolate out of her brother's hand and put it back in the dish. "Clients," she said. "Why aren't you in school?"

"Half day," he answered, popping the other Kiss in his mouth. "Mr. Graham wasn't feeling well."

"Not too attached to Mr. Graham, are you?" Shoe asked.

Jack dropped into Shoe's chair and swung his legs over the rolled arms. "I'm never going to use this stuff. I may as well be back in Nevis."

Shoe tossed the newspaper to him. "Curious you should say that. Big murder case and I've been offered a chance to investigate it. And it's good money too. Want to go back?"

Jack caught the folded paper but didn't bother looking at it. "I heard about it." His eyes shifted to the window.

Jack wasn't big on reading, but neither was he one to contemplate life from an easy chair. "Something happen at school?" Shoe asked.

Jack shook his head and mumbled something. "Got to go." He tossed the newspaper on the crate and headed out.

Shoe frowned. "Nevis. I didn't get a yes or a no. Would you like to tag along?"

"No, he can't," Fannie said. "He'll never get an education if he starts bopping in and out of school every time you think he might be entertained by something."

Jack didn't turn, but he said, "Is that all I was to you in Nevis, just a tagalong?"

"Of course not," Shoe said. "I never could have cracked the bootlegging operation without you. You have the instincts to be a first-class investigative reporter."

"If he stays in school and applies himself," Fannie interjected.

"Right," Shoe said. "What's really eating you, Jack?"

"Doesn't it bother you that there were two murder victims, but the best the paper can do is add a single line about the second one? Horse pukey—"

"Language!" Fannie admonished.

Jack hung his head. "They can't be bothered to name a local boy who lost his life down there? Was he that insignificant?" He choked up. "Who's out paying someone to find his killer? I ran those streets at night. What if that had been me? Would anyone have cared about *me*?" He flicked his balled up nigglywiggly from the Kiss toward the window.

"Well, to be precise," Shoe said, "they didn't identify either victim, but I get your point. Do you know something we don't?" he asked. "An educated guess who this kid might be?"

Jack shrugged. "I knew everybody. Don't know nobody here."

Shoe nodded. "Washington is a big, rough town. It's not for everybody. If we find the perpetrator, then it's a pretty good bet that we nab the one who killed the boy too. Does that help?"

Jack turned and fixed serious eyes on Shoe. "Small town or big city, kids matter. *Everybody* matters. I'll come with you. If it's the last thing I do, I want to know who killed him."

Shoe looked at Fannie and raised his eyebrows.

She slowly nodded. "All right. But if Mom says you have to stay in Nevis for good, I'm not going to argue with her. Go pack while Shoe and I work out the details."

"You start packing too, Fannie. Anything we don't want stolen comes with us."

"Got it, boss. Do you think they'd take these?" She waved the stack of overdue bills at him, but her Irish eyes were smiling this time.

He laughed. It was good to see her happy with him again. "Let's not press Lady Luck, okay? Pay half of what we owe to half of them today. And tomorrow, do likewise with the other half. That's when I meet up with Emerson again. I don't think we need to raise our creditors' expectations too much."

He retrieved his fedora from his desk and headed out, catching the door with his foot just as it was about to close behind him. He looked around the dumpy office with a nostalgic feeling that surprised him. Then it bolted for greener fields and he followed.

Chapter Three
Heaven Sent

Rudy Becker stepped off the train platform. The tiny booth that masqueraded as a train depot was already mobbed with discontented passengers pleading for assistance. A useless endeavor, if he had interpreted the train's high-pitched whining and unplanned stop correctly.

The sunset was coloring up all right—shades of scarlet and cameo pink streaking across the December sky. The landscape, on the other hand, was dismal—nothing but fields of stubby brown tobacco plant remains, no matter which direction of the compass he turned. Baltimore had its cultural roots, Annapolis an historic charm, but Clinton, Maryland? Ha! Bumpkinville. The value of the place was that it led to someplace better. Just ask John Wilkes Booth, who galloped through on his way from Ford's Theatre to possible sanctuary in the deeper South, or the conductor on the Chesapeake Railway Express who traversed the landscape daily to get to the nation's capital. Clinton was a means to the ends.

Rudy emitted a sound beyond a weary sigh and just short of a growl. If luck should continue to fail him, he would need to lay over until he could reach Nevis, Maryland. He gave the farmland one more look and pitied the children who grew up in this cultural wasteland. As he searched the line for a railroad worker, his eyes fell upon a grease-covered, bedraggled fellow rushing along toward him—the engineer's assistant, no doubt. "Excuse me, sir," Rudy said to him. "Will we be long?" He held out a dollar bill.

The worker swiped it and kept walking. "Dead, sir."

"And a replacement?"

The worker laughed.

Well, then, when's the next scheduled run?"

"Eight-thirty tomorrow morning. Bright and early."

Rudy vented his frustration in a longer, deeper sigh that sounded much like the death throes of the engine behind him. *Bright and early* would be *having a back-up train ten minutes ago*. He turned and re-surveyed his surroundings. Surely there must be—

And there it was. He took off at a brisk pace for the sad story of a buggy—JEFFERSON DELIVERY stenciled in faded white letters on the side—sitting quietly by the storage door of the depot. "Jefferson," he said, rapping the sideboard, "How much to get me to a place for the night?"

The sleeping driver pulled his flat cap from his face and pushed himself up into attention. "F-f-fifty cents, sir," the fresh-faced young lad said.

"Acceptable," Rudy said. Actually, it was atrocious, but given the circumstances . . . He dropped his valise into the wagon bed and climbed up next to Jefferson. "Do I have a choice in this godforsaken place, or is 'clean' all I can hope for?"

"Oh, you won't be disappointed," Jefferson replied, holding out an empty palm.

Rudy gave him half up-front, and Jefferson unhitched the horses and sallied forth.

As they bumped down the road, Rudy correctly assumed Jefferson would hit every hole between here and their destination. He clapped one hand down on his fedora to keep it from sailing off to adorn some godforsaken dead stalk. The fields of brown seemed to stretch on without abatement.

"Just so I don't fall off the map here," Rudy said, seriously reconsidering the wisdom of striking out on his own. "Where are we off to?"

Jefferson added a pinch of snuff to the already sizeable wad in his cheek and offered up the Sir Walter Raleigh can. Rudy waved it off. "Downtown Clinton," he said between chews. He appraised Rudy out of the corner of his eye. "There's two board houses, but I think the Surratt Inn will be a better match. That's as comfortable as it gets and that's plenty good. How often do you get to spend a night in a haunted house?"

Dear God. Rudy was beginning to yearn for the stiff coldness of his deserted train seat. "Haunted, huh? And who might the unfortunate soul be?"

Jefferson looked at him as if he'd just fallen off a tobacco truck. "Why, you've never heard about the restless soul of John Wilkes Booth, the assassinator of Abraham Lincoln? Forever doomed to walk the earth in search of forgiveness? They say he and Mary Surratt were in cahoots, but we know that's hogwash. The military screwed up and hanged her anyway. Not as smart as old Booth, no she wasn't. Where's a restless soul to go? It seems Dr. Mudd's house was full, so ole Booth moseyed over to Mary's house and has been there ever since. He haunts her rowhouse in Washington, too, but he ain't there near as much as the Surratt Inn. Might say *that's* his primary residence." Jefferson chuckled and let fly a stream of brown tobacco juice out to his left.

Rudy closed his eyes and bemoaned his decision to jaunt off to

Washington in the first place. He should have stayed in Nevis, where he was needed. He could have discussed the job later. Maybe.

The Surratt Inn was a tidy white clapboard farmhouse with a chimney at each end and a broad porch that ran across the front. There were three rentable rooms upstairs and a small public dining room on the first floor. A brick smokehouse sat just off the outdoor privy in the backyard. The accommodations would be satisfactory as long as they proved clean.

Signage just inside the door listed rates for rooms: forty cents a night or two-fifty for an entire week—meals included. To the left of the front desk he could see the long communal table in the dining room. The air was filled with the smell of cooked meat and garbled conversation.

"Would you have any rooms available?" Rudy asked the young brown-haired woman sitting behind the desk.

She stuck her spoon into the mound of mashed potatoes on the dinner plate before her and gave him a heavenly smile. "Yes, sir. Just one night?"

Sweet and virginal, she looked to be in her early teens. He got lost in her lovely blue eyes for a moment before fighting his way back to earth. He nodded and handed her the exact amount. In return, she slid the register toward him.

He gave the open book a brief review, chuckled to himself, and then scribbled *Tatum Shoemaker* across the first empty line. Private joke and he enjoyed it everywhere he went. What did it mean? He had no idea. Maybe he secretly desired to be Shoemaker. That Freud guy would find some deep-seated reason for it. Of all the reporters he had ever met, Shoe was the best. He crossed the second *T* in *Tatum* and looked up at the young girl, who was smiling at him. Ahh, to be a younger man. He took the proffered heavy brass door key to the bedroom that overlooked the front of the house and headed upstairs.

After he'd cleaned up and confirmed that the lock on his door was in good working order, he sat at the tiny secretary in the corner and jotted a quick message explaining his misfortune and whereabouts. Then he was off to find the post office. If he had any luck at all today, the missive would post to Nevis before he arrived. He didn't want to leave the love of his life dangling. His delay could not have been more ill-timed.

The center of town stood at the intersection of two roads. He supposed they had names—Main Street and Whatever—but there were no street signs. On the four corners of this little slice of paradise stood four buildings. On the Surratt's side of the street stood a small but stately brick building. There was no marquee on the latter, but considering the vertical iron bars across the windows, he assumed it to be the bank. A single chestnut nag stood tethered outside. Across the road from the inn stood an unremarkable one-room, white clapboard building housing both a post office and a school. A discreet plaque affixed just to the right of the black twin front doors proclaimed it so. On the diagonal, which he would guess to be north by the sun's direction, sat B.K. Miller's Market—easily the largest structure in town. If he somehow got into trouble, that would be the name he dropped. On the diagonal to the bank stood a stable, a blacksmith's hammer tapping and ringing out a practiced rhythm.

There was little else in the thriving metropolis. Beyond Miller's stood a white building with a barber pole prominently displayed. And past that on the same side of the street, the Clinton Inn, which looked more like a booze joint than a respite for the weary traveler, and lastly, a fair-sized church. He walked far enough to see that its denomination was Catholic and that confessions were heard on Monday through Friday from 9 a.m. until 4:30. It seemed Clinton did quite a bit of sinning.

He crossed over Main Street—or Whatever, if one preferred—to Gwynn's Ford car lot. Out front, two brand-new black Model Ts glistened in the sun, and out the back several decent-looking horses munched weeds from their short tethers.

And that was it. He could stock up on provisions, get his hair cut, bend elbows with the local boys, or confess his heart out. Clinton was tiny and as unexciting as he'd imagined—the kind of place its youngsters no doubt dreamed of escaping one day.

In a small backwater like this, keeping to oneself was always the wisest choice. He returned to the inn. Supper was well underway in the dining room, but there were only dregs to be had in the various communal serving dishes. He made an about-face, nodded good-night to the lovely angel at the counter, and headed for bed.

"Wait, Mr.—" The angel paused to consider the register. "Mr.—"

"'Rudy' is fine."

"I think I might be able to find something for you, Rudy," she said with a wink. "Just go on about your business and I'll bring it up shortly."

He was inclined to tell her not to bother, but the aroma of good food lingered and his stomach was grumbling. He agreed and retired upstairs.

After an hour or so, without his promised meal, Rudy began to doubt her word. It was the perfect ending to a perfectly miserable day. He hung his trousers and suitcoat neatly over the brass clothes valet and climbed into the spindle bed in his skivvies. The bed was firm, but comfortable. With the heavy, warm patchwork quilt pulled up tightly under his chin, he slipped quickly into sleep.

He jerked awake just as quickly at the creak of the heavy bedroom door. A sliver of light from the hallway sliced the dark space and grew wider as the door opened. He remained silent and still, bemoaning the fact that his pocketknife and pistol were snugged away in his trousers.

"Mr. Rudy?"

The form was feminine, the voice that of the girl at the inn's desk.

"Yes, sorry." He sat up and fumbled for the light on the bedside table.

"Don't," she said. "I've enough light. I'll switch on the light by the door as I go." She deposited a tray on the writing desk under the window. She then went back to the door and closed it, once again returning the room to total darkness.

And then he heard the lock on the door click, which was peculiar, because he was fairly certain it could only be locked from the inside. Before he could swing his legs out of bed, Rudy felt the bed sway and the touch of a soft hand against his cheek. It was one of those rare sweet moments that did not need to be explained or rejected. He didn't need to say a word, just pull her into his bed and accept all the hospitality she could offer.

He politely escorted her out the door and locked it. He had but one love these days, and he would never betray her.

He fell into a deep sleep, and the next time he awoke, morning light was streaming through the window. He discovered the angelic desk clerk asleep on the floor next to his bed, a room key still clasped in her hand. She—they'd never gotten around to formal introductions—was as beautiful as the first time he set eyes on her. He took a moment to admire her face. His only complaint would be her chubby physique, but to dwell on that would be unkind.

He got up and dressed quickly, struggling with a difficult question of protocol. Did she expect him to leave some sort of payment on the nightstand? Or should he chalk this up to his charm and dashing good looks?

He didn't get a chance to decide.

"Arlene?" a man's voice called out, followed by insistent knocking on doors, including his. When the doorknob began to rattle, Rudy grabbed a roll off the tray of untouched food and scampered out the window. He managed a controlled slide down the porch roof and perched there a moment to see if the coast was clear. Why, this was a lucky day, he decided, spying Jefferson looking up at him from his wagon directly below.

"Any chance you're going to the depot?" he asked, checking to see if anyone had climbed out of the window behind him.

Jefferson threw aside the apple he had been eating and nodded. "Two bucks will get you back there."

"A bargain at any price," Rudy said. He jumped off the roof and landed onto several hay bales in the wagon bed. "Bonus for you if you can get me there in time to catch the 8:30."

"No problem," Jefferson said. He lashed the horses and set off lickety-split.

Thank God for this man, Rudy thought as they jounced back to the depot. It seemed good fortune had decided to keep him company once more. What were the chances of him being right there? "If you can keep all of this among friends, it would be most generous of you."

"Yes, sir, not my business."

"Much obliged. It was all a small misunderstanding, you see. I paid in full." He looked at Jefferson, who was smiling pleasantly, and suddenly he knew exactly what Jefferson's business was all about. "Something tells me this isn't a new experience for you."

Jefferson's smile broadened and he winked at him.

"Just you, me, and Arlene."

Chapter Four
Tobacco to Cabbage

Rudy checked over his shoulder several times. Once or twice he thought he saw a dusty cloud kicking up behind them, but if Arlene's outraged menfolk were in pursuit, they didn't manage to close the distance.

As they neared the depot, Rudy could see a four-car blue passenger train already at the station, its engine billowing steam and its whistle wailing impending departure. "Can't you go any faster than this?" Rudy asked. It was a rhetorical question, of course. Jefferson was already laying heavy on the lash, the wagon bouncing and creaking along the dirt road as if it were going to fly apart at the joints.

When they hit the station yard, the wagon jerked to a halt as close to the tracks as the horses would let it. If there had been a milling crowd, Jefferson would have mowed them all down. Rudy thrust a five-spot at him and bounded straight for the first carriage. The conductor was already preparing to give the all-clear signal.

"Wait, wait," Rudy yelled at him.

"Ticket?" the conductor called back.

"Yes," Rudy said, fumbling through his pockets for yesterday's paperwork. He mumbled a curse. It was stuffed in his suitcase back at the inn. He stopped at the bottom of the stairs and tried to catch his breath. "Yes . . . I'm afraid . . . I've misplaced it since yesterday's mishap. I had to overnight in that godforsak—Clinton."

The conductor gave him a disgusted look and pointed toward the depot. "Next train, ten o'clock."

"That's impossible," Rudy said, watching a billowing dust cloud growing ever larger on the horizon. He broke out into a sweat. "Surely you have a master list of last night's passengers? *Rudy Becker.* Check it."

There was a bit of jostling and rearranging of bodies at the top of the stairs. A dapper older man in a fedora squeezed past the conductor and gave him the once-over. "*Rudy Becker?*"

"Yes, sir," Rudy said, wondering if certain offended parties in Clinton had wired ahead about his ravishing of a virginal member of the household. The gentleman didn't resemble any railroad dick he had ever encountered. "Have we—"

The new man turned to the conductor and said, "I can vouch for this man. Let him board."

There may have been an exchange of money, but at the moment, Rudy didn't care. He hustled aboard, followed his benefactor to the rear of the car—which was virtually empty—and sat down across from him. "How do you know me?"

"I was in Washington yesterday looking for you. I'm Douglas Emerson."

"Emerson . . . Emerson . . . Emerson?" Rudy shook his head.

"No worry. We have never met, but I'd like to discuss with you a very important matter of the utmost sensitivity." Emerson handed him a business card that indicated he was a lawyer. "I can only assume that our serendipitous meeting this morning bodes well for both of us. I have a proposition for you."

Rudy held out his hands in protest. "I think I've had enough propositions for a while."

Emerson leaned forward in his seat as if he didn't wish to be overheard. There was a no-nonsense intensity in his gaze. "Rudolph initial *S* Becker. Investigative journalist. Born out of wedlock in Baltimore, Maryland in 1903. Other than that, your personal life is immaterial, Mr. Becker. I just need you to do a little investigative work which, if done satisfactorily, will net you a handsome profit. Still not interested?"

What was Emerson all about and why was he poking around in his personal life? Seeing as how he was momentarily beholden to the man, Rudy decided Emerson's comments were more curious than offensive. If he had more thoroughly snooped, he'd have known Rudy had recently moved on to a more lucrative line of work—one which he was not at liberty to discuss. For now, "investigate reporter" would continue to suffice.

"No," Rudy said, watching a wagonload of trouble pulling up to the departing train with baseball bats and sticks. He looked at the raging face of the driver. It was a face he wouldn't soon forget. "I think you're talking my language. What did you have in mind?"

"I have a murder in Nevis that I need you to investigate. There will be substantial resources at your disposal, and provided you can remain discreet, free rein to carry out your business."

Why did things always boil down to money? The short answer was, because journalism had never paid well and his new position hadn't paid *yet*. The long answer . . . well, as might be expected of him, it involved a woman. But this time, he was attempting to do the right thing. And to do the right thing took money. Lots of money. Probably more than he could ever accumulate, but he was trying. He assessed Emerson: well-cut clothes; expensive shoes, albeit needing a good polishing; and manicured fingernails. How fortuitous to have a well-heeled total stranger offering to fill the much-needed kitty. This could be a windfall. Rudy eased back into his seat. A little more jingle in his pocket would make it all turn out swell, quicker than they had ever thought possible. "I'm your man, sir. Give me the particulars and I'll start immediately."

"Not here," Emerson said, taking in their surroundings. "Somewhere a little more discreet. Meet me at the Bayside later today at three o'clock sharp and we can discuss it further. If you're late, I'll assume you're not interested."

Rudy gazed out the window and saw trouble disappearing into the distance. At least for the moment. He'd worry later about all the identifying information in the suitcase he'd left behind.

Chapter Five
A Convenient Cover

The Chesapeake Railway Express pulled into the Nevis train station right before 8:30 a.m. Shoe alighted from his coach a much different man from the naïve green reporter who had arrived in town two years earlier. Back then, he had nothing but a pedigree, a snout for news, and an abundance of ambition. To that he could now add experience and investigative skills that could make things happen. He was tired of living paycheck-to-paycheck. Douglas Emerson could fix that. Then he would be choosy about the cases he took.

He looked around, taken aback at the number of people pouring out of the train. He checked his watch. Even in this fine December weather, it was odd to have patrons rushing the gates to Bayland Amusement Park. He flagged a railway porter with the name tag PARNELL and requested their luggage.

Jack immediately disappeared into the crowd. By the time Shoe saw him again, he suspected Jack would have more leads than a barnful of thoroughbreds. He turned and offered Fannie a hand. She'd kept her nose in *The Sheik*—her most recent escape into romance novels—until they had rounded the great curve on the outskirts of town. She was either truly enjoying it or giving him the silent treatment. He wasn't sure on that one. She kept him off balance all the time. Currently, she was smiling and her eyes were bright, almost sparkling. She inhaled deeply as she reached the bottom of the stairs.

"Are you coming with me or shall I engage you a ride?" he asked.

"No need," she said. "All I want is fresh air, a brisk walk, and Mom's darb raisin bread. What time is your meeting with Emerson?"

"Eleven o'clock. Jack can take care of himself, but I'm not so sure about letting you wander around by yourself."

"My hometown and the middle of the day? Pfft. I'll be fine. Now you . . . don't wander into any alleys and I'll meet up with you later at the Bayside Hotel. Noonish?"

"Sounds about right."

She raised up on tiptoes and smooched his cheek. "Now breeze off."

Shoe chuckled. This was the Fannie he enjoyed—happy, with just a little bit of sass. "Will do. Soon as they find our suitcases."

"Right here, sir." It was Mr. Parnell, pushing a cart of luggage.

Shoe gave him a tip and asked that his bags be delivered to the Bayside Hotel and hers and Jack's to Betty's diner. "Mr. Parnell," he said, motioning toward the throng milling about. "All these people here to get a jump on the park line, or are they giving away something that I don't know about?"

The porter arched a bushy gray eyebrow. "It's the visitation, sir."

Shoe racked his brain, scanning it for any political or diplomatic mission that would somehow consider it important to include backwaters such as Nevis on its itinerary. Goose eggs. "Sorry, which one would that be?"

"Why, the visits by Mother Mary down at the waterfront, don't you know."

Parnell pocketed his tip and crossed himself.

Shoe was unsure of whether the hand gesture was one of reverence for the Virgin or appreciate for the money. He wasn't particularly religious—a quick prayer requesting assistance when he was in trouble, appreciation for a particularly lovely azure sky, or giving thanks for a sudden, inexplicable influx of money when he was short. He'd never been a member of a church, and he wasn't planning on joining any time soon. "All these people?" he asked. "Must have been quite a show to attract this kind of attention."

Parnell gave him a quick look. "Does everything have to be flashy to be important? These are true believers." He tipped his hat and headed off toward a group of older women struggling with big suitcases.

"Parnell," he called, turning the old man around. "Where can I find out more?"

"*Evening Star.*" Parnell flashed a quick smile and disappeared into the throng.

Shoe nodded. If anyone knew their onions, it was the local newspaper. He could handle that. Just so happened the newspaper was his next stop anyway. He collected his bag and fell into step with a herd of people traveling downhill toward the waterfront.

Less than a week until Christmas and the town had gone all-out. Wreaths hung on the doors of many businesses. Lampposts were festooned with big red bows and more than a few had posters advertising Winter Wonderland Friday night dances at the pavilion. More like Winter Wonder-*out*-land-ish, he mused. He could never quite find the rhythm to be a good dancer. He fought the strong urge to pluck each advertisement from its place and chuck them all into a nearby trash receptacle; Fannie would want to drag him there if she could. It gave him even more incentive to get things tied up here and get back to D.C. in time for President Coolidge's Christmas tree unveiling. No dancing there.

As Shoe hit the first intersection—Third Street and Bayside

Avenue— he scrutinized his surroundings. He could put up a good front with Fannie, but honestly, returning to Nevis gave him the shivers. The bootlegging network he had here had been but one facet of a massive illegal operation extending clear back into Philadelphia and the Delaware Valley. The resultant scandal touched the highest level of local government, and not all of those people were currently doing time in the Big House. The Volstead Act had no teeth. First-time offenders got off relatively easy. With juries rare to convict, most arrestees walked away with no jail time. Oh, there was public embarrassment to contend with, but considering that most citizens were partaking in illicit sippy-sippy, the only ones who cared were the temperance people.

When he decided no one was paying any particular mind to him, he continued on down to the *Evening Star*. He ignored the newspaper's main entrance and headed for the side door in the alley; old habits were hard to break. It was unlocked, so he walked right in.

Perkins was hunched over his linotype looking as if he had not gone home since the last time Shoe had seen him. Shoe gave him a nod as he threaded his way around boxes of printing paper, machine parts, and other printing paraphernalia. Riley Tanner's office was closed. The old Shoe would have considered it a blessing and crept quietly away. The new emboldened Shoe rapped several times. "Too busy for a quick howdy?" he asked, peeking in.

Tanner looked up, startled. "Well, I'll be." They shook hands and Tanner seemed quite pleased by his old employee's interruption. "Never thought I'd see your face this way again." He pointed to an empty chair across from his desk.

"Yeah, well, there's a certain charm about the place," Shoe said. He pulled his fedora from his head and looked about the editor's paper-filled office—same clutter as before, newer publication dates.

Tanner offered him a cigar. "You know I'll never forgive you for running to the *Washington Evening Star* to publish that political piece of yours."

Shoe didn't smoke, but he took it anyway. It might serve as an excellent source of barter later on. "And if you'll remember," he said, sitting down, "I tried several times to sell you on that story . . . from early on. But in all fairness to you, I guess it is unusual for someone so green to crack a story that big."

Tanner sighed wearily as he trimmed the end of his fat cigar. "The one time in my life when I sell someone short and they come up with *that!* I'm such an old donkey's rear end, Shoemaker. But now you're back. All is forgiven. I have an empty office right next door. Assistant editor if you'd like."

"Don't think Buck would like that much."

Tanner shook his head in disgust. "Ole Buck Hooley traded in his newsman's cap for manufacturing typewriters. I tried to tell him, *once a newsman, always a*—anyway, when can you start?"

"You're serious?"

"Of course. Best reporter I ever had. Can't fathom why Washington would let you slip away, but their loss."

Shoe nodded. The Nevis paper would be good cover . . . free access to insider information and extra moola in the pocket, who wouldn't run with that? "I, er, when do you want me?"

"Yesterday, kid."

"Uh, that'd be swell," Shoe said, trying not to sound overeager, "but I have a story I'd like to follow up on. Free rein to do that?"

"Can I get first crack at it?"

Shoe rotated his hat around in his hands, studying the brim. "Well, sure . . . yeah, I suppose you can. I've just got to make sure I don't step on any toes. I'm not planning on catching any more midnight trains out of town to save my skin."

"Done. I'll get you with Conrad and we'll blow your horn a bit. He's been writing our human-interest stories since you ran out on me. We'll splash it across the bottom of page one. *Pulitzer Prize-Winning Hometown Boy Returns*," he said, trying to paint a visual picture with a sweep of his hand. "It'll be good for business, good for you."

"*Nominated.* Didn't win, actually," Shoe said, blushing. "And I don't know about all that. I'm sure there are more than a few who'd like nothing better than to boot my rear end right back to D.C." He picked up a galley proof from several on Tanner's desk. "But look at you! Business seems to be rolling right along. Like that bloody killing on the wharf. The *Washington Evening Star* picked up your story. What's the scoop on *that?*"

Tanner shook his head. "Wish I knew. We can't get a word out of anybody. Chief McCall just about ripped off Ed Nugent's head when I sent him for a comment. All we know is what we printed: a woman and a boy whose names they are withholding. The young'un probably a local. They found his bike nearby. Snake-eyes on the woman. I guess they'll provide more information when they get positive identification."

"Why would the cops withhold information? Somebody might have seen something."

Tanner shrugged. "You know these police. Everything is held close to the vest until they build a case."

"Fingerprints?"

"Afraid not. Not enough left . . ." Tanner's voice trailed off in disgust.

"Witnesses?"

Tanner gave a half-shrug. "If there are, they've got 'em on ice somewhere. But hey, don't go blabbing, okay? This is strictly on the down-low. With all the hush-hush you'd think it was someone important, but down in that section of town . . ." He shook his head. "Rough and dirty."

Shoe's eyebrows went up. "Really? And how does all this religious—the visitation by the Virgin Mary? A porter up at the depot said it was bringing in boatloads of people. Saw it for myself getting off the train this morning. That story getting good traction?"

Tanner laughed and rolled his eyes. "Too much. If you can get me a deal on cheap rosaries to hawk down wharfside, I'll cut you in on nice little side job."

"Creative advertising from Bayland Amusement Park?"

"Oh, no! Couple of Irish nuns decide to spice up their American visit with holy people floating around the warehouses like specters. Suddenly, we've got nuts-o's coming from everywhere. If I wanted to give it momentum, first thing I would ask them is why they were down in the red-light district in the middle of the night." He studied the end of his smoke and then tapped the long column of gray ash into a nearby ashtray. "No, the amusement park folks didn't dream up that one, but they're sure reaping the benefits. The last thing in the world this town needs right now is a bunch of people poking around in bad places. We don't want any more of them getting sliced and diced down on the waterfront."

Tanner suddenly preoccupied himself with snuffing out a perfectly good cigar and lighting a fresh one. There was a tremor in the editor's hand. Things were really bad when a battle-hardened newshound ran scared.

Shoe stood up. "Could talk to you all day, Riley, but I do have my other business to complete." He settled his hat back on his head and pushed it well off his face. "Maybe I'll nose around a bit. If you don't mind, of course. And my assistant, Miss Byrne—would you mind if she poked around the news morgue so we can catch up to speed on town goings-on?"

"Betty's daughter? Tell her to have at it." Tanner pointed towards a rear corner of the building. "Same place as when you left. But tell her to avoid Jenkins. He has an eye for pretty young ladies. And you," he said, pointing at Shoe now, "you be careful. Still a load of townspeople holding a grudge. Best watch your back. And watch yourself along the pier, especially after sunset. They don't care who you are down there."

Shoe laughed. "Yeah, I heard. I might be safer where they don't recognize me. Doesn't say much about the electorate, does it?"

"Oh, I think it speaks more to man's unwillingness to give up the fruit of the vine, and Volstead's inability to stick violators where it hurts. Six months for Prentis Gant, that's all he got. If he could have weaseled out of the manufacturing charge, he might have walked with a simple fine. He's still a god of the common man's plight. Hard liquor sooths everything."

Tanner was thoughtful for a moment. "Ahh, I could yap about this all day long. Get out of here so I can get some work done."

Shoe skirted the group of reporters kibitzing near the front door and headed for the Bayside Hotel and his appointment with Emerson. He had no intention of permanently hanging out his shingle here. He didn't think Tanner knew much more about the murders than he did, but whatever the old goat found out, Shoe was certain he'd share.

Were the Marian visions and the murders related? He would get Fannie into the news morgue to nose out any patterns. It was possible someone was making murder their religion. He aimed to find out who . . . and why.

Chapter Six
Forget the Why

The Bayside Hotel was the grandest of the lodgings in Nevis, a vision of octagonal towers, wide wraparound porches, and gables dripping in Victorian vergeboard. It was impressive, but Shoe much preferred the uncluttered look of some of the newer buildings in town.

He pushed through the stained-glass paneled doors of the grand entryway and entered into a microcosm of high society. This was a leisured, wealthy clientele for the most part, with a few barnacles who, whether through charm or striking good looks, had attached themselves to a free ride. They strutted. They posed. They scrutinized him fiercely.

He crossed the dark, polished floor and headed for the maître de standing guard at the double-doored entrance to the glass conservatory. Mentioning Douglas Emerson's name brought him instant curry-favor. He hadn't received this much consideration since he'd been nominated for the Pulitzer. He was swept immediately into the room and seated at the best table, which was tucked cozily into a corner underneath a potted evergreen festooned with enormous red Christmas bows and silver bells. Close by, a fire crackled in a fieldstone fireplace with a hearth stretching the length of the wall. Here, the most powerful and rich could be admired but not inconvenienced by the lesser folk.

He ordered a Klondike Fizz and reminisced about his last visit, right before he broke his big story. He had been stalking Nathan Tarkington, a charming bootlegging middleman out of Delaware. Shoe wondered if his exposé had sent the man to prison. Probably not. He had seemed like an adaptable chap who would land on his feet no matter what life threw at him. No doubt all the notoriety had launched him into a new career—maybe something honest like selling shoes at Hahn's. He'd check with Fannie.

"Mr. Shoemaker?" Douglas Emerson's quiet voice stirred him from his reverie.

Shoe rose and they shook hands. "Glad to see you made it back to Nevis safely."

"And you also, Mr. Shoemaker. If this is too public a place for you, we can procure another room, but I though the privacy adequate. The staff will make sure we aren't disturbed." When Shoe offered no objections, he took a seat.

"What he's having," Emerson said to the waiter. And when the waiter returned with his drink he said, "I'll let you know when we need you again."

The waiter discretely disappeared.

"Have you settled in yet?" Emerson asked, turning back to Shoe.

"Not yet. Thought it best to see what I've gotten myself into. Who, exactly, am I working for? And the unidentified victim? But please, no more pictures."

"Oh, I intend on telling you everything, Mr. Shoemaker. And I'm fairly certain that when I'm done, you won't walk away disinterested. As for the pictures? Just these." Emerson handed him a buff-colored folio of heavy cardboard.

Shoe unwound the string from the button and opened it. Inside was an old, formal family portrait in the typical American style of yesteryear: a studio setting with a man and woman seated next to one another, a boy of about twelve standing beside them with his hand on his father's coat sleeve, and three younger children sitting primly at their parents' feet. Shoe noted the close, conservative cut of the gentleman's coat with its wide, notched lapels, and the heavily beaded ruby-red dress of the elegant woman. This was a family of considerable means.

"Wilhelmina Barton Weathersby," Emerson said, tapping the face of the youngest in the picture—a curly-haired brunette beauty with rosy cheeks and doe eyes. He produced a second picture of a little girl clutching a bouquet of flowers. *"Mena,* beloved daughter and last surviving child of shipping tycoon Benedict Weathersby. She's also the granddaughter of Edgar Tuttle Barton, former advisor to the President. Benedict Weathersby is a gentleman—to be most blunt—on whom the rain does not fall, Father Time does not ravage, and certainly, no one has ever thought of crossing."

"Benedict Weathersby? Now that's some money!" Shoe studied the pictures a moment, then Emerson. "How does the little girl fit in with what happened to the woman on the wharf?"

Emerson lit a cigarette and glanced around them. "They are one and the same."

"Her?" Shoe picked up the girl's photograph and studied it more closely. "I take it they found identification on the . . ."

Emerson looked at his cigarette and studied the wisp of rising white smoke as if he would find some answer there. "None."

"Then how do you know—how long had she been missing?"

Emerson shrugged. "She was never missing. Just displaced. She cut herself off from family and kept a low profile in the Bowery in New York. Good stock but ill repute. A heroin addict. Her family kept tabs on her general whereabouts just so there were no surprises. The day before the murder, she checked into the Bayside under her stage name, Mena Beebe. Room 29."

"'Stage name'?"

Emerson shook his head at this. "Mena ended up about as far away from Broadway as one can get, and in the end resembled nothing of the sweet little girl in that picture. Have you ever known someone who has more money, Mr. Shoemaker, more money than they know what to do with? So much money that they build an ocean-view mansion on a cliff in Newport, Rhode Island with no intention of spending more than three weeks a year living there? Children of such wealthy families often find themselves with too little to do and too much money to do it with. Women move so fast now," he said with a sigh. "If they knew what was good for them, they'd find a nice fellow and stay home and have babies."

Shoe wondered what Fannie would say about that. He stared at the photo and tried to imagine the little girl without a face. It brought up bad memories and breakfast. He flipped the picture over. "If they haven't found identification, how do you know the body is Miss Beebe's?"

"From the moment she alighted from the train at the Nevis depot, her father had her followed. She went directly from the train to Betty's, where she ate alone. As I'm sure you know, it's a well-established place, nothing out of the ordinary."

"And she never slipped away?"

Emerson shook his head.

"Did your man get any feel for whether she was expecting to meet someone there?"

"Mr. Henderson noted nothing definitive. He described her

demeanor as *uncomfortable*. She insisted on a table away from the door, sat with her back to the wall, and eyed the doorway throughout her meal."

"Mmm. As would anyone relocating to a new place. And how did she look? Physically debilitated?"

"Actually, he thought she looked better than usual."

Shoe shifted back in his chair and mulled over the information. Coming all the way to Nevis didn't make a lot of sense. The main appeal of the small town was the Bayland Amusement Park. If she wanted that sort of thing, Coney Island was closer and much bigger. "Any ties to Nevis?"

"Weathersby is part owner of this very hotel. The family has spent time here over the years."

"Oh, now we might be getting somewhere," Shoe said, sitting up straight again. "She had to be seeking something else, meeting someone. Your man Henderson, he's sure she traveled alone?"

"He believed so. She sat alone and never spoke to anyone. She made contact with a gentleman who helped her descend the train stairs at the station. And when she headed for the pier, she disappeared into a group of apparition seekers. After that, he lost her."

Shoe made a note on his writing pad. "He didn't by any chance provide the man's description, did he?"

"Certainly," Emerson said. "Everyone Mr. Weathersby employs provides their money's worth, Mr. Shoemaker." He then closed his eyes and recited as if reading notes scribed onto the inside of his eyelids: "Handsome; well-made dark suit, possibly Brooks Brothers; spotless oxfords—"

"A gentleman," Shoe said, tapping his pen on the table. "That certainly narrows things down."

"And a subtle limp," Emerson said, glaring at him. "He favors the right leg."

Shoe wrote that down and circled it. "Any indication where he went?"

"Towards town. I'm sure you'll find out."

Shoe nodded. "So where else did she go?"

"She shopped along Main Street, stopping to peer in the window of three establishments: Wockenfuss Confectionary, Francine's Salon, and a Dr. Thurber's."

"Thurber? He must be new."

"He's a charlatan quack."

Shoe marveled at the preciseness of Emerson's information and wondered why they even needed him. He might not even be able to meet the high standards that would be expected of him.

He reviewed his notes. "So, to summarize: she was an addict, appears to have traveled alone, liked chocolate, valued good looks, and may have had some ailments. Anything else?"

"None. She arrived on Thursday and remained in her room all the rest of the first day. She stayed in all day Friday, ordering room service in the morning and once again at midday. Friday night, she sashayed down to the rough section of town and never came back out again. It was Henderson who found her lifeless body behind a trash bin. He recognized her clothing."

"Hold up," Shoe said, motioning for him to stop. "This Henderson guy watched her waltz down into the bad part of town and did nothing to stop her?"

Emerson nodded.

Shoe arched an eyebrow and scratched his head. "And you don't see anything ethically wrong with that?"

"Of course! Everyone can see what's wrong with that, but who could predict . . ." Emerson heaved a sigh. "Mr. Weathersby's employees quickly learn what their duties and responsibilities are, or they are quickly seeking employment elsewhere. Mr. Henderson was to follow at a discreet distance but not interfere in any way. Unfortunately . . ."

"I'd like to speak to him."

"That won't be possible. He's no longer in Mr. Weathersby's employ."

The thought suddenly occurred to Shoe that he should get as much money up front as possible. "What about the kid?" he asked, shifting subjects. "Have they identified him yet? I take it he's not a Weathersby?"

"As far as we can tell, just an innocent local. Mr. Weathersby has offered to pay for final arrangements. Anonymously, of course."

"And why would he do that? Feeling guilty? Should I be looking at him too?"

Emerson gave him a sharp look. "Absolutely not. Feelings of guilt often accompany loss of a child."

Shoe let it drop. If Weathersby had something hidden, it wouldn't stay so for long. "Okay. Was she still in the will?"

"Of course. Underneath Mr. Weathersby's steely business exterior is the shattered interior of a loving father, Mr. Shoemaker. He never gave up on her and regularly provided a modest—*very* modest—stipend that was picked up from an intermediary down on the Bowery. He would have given more, but he realized that anything substantial would have been frittered away. Mr. Weathersby is a complicated man; both blood and dignity run deep."

Shoe nodded. Emerson pulled an envelope from his breast pocket and pushed it across the table. "Mr. Weathersby isn't as interested in the *why* as the *who*. Confidentiality is crucial. As he's rumored to be entering the next gubernatorial race, he wants as little information spilling out into the press as possible. One slip of the lip and you're out. Understood?"

"Certainly." Shoe palmed the envelope closer. It seemed to warm to his touch. "What did they pull from her room?" he asked, casually fanning his thumb across the wad of bills in the envelope. From what he could tell without appearing greedy, the bills seemed to be of small denomination.

"The room has been left untouched for *renovation.*"

Shoe stopped thumbing. "And the police let him get away with that? I *am* impressed. You have the key?"

Emerson shook his head. "At the desk. I'm sure you can handle that. And it's not a question of getting away with anything. There was no identification on the body, no connection to the hotel, and thankfully, nothing to connect the deceased with Mr. Weathersby. Not yet, at least. Keep it that way."

"Any current or past beaus I might need to consider?"

"She had a brief fling in Newport before she took off. A ne'er-do-well that the family chased off. He hasn't been seen since. We don't think he's involved."

"You mean, 'paid handsomely'? Isn't that the way it's done?"

"He was a bounder, sir. He was sent off with enough cash to make him happy and a warning to not approach her again."

Shoe stifled a chuckle.

Emerson gave him an indignant look. "Why do you find that amusing?"

"Ahem, sorry," Shoe said, trying to pull himself together. "Where I come from, there's no reward for that kind of behavior. They just chase you off with a baseball bat and that's the end of it."

"If you had children, you would no doubt think it all less funny."

"Fair enough," Shoe said. "What was his name?"

"Looking him up is a waste of time. He never showed his face again. Concentrate on other things."

"What about business, political rivals? I'm sure Mr. Weathersby has made quite a few enemies along the way. Any of those despise him enough to seek revenge? Maybe not so far as to murder someone. Kidnapping, perhaps, with things gone terribly awry?"

"What you have to understand is the politics of *old* money. They form business partnerships, lavish one another with entertainment, and their children get along well enough to marry each other. All goes extraordinarily well until there's a falling-out. Unfortunately, those happen quite often, part and parcel of business. Mr. Weathersby is troubled by only one such relationship. Carlton Donaldson."

"The shipping magnate?"

"The same. Long ago, Missus Weathersby and Mr. Donaldson's son, Theodore, were betrothed. Healthy business competition between Messrs. Weathersby and Donaldson became a heated personal competition, driving a wedge between the intendeds. They went their separate ways. Thus far, Carlton Donaldson is disinclined to back Weathersby on anything."

"Where might I find this Donaldson?"

"You don't. Arouse his suspicions and it affects Mr. Weathersby's business dealings as well as any future political aspirations."

"Well, surely Carlton Donaldson knows about Mena's downward spiral."

"Oh, most assuredly, and his son's breaking of their engagement no doubt led to some of the poor choices she made. But feeding the flames of curiosity surrounding a recent sensational murder could provide unnecessary fodder on an already toxic relationship."

"So, no Donaldson."

Emerson didn't respond but crushed the last of his cigarette in a nearby ashtray as he exhaled smoke through his nose.

Like the cigarette, Shoe's time was up. He closed the folio. "Can I keep these?"

"Certainly not," Emerson said. He slipped the pictures back into his jacket pocket and handed Shoe a slip of paper. "This is her last known address in New York. Grief is a private matter, Mr. Shoemaker, and Mr. Weathersby would like to keep it that way. Find out who killed his daughter and keep the family name out of the press, and he will be most grateful."

With that, he slipped money under his glass—a sizeable tip for the waiter's discretion, no doubt—and left.

Shoe sat a moment longer, transferring the New York address into his reporter's notebook. There would be no trips to New York until he exhausted the leads in Nevis, slim though they might be. He checked his watch. Fannie was probably wandering around the lobby waiting on him. He could only hope that the latest scuttlebutt from her mother's diner was more straightforward than some of the malarkey just dished out to him. Emerson wasn't playing it straight. Too many secrets and *don't go there*'s. So, what of it *was* true, and why bother to throw a boatload of money at him and then play games?

He pocketed the envelope. This case was getting better all the time. It would be interesting to use someone's own money to call them out.

Chapter Seven
Room 29

Shoe didn't see Fannie. He dinged the gold bell on the check-in counter and in exchange for a room signed away three days' pay on the Bayside Hotel's guest registry. In return, the concierge gave him a disapproving head-to-toe, a celluloid smile, and a bronze room key.

"This is overlooking the water?" Shoe asked, running his thumb across the *28* on the brass key.

"No, sir. It's parkside."

Shoe tipped his head, beckoning the desk clerk closer. "This puts me in a bit of a bind with the little lady," he whispered. "Foolishly, I promised her a suite on the bay side. Nothing else available, Mr. . . . Waddell?" he asked, reading the gentleman's name tag. He slid a twenty across the counter.

"Hmm." The gentleman turned and consulted the key board, which was empty save for one key hanging below the number *29*. "No, that would be all, sir."

"What about 29?" It was Fannie, fluttering both eyelashes and a dainty hand at the rack. "I believe we've stayed there before. Right, sweetie?"

The concierge blanched. "Oh, no, that one isn't available at the moment. It's being renovated. Perhaps on your next stay?" Waddell lifted the key from its hook and slid it into his pocket. "Do you want 28?" he asked, honing an edge on his voice.

"Very well," Shoe said, sighing dramatically. "I'll make it up to you later, baby." He put an arm around Fannie and guided her toward the elevator.

"Why do we want to stay in 29?" Fannie whispered, giving the bellhop a wave and a smile.

"It's the victim's room, only nobody knows it."

"Then how come you know it?"

Shoe held the elevator door open and followed her on. "Because I know all the right people." He punched the button for the second floor and when they got off there, he ignored room 28 and rattled the handle on 29 across the hall. It was locked.

Shoe studied Fannie's glossy short hair a moment. "I wish you hadn't bobbed your hair," he whispered.

Her face fell. "I thought you liked it," she said, fingering her soft waves.

"Oh, I do," he said, turning his attention back to the door, "but I need a hairpin to work this lock."

Her smile returned. She dug down through her handbag and pulled out a metal tin stuffed with hair clips. "All you had to do was ask." She hung over him as he jimmied the lock. "Where'd you learn to do that?"

"Your brother." The lock clicked and Shoe pulled her in behind him and closed the door. The room was actually a suite, spacious and well-appointed with white furniture he'd be afraid to sit on. The window curtains were pulled back to reveal a sweeping view of the sparkling Chesapeake Bay, its glassy surface dotted with tiny fishing vessels. This was a life he'd never have.

Shoe moved to the bedroom, Fannie right behind him. In this room stood a four-poster bed, dresser, chifforobe, and a small writing table. Near the bed were several leather suitcases stacked one on another. Fannie pushed past him and scooted to the mahogany chifforobe on the far wall. She pulled open the long, mirrored door on the right side.

"Look, but don't touch," he whispered. "Unless you want a nice little interview down at headquarters. At some point the police are going to be in here."

Fannie rolled her eyes at him and opened her hand to reveal a lace handkerchief wrapped around her fingers. She poked around a moment before switching to the left side of the cabinet. "Empty," she said, taking in the rest of the room. "I wonder why room service didn't unpack her? She spent a whole night in here and never unpacked?"

Shoe walked over to the three suitcases—two matching dark leather-edged Louis Vuittons and a smaller Pullman of tan vellum—and popped the latches on the top one. "Empty," he said. And so it was with the second. The third, the largest of the three, was locked, with no sign of a key.

"Can you spring it?" Fannie asked.

"Sure, but that's evidence-tampering." He stepped back and stared at it for a moment. He shrugged it off. "Leave it be for now. If we get desperate . . ."

"Why would someone take her clothes?" Fannie asked. She pulled up the bottom of the bedspread and looked under the bed. "Nothing."

Shoe checked the desk. The writing pad was blank. He ran his fingertips across the top page, feeling for indentations. There were none. He put it back and pulled out a burgundy leather-bound book from the same drawer. "Well, she can't be too bad a character. She unpacked her bible."

"It's a Gideon."

"No, *bible*. Says so right across the front."

"It's a *Gideon Bible*," she said, taking it from him. "From the traveling evangelists, named after the biblical figure Gideon in Judges. They gave them away to students at Drexel." She stared at him a moment. "You don't know your Bible, do you?"

"Judges 6," he countered, throwing her a smug look. "So, we might have a hooker who's found her way back to the righteous path?"

She shook her head. "It's not hers. Wherever the Gideons go, they leave them for other people. It's their mission." As she fanned through the book, something blue flipped out of the pages and spun to the floor. She picked up the crinkled slip of pleated paper and smoothed it out into its circle shape. "Blank," she said flipping it over. Then she sniffed it. "Mmm, chocolate. And not your penny candy stuff either. Heavenly," she said, enjoying a second whiff.

"Something you could buy here?"

She shrugged. "Here as in the Bayside or here as in town? Probably no to the first and yes to the second. The wrapper is lovely. Wockenfuss Confectionary down on Main Street could probably tell you. I could do that if you'd like."

"Actually, I have something else for you," he said, not trusting the dent she might put in his wallet in a heavenly chocolate shop. He slid the paper into a breast pocket and took in the rest of the room. "So, she was a sentimental type and she liked to squirrel away her mementoes. Take one more look, Fannie. What else can we learn here?"

Fannie took her time, starting at the door and gradually working her way around the room. "Nothing," she said with a sigh. "Either someone's taken all her things, or she traveled light because she was in a hurry and she was keeping up pretenses." She shook her head. "Doesn't make sense."

"Faceless corpses never do. Come on. Let's get out of here." He cracked the hallway door open and listened a moment. It was as quiet as a morgue on Sunday night. They slipped across the hall.

In the three strides it took to switch rooms, Fannie and Shoe crossed from the domain of the excessively rich to that of the moderately comfortable. Whereas room 29 was an opulent bayside suite, room 28 was a single small room, although still well-appointed with two nicely carved beds, a small table separating them, and an adequate chifforobe opposite the window. A view of Bayland Park replaced the glorious bay panorama.

Shoe walked over to the window and drew up the shade. The view wasn't bad if you liked looking at treetops and the summit of the Derby roller coaster. He wondered how much clickety-clack he'd have to listen to.

"Where are my bags?" Fannie asked, making a quick visual sweep of the room.

"Where—I had them sent over to your mother's house." He turned around to get a better look at her. "Surely you didn't think you were staying with me?"

"Well, er . . ." She cast her eyes down and refused to look at him.

He chuckled. "Well, I appreciate the trust, but think of your reputation, Fannie. How good would that look?" Two unmarried people sharing . . ."

"But you signed us in downstairs as married?"

"Well, yes, but that was just for show. So we could come and go without the clerks gossiping."

Fannie didn't look pleased. Shoe walked over to her and tried to put an arm around her. Apparently, he read that one wrong. She pulled away with a huff and decided to check out the window view herself.

Somehow, he didn't think she'd be giving him the lowdown on how the roller coaster was doing.

"How's your mother?" he asked, casting about for a more amicable topic.

"Quite well. Kids," she said, pointing out a pair of boys engaged in a friendly wrestling match on a patch of grass on the other side of the boardwalk. "Some of Jack's friends, I think. Maybe we shouldn't take Jack with us when we leave. He needs more of that and less of us."

He joined her at the window. "What, leave him in a town where someone's butchering women and boys? Where is that coming from? Your mother said something?"

She shrugged. "It's just me. Everybody at the diner treated me like I was Medusa. I don't fit in here anymore. I feel like an outsider. And I'm not making any headway in Washington either."

"Listen, doll. Nobody in Washington wants Medusa to make any headway."

A single tear rolled down her cheek and disappeared around the curve of her jawline. Why did he have to be such a wise-ass? He reached for her and this time she let him pull her close. "I'm sorry. It'll be okay. By the time we wrap things up here, I'm sure you'll have a better understanding of where you should be. Okay?"

She nodded and brushed across her cheek with the back of her hand.

He gave her a squeeze and let her go. "Good, because I don't want you to go all girly on me right now. I have something important for you to do."

"Girly?" She bristled.

He raised his hands, palms out. "I'm sorry. Bad word choice. I'm trying, okay? Do you want to search the *Evening Star* morgue for past murders? I'd do it, but I have to run a lead on some of the businesses downtown."

"Yes."

"Great. Tell 'em I sent you. And avoid Jenkins. He's a bit of a letch."

"Pfft," she said. "I can handle it."

"I'm sure you can," he said. And with a bit of relish, he thought. "Look for me outside the building when you're done."

Chapter Eight
Running Scared

Jack Byrne had mixed feelings about being home. D.C. was okay—plenty to explore, but the turf was unfamiliar and hustle in short supply for someone without the appropriate affiliations. Not to mention that a turn around the wrong corner could be his last trip anywhere. He once swore that if he ever escaped this backwater, he would never come back. That oath had lasted less than a year.

At the main pier he fell in amongst the laborers and merchants and rode the bustling flow of human traffic past the old Millman glassworks and other businesses into the seedier section. These were mainly flophouses and dens of iniquity. He had never been in any of them, but he'd heard a good tale or two. As he approached a break in the buildings, he found the culvert that channeled the Little Poni Creek out into the bay. When he thought no one was watching, he scrambled down the bank of dirt and oyster shells and swung himself into the tunnel by the top rim of the pipe. He landed with a splash in slow-moving, ankle-deep water. It was numbingly cold. His sudden entrance startled the three boys lounging on a makeshift platform made of scrap wood.

"Ho, there," the tallest among them challenged.

"Ho, there, yourself, Dermott," Jack shot back. He splashed out of the water to the higher, dryer side of the tunnel. The place had a fishy smell like bad oysters. "It's me, Jack."

"Byrne? Well, I'll be," Dermott said, edging his way down the mound of shells the fort sat on. "We thought you'd escaped for good."

"Not here long," Jack said, meeting him halfway. He nodded to the rest of the gang. "Chester, Spence. Thought I'd catch up while I was in town." He motioned for Chester's cigarette.

Chester forked it over. "You first. Washington, what's it like?"

"Yeah, what's D.C. like?" Spence said, pushing his flat cap back on his head. Jack could see his eyes now.

"Big," Jack said. He sat down with his back against the tunnel wall and they gathered round like disciples at his feet. He smoked the rest of the cigarette and regaled them with the twists and turns of every Shoe case he could remember, throwing himself into the mix wherever it was convenient.

"So enough about me," he said, flicking the butt down toward the water. "What happened down at the wharf? Anybody I know?"

The others were silent for a moment. Spence began sorting oyster shells at his feet and Chester pulled his knees tighter into his chest. It was Dermott who finally spoke, his voice low and intense. "Bad, Jack. One minute the guy's here and the next he's chopped up like Mr. Nick's butcher special. Real bad."

"They don't make 'em like him anymore," Spence offered. Chester murmured agreement.

"Who was it?" Jack whispered.

The other boys exchanged glances.

Dermot finally spoke. "They haven't said."

"But you got a good guess," Jack said, eyeing each of them in turn. When no one offered anything else, he stood up. If he had an idea,

Dermott wasn't giving it up easily. "I'm gone six months and you don't you trust me anymore? Guess I'll see ya 'round."

"It was one of the Koenigs."

Jack tried not to react, but it was like a punch in the gut. Everybody liked Charlie. His brother, Butch, was a close friend. "Funeral?"

Dermott shrugged. "Nobody knows nothing. They won't even talk about it."

Chester took a shell and launched it like a dart into the flowing water below. "Yeah, well, wherever they got 'em, it must smell something awful."

Dermott elbowed him in the side, eliciting an *oof* and a retaliatory swipe that missed. "Charlie's our educated guess. But you didn't hear it from us, all right? You can hang down near the jail and get bits and pieces. We tried to get down to where he took his final breaths, rest his soul, but the cops wasn't having none of it."

"What do you think he was doing with the lady who died?" Jack asked.

Dermott shrugged. "One body was on the wharf just before you hit the dives, and t'other a few feet away on the path leading back to the amusement park. They found a bicycle and a Western Union cap."

"Sure proud of that cap," Spence said, staring up at the pipe ceiling.

Dermott nodded. "Yeah, that's all you heard from Charlie and Butch . . . how important they were running messages, and how much money they made."

Yeah, like Dermott never laid it on thick or spun a tail, Jack thought. "Anybody seen Butch?"

"That's the weird part. It's like he vanished into thin air."

"Dead too?"

"Don't think so. I knocked on his door, but his mother said he was staying with relatives in Solomons. Right away I called BS on that one—not directly, Mrs. Koenig is a nice lady. But Butch never mentioned nobody in Solomons."

"Guess we'll never know what happened."

"Guess not," Jack said. He looked toward the water where oyster boats had dropped anchor just offshore. He'd never noticed before how beautiful they were, bobbing out there on that glistening water. Not a dredger in sight. To avoid turf wars, the town awarded permits that rotated among the local fishing interests. The older oystermen said the dredgers tore up too much of the bottom. Why would anybody want to destroy a good thing?

He shifted his focus back to Dermott. "Any changes down at the precinct house?"

"Same place, same faces. Only Chief McCall is making life miserable-worse than usual. Ya can't do this, ya can't stand—"

"Bet they keep the evidence in there somewhere," Jack said. "I'll bet we could—"

Spencer stood up. "Count me out." He jumped off the platform. Hugging the narrow, dry ledge that ran the length of the tube, he worked his way out of the culvert on the land side.

When he had disappeared from sight, Dermott sighed and said, "Jack, it's bad. Everybody's scared. You should stay in Washington where it's safe."

Jack pictured the assemblage of shady characters he had to work his way through just to get to Shoe's office. "It ain't no end of the rainbow, Dermie. And it wouldn't be right for me to go back without getting some answers. How many times did Charlie sit here, just like this, shooting the breeze? We owe him."

"Maybe. And if you come up with something good, we're probably in. But it'd have to be in the middle of the day, because there ain't nobody insane enough to be sneaking around at night no more. Everybody's quit Western Union. They're pleading for bicycle messengers."

Jack bounced a particularly large oyster shell off the opposite wall and listened to the sound echo down the pipe. "That so? I need a job."

"Pick a job you can grow in," Dermott said. "That one's a dead end." He got up and headed after Spencer. "If you're here a while, give us a shout," he called over his shoulder.

Chester got up as well. "Good to see you again, Jack." He dusted off his britches and took off after his friends.

Jack watched them go, his insides bubbling up with feelings he couldn't put into words. He hadn't been gone that long and already he'd lost his friends—friends he'd known forever. And Charlie, gone less than a week and already forgotten. Didn't seem right. Didn't seem fair. Not in Jack's world. He'd give a hoot, all right. As soon as he got himself a bicycle and figured out how the police barracks operated. He clambered down the mound of shells and headed for Main Street.

Chapter Nine
Penny Candy, Dollar Bribes

Shoe took a seat on the sidewalk bench outside Mac's Pharmacy. He skin wasn't prickling, nor had he noticed anyone dogging him, but his father hadn't raised a fool. He checked his surroundings. Sooner or later, one of his liquor *friends* was going to catch wind of him being in town and make his life difficult.

He studied two nearby gentlemen engaged in animated conversation. They seemed indifferent to him. And likewise, the man kneeling curbside was legitimately poking around at a Lizzie's front tire. Satisfied he was still anonymous, he crossed the street to Wockenfuss Confectionary.

The intoxicating scent of sweet, rich milk chocolate rolled over him as soon as he pushed open the door. The proprietor was preoccupied with a young woman at the counter, which gave Shoe a chance to inventory the shelves and glide along the showcase. Yellow boxes of Whitman Samplers and other prepackaged chocolates were artfully arranged along the upper shelf behind the cash register, while enormous jars of fruit bonbons in every color of the spectrum occupied the lower. On the counter near the register stood jars of striped candy sticks and rock candy, Reese's Peanut Butter Cups, Jujyfruits, and Goo Goo Clusters. And before it all, at waist height—or more accurately, at a youngster's reach— stood floor-stand baskets heaped to overflowing with Beemans gum and penny candy. The penny candy looked like an afterthought to compete with the inexpensive selections at Mac's Pharmacy and Tanner's Mercantile.

The confections in the showcase were certainly finer than anything to be found at any of the local competitors. They were divided into sections by variety: fudge in varying shades of brown and cream at the near end, mounds of chocolate-covered nuts and such at the other end, and hand-dipped chocolates—light and dark— in the middle. At least, he thought they were chocolates. Did chocolate come in greens and pinks? He perused them before settling in the center of the case. All the delicate morsels were nestled in little paper nests —he should have asked Fannie what they were called—but none as fancy as the blue paper he was looking to match.

The customer left and he moved forward to take her place. "Good afternoon. I'd like four of those," he said, pointing directly before him to the milk chocolates adorned with pink flowers. He watched the confectioner limp over, place them in a little box with white tissue paper, and tie it off with a ribbon.

"I'm in a bit of a quandary," Shoe said, taking the box. "I'm trying to impress a certain lady and I secreted this away when she wasn't looking." He passed the blue floral paper over the counter. "Can you tell me what sort of candy might be wrapped in this? I thought it was purchased here, but I don't see anything like it in the case. You don't carry it anymore?"

The confectioner shook his head and handed it right back. "Special order."

"Oh! So you can order it for me? And what, pray tell, would I be ordering and where would you have to go to find it?"

"Swiss chocolate. Mr. Sass in Baltimore. Expensive. You want to order?" He picked up a short, fat pencil and a receipt pad. "How many?"

"Well, actually, maybe I shouldn't trouble you with that. I'll be up that way soon. Is Mr. Sass located in Lexington Market?"

Wockenfuss nodded.

"I'm not trying to stick my nose in where it doesn't belong, but perhaps I could bring back extra for your other customer?"

"Not a regular. Don't know his name. He paid. I don't need to know more."

"Yes. I've overstepped. My apologies." Shoe leaned over the counter far enough to read the amount on his receipt. He doubled the amount, added a bonus, and pushed the adjusted amount across the counter. "Was this recently? Just so I know they're still making them," he quickly added. "You know, who wants to waste a trip?"

Mr. Wockenfuss studied the money. "Last week. Young established fellow, but he didn't give a name. He wasn't from around here."

"New York?"

"Pfft. Balmer if I ever heard one." He put the money in his cash register drawer and pushed it closed with a bang. "Anything else?"

That fiver bonus evidently had bought everything he knew. "No, sir. Have a good day."

Halfway to the door, Shoe turned. "This gentleman from Baltimore, he was alone?"

Wockenfuss swiped a hand across the counter next to the cash register and began to rearrange the penny candy.

Shoe sighed wearily and walked back over. "I think I may have underpaid you." He placed two one-dollar pieces down next to the candy straws.

"Alone. When the chocolates arrived, he instructed me to have them delivered to the Bayside Hotel. Gave his name as Lewis Ware."

"Delivered to whom?"

"*Miss Della.*" He pointed to his arm, just under his cuff. "Tattoo. That's all I know. Now if you pardon me, little elves don't make the bonbons."

Shoe took his chocolates and left.

Lewis Ware? The name itself brought no one to mind. But he was someone who had fallen hard enough to have his heart's desire permanently inked on his person. That didn't smack of a gentleman at all. And he had enough money to buy expensive chocolates. And *that* didn't sound like someone who frequented the New York City slums. His guess was an older acquaintance from somewhere other than the Bowery. Newport perhaps, where the Weathersby family of Baltimore summered. Mr. Emerson might be able to shed some light on that, but it was a notion Shoe quickly rejected. Giving up too much information too soon was ill-advised. He had no guarantee the information wouldn't be shared with Rudy or other potential rivals. No use making himself obsolete.

Chapter Ten
No Dumb Dora

When Shoe got back to the *Evening Star*, there was still no sign of Fannie. He spent a jitney on a fat red apple at Trott's produce stand and settled on a nearby bench to wait. It shouldn't take too long for Fannie to search the past issues and reporter notes for any major crime cases in the last few years. He could have done it in short order, but he wanted to dodge any work Riley Tanner might consider throwing his way.

He didn't wait long, had barely thrown the apple core in a trash can, when she walked out. With her hat pulled down low, Shoe couldn't get a good take on the eyes, but the body language was all there for Fannie having a good day. The shoulders, hips, and flashy new red shoes were all working in a graceful rhythm that would have made Theda Bara proud. She had either hit pay dirt in the archives or just stuck him with another pricey bill for haute couture. What had happened to the sweet ingenue who would once have settled for a boring life as a merchant's wife?

She sat next to him and flipped open a stenographer's pad.

"Before we get into that, I wanted you to know I was thinking of you," he said, producing the box of chocolates. "These are for you."

She eyed the box suspiciously before giving it a sniff. "Wockenfuss? Oh, you clever boy!" She nibbled a pink flower off one of them. "You do realize these are chocolate creams and the paper smelled like chocolate-covered cherries, don't you?"

"Of course," he lied. "If you'd like to wait for the cherries, I can finish these up myself." He tried to take the box but she pulled it free and slid it into her handbag.

"Very thoughtful to bring them," she said. "Did you get a name?"

"They were bought by a man named Lewis Ware from Baltimore. And the cherries were a special order from Baltimore. Wockenfuss' s instructions were to deliver them to a *Miss Della* at the Bayside. Mena, I presume."

"And maybe his name wasn't Lewis? If he's from Baltimore, why didn't he bring them with him?"

"Maybe he didn't realize he would need to flatter her until after he got here. Either he wasn't expecting her to be in Nevis, or they had a row and he had to make amends. Thoughts?"

He watched her as she sucked the last morsel of chocolate from a fingertip.

"No need to woo her or apologize. Those were *I love you* chocolates. They're already in a committed relationship."

"Such conviction, Fannie. How did you get *that* out of *that*?"

"Too expensive to waste on an insecure relationship." She leaned over and bussed him on the cheek. "Thanks for the chocolates."

He wanted to tell her they were less expensive than a pair of Hahn's best, but that would leave him on the hook to make up the difference. "Okay, that's what I accomplished. "Now let's see what you got. Anybody give you any lip?"

"No, just some lunch offers and a little innuendo," she said, matter-of-factly. "I don't think they're used to rubbing elbows with women at work."

"One word, Fannie, and I'll—"

She ignored his chivalry and consulted her notes. "When I lived here, I didn't realize what a dangerous little town Nevis was. For the eleven years prior to this one, the murder rate held steady at around ten annually. And then you have this inexplicable change . . . want to guess how many in the twelve months?"

"Twenty?"

She held up two fingers. "Just Mena and the bike messenger. Seems everyone's giving up their wanton ways. Either that, or they're burying the body so deep nobody can find it."

"Or they throw it in the bay with cinder blocks tied to the feet."

"Exactly," she said, cracking a smile. "Anyway, ten seemed a bit high. Most violent crime in Nevis involves altercations between longshoreman or day laborers on the waterfront—arguments while unloading freight, or bar fights. There were only four stranger assaults. Those were on the wharf, and all but one was solved. That'd be little Billie Peaden, a ten-year-old townie who snuck out one night to play hide-and-seek with his friends down on the wharf. They found him with his throat cut ear-to-ear. No suspects. Poor kid. But that was five years ago," she added, looking down at her notes again, "and nothing remotely like it until Mena's assault. All the other brouhahas were rows between family members, usually on Saturday evenings after a bout of heavy drinking. With Prohibition . . ." She shrugged.

"Mmm," Shoe said. He reached over and pushed a wayward piece of hair out of her face.

"Stop. I like it short," she said, pulling away.

He smiled at her independence and dropped his hand. "That gives me a whole different picture than the one Riley Tanner gave me earlier. He doesn't seem to think it's safe. Told me to watch my back." He thought a moment. "What about a year back—was there a record of the two bodies found under the wharf?"

"I skipped that one. It was about bad booze. Comments? Suggestions? About the murders, not the hair."

"It seems unlikely an acquaintance would have followed Weathersby here from New York and done her in. Why not do it there, in the Bowery? That stuff goes on all the time. Besides, the circles she lived in wouldn't have the wherewithal to follow her to Maryland. No," he said, shaking his head. "Too far. Maybe it was just a case of bad judgment on her part, and she thought if she could survive in the Bowery, Nevis would be a Sunday stroll. Emerson said her father watched over her from afar. It's hard to picture him letting her wander freely on the questionable side of town."

Once again, the feeling crept over him that there were eyes on him. If Weathersby kept tabs on Mena, why not keep tabs on him too? Shoe considered his surroundings: an older couple holding hands as they window-shopped, a gentleman walking a small white dog, and a shopkeeper collecting his mail from the mailbox mounted next to the door. No one seemed to give them a second glance.

"By the way," he said. "Weathersby's considering a run for office."

"Are you thinking family did it? To protect their reputation? I can't even fathom a family like that."

Shoe ran the tip of his shoe across the ground, smoothing out the dirt in front of him. How much should he share with her? Her help was beneficial, but she'd burned him before—a little too independent for her own good and the potential for going rogue if she thought it would help him. "Doubtful. If the truth were ever revealed, political opponents would have a field day with the scandal."

Fanny flipped the steno pad closed. "Where does that leave us?"

Shoe considered, for a moment, Lewis Ware, the only lead he had. Was he a do-gooder out to rescue a trollop—as Emerson referred to Mena—and dime-a-dozen streetwalker? It seemed *off*, a bit far-fetched. "Based on the viciousness of the attack, I'd say it was a crime of passion."

Fannie studied her bright red shoes. "So, she knew her attacker. Jealous lover? Someone with kinky habits who got possessive."

Shoe gave her a double take. "Miss Fannie, that certainly didn't come from your Emily Dickinson days. What on earth have you been reading?"

Fannie blushed and hung her head. Shoe loved to make her blush, but he didn't get to revel in the moment. His attention was drawn to a rattling flivver that pulled up to the gasoline pumps in front of Spitlers Auto Supply. A dandy in a tweed jacket hopped out and cranked up gasoline on the pump while his passenger remained in the car.

"Jeez, Maries," Shoe said, turning away and shielding his face behind his hand. "Ten o'clock—Rudy Becker. No, on second thought, eyes over here. His investigative skills are outdone only by his extraordinary good looks. Why does he keep following me around?"

Fannie looked up and flashed her brightest smile. "Consider it done," she said.

"Done? I've not said a word about doing anything. When did you suddenly turn into this free-spirted femme-fatale flapper?"

"When I found out how much fun it is." She patted his hand. "Think he's here for the reward?"

"Most assuredly. What else would bring him out of his comfortable Washington office? I'm beginning to wonder how many people Emerson's paid to sleuth around. Clearly, he's not been entirely forthwith." Shoe parted his fingers and took a peek at his nattily dressed competition. Shoe didn't get how Rudy could take the same Roman nose, chestnut hair, and dimpled chin he himself had and turn them into something swoonworthy. "Oh, dear, the weasel's heading this way. How about you go powder your nose somewhere?"

"Nonsense," she said, poufing her bob. "I think I'd prefer to sit here and shine."

"Shoemaker!"

"Becker!" Shoe moved away from Fannie. "What a surprise!" He dodged a playful right hook Rudy threw at him. He offered his hand, which Rudy grasped and crushed in his own.

"Still boxing, I see."

"Of course," Rudy said. "Dempsey's the greatest. Babe Ruth, eh, maybe a distant second when it comes to heroes." He leaned around Shoe and smiled at Fannie.

"What brings you out of Washington?" Shoe asked, leaning slightly to block his view. "If you're looking for a position, I'm on good terms with the editor of the newspaper here. Shall I give Riley Tanner a reference?"

"Business is good in D.C., but a little collegiality never did newsmen any harm. You?"

"Vacation."

"Good for you. It's all about pacing. All work and no play makes Shoe a dullard. "Am I right?" Rudy asked, looking at Fannie again. "When I saw you sitting here, my first thought was that you had given up trying to make it in the big city. It gets rough, spending your day dodging creditors."

Fannie crossed her legs and gave him a radiant smile. "Actually, Shoe is being modest. He's working on a big case."

"Really? Care to share, Miss . . .?"

"Fannie Byrne," she said, offering a hand.

"Rudy Becker," he said, walking over and taking it.

"Oh, look, dear," Shoe said, taking Fannie's hand from Rudy and pulling her to her feet. We're late." He turned to Rudy and said, "Maybe catch you about. Staying long?"

"As long as it takes," Rudy said. "No vacation for me. I'm on a great case. I'll be at the Calvert. Give me a ring when you're able to make some introductions." He smiled at Fannie. "If you get bored, Miss Byrne, give me a call." With a wink and a tip of the hat, he was off.

"My case," Shoe muttered. "As soon as Emerson offered me the case, he made a beeline for Rudy's place. I wonder what he knows, that scoundrel!" He turned and gave Fannie a sour look. "*Big case?* I wanted to keep this on the down-low."

"Then why did you offer to show him around the *Star*?"

"Well, ah, I didn't think he'd take me up on it, that's why. Somehow that scoundrel always seems to get the best of me." He took off his hat, smoothed the brim, and resettled it on his head again. "And don't think I didn't see you flirting. Care to explain that?"

Fannie's lips pulled up into a pouty little bow that almost always drove him nuts. Sometimes it was anger, but more often than not it was lust. "Well, he seems to be as low as they get. Maybe I'll see if he's free for cocktails later."

"Over my dead body! What happened to the naïve young woman who followed me to Washington?"

"She bobbed her hair, picked up some worldly girlfriends, and learned not to be beholden to anyone for what she wants."

He gazed at the eyes. He thought they had a loving light, but it might have just been the delight of tormenting him. "And what would that be, because I'm not sure anymore."

"What every woman wants. Now if you'll excuse me, I'm going to

73

visit Miss Francine's beauty salon and get my nose powdered."

Shoe watched her float off. "Do you think you could fit a little reconnaissance into your visit?" he called after her. "Find out of anyone knows a young gentleman named Mr. Ware. And stay away from Rudy Becker!"

She fluttered her fingers over her shoulder and threw in an exaggerated wiggle to her walk. Only God and women knew what the fairer sex wanted. If he could crack that code, he'd be ruling the world. If she was setting her sights on Rudy, the man would never know what hit him. It suddenly occurred to him that if God were a woman, it might explain a lot of crazy things in this world.

He sat back down on the bench to cool off and regroup. Where was Jack, the other member of their merry little trio? Fannie's brother might be only thirteen, but he was experienced way beyond his years. Right about now, Shoe pictured him working his connections down at the wharf. Pulling information from the lad would be relatively easy if Shoe threw money at him and framed his questions carefully.

Chapter Eleven

Sparrows and Chickens

Dermott flicked away the half-smoked remains of his third cigarette. The area behind the police barracks was littered with old smokes. "Jack, I don't know why I let you talk me into these things."

Nobody could make smoking look more boss than Byron Dermott, but the chain smoking gave it away. Old Dermie was fighting his insides. Imagine that.

"Ssst! Hey, kid!" It was one of the jailbirds watching them through the iron bars of the lock-up next door. The voice was chipper, hopeful, but the words a bit slurred. He stuck a crooked finger through the grille. "If you're gonna waste 'em . . ."

Dermott shoved his pack deeper into his pocket and turned away.

The voice took on a mean edge. "What're you doin' out there? Up to nooo good. Gonna end up in here with Jimmy and me. Good times."

Jack didn't need to look him in the eye to know there was a leer there. He also knew the fellow was full of it. The jail wasn't a long-term lock-up but mostly a drunk tank. The boozehound would be out in a few hours when he sobered up.

"Gimme one. A *new* one and I won't start hollering for the coppers . . ."

"Christmas, Dermott," Jack muttered. "Give him one. Shut him up."

"Sss." Dermott tapped one out of the pack and made the fellow stretch hard for it.

"That'en too," the jailee said, pointing to one on the ground.

Dermott gave him that one at arm's length also. Apparently satisfied and tired of the game, the inmate disappeared with his booty.

Dermott moved quickly away from the window. "Hurry. I'm not giving any more away, and I ain't doing time for breakin' and entrin'." He laced his fingers together and got down low against the back wall of the barracks. "Up you go."

Two quick steps—one into Dermott's hands and one for traction against the brick wall—and Jack caught the edge of the metal gutter. A couple of swings and a heave-ho rolled him up onto the roof. He rotated around and offered Dermott a hand.

Only, Dermott stood staring, hands on his hips, disinclined to follow. "You see the problem," he said. "Right? You're gonna slide off of there."

He did have a point. Without any way to hook his feet, Jack was coming off head-first. "Running start," Jack said, directing him away from the building.

"Yeah. Maybe." Dermott trotted back until he hit the wooden fence at the end of the lot. He spent a moment sizing it all up and then came full-steam at the building. About three feet from the wall, he launched himself upward and lunged for the top of the drain spout. He latched onto the metal pipe about halfway and began to shimmy his way up—a superb effort.

Who woulda guessed the gutter wouldn't hold? The metal trough detached with a squeak and a pop, dropped down, then toppled earthward with Dermott still attached. He hit the ground with a yelp and a thud. Then, not a wiggle, nor a whimper, nor an oath.

Sweet Jesus, he'd just killed his best buddy. "Derm! Talk to me, Derm!" Jack hung over the edge of the building, waving his hands like a madman. "Say something," he hissed. He started off the roof and then thought better of the drop.

"Do it, dammit!" came a faint voice from the ground. "Get on with it. And then I'll help you down."

Jack clambered up the sloped roof to the chimney and waved his hand around the flue cap. The ventilation coming out was cool air, no fire. He eased the cap free and put his ear close to the flue opening. The room below was silent.

After a bit, his neck muscles began to burn. Maybe this wasn't such a good idea. He could be here awhile. He switched ears, closed his eyes, and thought of other things. Like bananas. *Yes, We Have No Bananas.* Why didn't the Greek guy have any bananas today? And what about yesterday? 'Course, if he was singing the song yesterday, that would make it today and he already said he didn't have any. It was a dumb song. He was humming it, so his brain didn't seem to think so. He shushed himself. The sound of voices rising up through the flue jolted him back to reality. *Huh?*

"Lots of trouble down on the wharf."

"What now?" The voice sounded weary.

". . . murder the other night? People's telling me it's not your average murder. Chief McCall's put a lid on things. Told those in the know to keep things real quiet. It's a political thing. Nobody's going to want to come here if we have a Jack the Ripper terrorizing the town."

"Politics? McCall's a Donaldson boy. Why would Donaldson care?"

"Boy?"

"Aw, you know what I'm saying."

Whatever they were saying got lost in the blast of a car horn on the street below.

The weary voice again. "What about the Koenig kid?"

"Which one?"

There was some chuckling.

"Always the smart aleck. The one that's left."

"Gonna go get him, scare a little silence into him, and cut him loose."

"Well, when you do, make sure you give him his brother's effects. They're locked in the evidence cabinet. Pocket stuff, you know? Marbles, penknife, buffalo nickel."

The conversation ceased. Maybe the coffee break was over. Jack leaned as far as he dared into the shaft.

"Sad, real sad," one of the voices continued. "Even McCall got misty-eyed. But don't tell 'em I said that."

"Not me," the other chortled.

Another moment of silence. Jack's legs were cramping. He changed from a squat to a sitting position and stretched out his legs. The voices began again, but the conversation was indistinct. He huddled closer.

". . . land speculation. Not much chit-chat but they say—"

"You ladies plan on drinking tea all day?" A third voice.

A couple of *no sirs* and that was it. *Sheet,* Jack thought. He stretched out on his back and pondered it all. A definite cover-up, someone named Donaldson, and land speculations. And the boys had been right. The other victim was one of the Koenig brothers. As his fourth-grade teacher often preached, 'Who, what, when, where, why, and how?' He couldn't give her a satisfactory answer then, and he could only partially answer the question now, but Shoe should know. For all the quibbles he had with the man, Tatum Shoemaker knew how to use his noggin.

He slid to the end of the roof and peered out into the woods. *Dermott?* He puckered up and gave his best rendition of a house sparrow. No response, no Dermott. Be damned, the great Byron Dermott cut out on him. Dad-burn chicken. Jack gauged the distance from the roof to the ground. If he dangled, then dropped, it might not be too bad . . . He needed to think on it. It wasn't being chicken, just cautious.

A moment later, he swung off the roof and let 'er go.

Chapter Twelve
Betrayal and Revenge

Rudy thanked his driver and hurried up the steps of the Bayside. Why was Shoemaker in town? He'd heard Shoe's girl was a local—maybe for her. Given the hullabaloo Shoe's reporting had stirred up, it was foolish to come back here and risk retribution, especially now. After months of upheaval, the Nevis political structure was calming down and settling back in with the same group of political figures previously swept up in the liquor raids. Rudy had to shake his head at that one. When was the populace ever going to learn that you could never trust a crooked man?

He paused in the lobby, searching for the conservatory. He'd long ago become jaded by the spending of the super-rich. Still, this place was a doozy, dripping in opulence: gilt wallpaper, crystal chandeliers everywhere, and an expansive sitting area filled with palms and other exotic flora. It seemed the approaching winter hadn't slowed down business; the lobby was full and bustling. He knew how it went with these places. Find one influential high-society benefactor to be belle of the ball—all amenities gratis, of course—and all the friends and wannabees would follow. The season would be a successful draw. This winter, it would be a Vanderbilt. Next year, an Astor or the like. Rudy shook his head. He was in the wrong profession.

An effervescent uniformed bellhop in a round brimless hat—perhaps seizing on Rudy's hesitation as a chance to earn a quick gratuity—skittered toward him. "May I be of assist—"

Rudy spotted the conservatory and shook his head. From there, his eyes shifted to the staircase across the hallway. No doubt a gentleman such as Emerson valued timeliness, but surely he would excuse a few minutes of tardiness and allow a gentleman to reassure the love of his life that he would soon be safely by her side. And maybe assuage his guilt for flirting with Shoe's lovely Miss Byrne, however innocent it might have been. Getting Shoe's billy goat was a difficult habit to break.

He was almost to the door when a heavily laden luggage cart rolled off the elevator and cut him off. The porter parked it directly in front of the stairs and took up residence next to it. Behind him waddled a well-dressed dame in black, the sloth-like quality of her progress caused, no doubt, by her substantial girth, great array of diamonds, and more than a little self-importance.

"Excuse me," Rudy said, motioning toward the stairs. "If I might get—"

The porter ignored him and proceeded to open the top train case for the lady to inspect. Rudy watched as she closed that one and indicated a need to plough through the checkered Louis Vuitton at the bottom of the stack. Rudy muttered an oath that would have brought color to her cheeks. His limited time now frittered away by the search and his own petty bid to stick it to Shoe, he turned and headed for his meeting.

Emerson, approaching from the opposite direction, quickly intercepted him and greeted him cordially. They set right to business at a quiet table away from the conservatory door.

"Are you staying here?" Emerson asked.

"The Calvert."

"Excellent choice. I suspect you won't be there long. This case is not that difficult for someone of your caliber." Emerson opened the briefcase at his feet, withdrew a sheet of paper, and handed it to him.

It was a nondisclosure form. That told Rudy two things. The parties involved had money, and he was about to get paid a hefty sum. He could be bought. Emerson proffered a pen and he signed it without question.

Emerson next handed him several pictures.

"Oh, dear God," Rudy said, handing them right back. "Yes, a most heinous murder. Who's the deceased and who do you think did it?"

"There's no guesswork here, Mr. Becker. The perpetrator is someone quite familiar with the town but not originally from Nevis. Someone with a public persona but not a terribly high profile. *A rising star,* if you will. We have no doubt."

"*We?* And who would that be?"

"You don't need to know the *who* to do your job. I'm going to give you the name of the killer. All you have to do is work your way backwards."

Rudy scratched an itch on his cheek that wasn't really there. He'd heard some strange ones, but this outdid them. "I can respect that, but if you know who did it, why hire someone at all? Take it to the police. That is their function. They'll apprehend the man . . . I am assuming it's a man . . ."

"And you would be correct."

"They'll immediately nab the scoundrel and he won't be able to harm anyone else."

Emerson raised a finger to stop him. "Because *knowing* and *proving* are two different things."

Rudy nodded. "Sounds straightforward enough." He pulled out a pen and reporter's pad. "Can I get some names here?"

"Tatum Shoemaker."

Rudy blinked several times. "Begging your pardon?"

"I believe you heard me right. An acquaintance of yours who now resides in the District."

"Shoe? *Shoe* Tatum Shoemaker?" Rudy realized his mouth was gaping. He closed it and continued staring at Emerson as if he'd just told him God had died. "We have a healthy professional rivalry, but, but, but . . ." He stopped a moment to consider it. "He scarcely strikes me as the type. An accusation of this magnitude, uh . . . you must have *some* evidence?"

"He was romantically involved with the victim."

Shoe was cheating on Miss Fannie? Rudy took quick inventory. No, he had no recall of Shoemaker recently being linked with someone else. In fact, his perpetual abstinence from the opposite sex had invited intense gossip and made him somewhat of a joke among some of the young journos . . . Rudy shook his head to get back on track. "And the victim?" he asked, picking up his fountain pen.

"Wilhelmina Weathersby."

Rudy's pen stopped its scratching. He looked quickly at Emerson and then over his shoulder, out the door, and across the hall to the stairs. "*Weathersby*," he repeated in a flat voice. "I'm sorry," he said, frowning at Emerson. "I should be able to put this in some sort of context, but at the moment, I, uh . . ." He leapt to his feet. "Excuse me . . . pictures . . . corned beef . . ." He bolted out into the grand entranceway, located the lavatory, locked himself in, and promptly vomited.

When the retching stopped, he eased away from the commode, sat down on his buttocks, and leaned against the cool wall of the water closet. When was their last communication? Two days ago? Yes, that would have been the day before he was stranded in Clinton. She had sent word that she would meet him in the evening down on the promenade. The same day as Emerson's murder case. Hideous images of the brutalized corpse came roaring back at him. He vomited again.

Oh, Mena.

He babbled as he tried to sort out an explosion of thoughts and emotions raging inside. He recalled their last meeting: she arriving in Nevis and he heading to Washington—a brief touch of the hands, a fleeting smile at the bottom of the train stairs. How he had wanted to stay with her! He couldn't handle any more. He visualized walking out of the hotel and leaving Emerson to handle the mess. Money had yet to change hands. Rudy owed him nothing. Who needed money if he couldn't spend it on Mena?

Mena cheating on him—it made no sense. There was nothing they didn't know about each other. They were running from her father together. Another day and they would have been out from under that overbearing tyrant's thumb. *Shadow of a doubt. Shadow of a doubt.* Powerful men like Emerson often knew more than they vocalized. He would have to put up or shut up.

He flipped on the gold faucet and splashed his face with water. The icy shock made him gasp. He watched his tears drip into the sink and mix with the water from the tap and wondered why the color hadn't changed to the red of a wounded heart or the black of his bleak, hopeless future without Mena.

He took several long, slow breaths. With control came clarity. If there was one thing he had learned as a journalist, it was to follow the money. Without a doubt, the money Emerson was waving at him belonged to Mena's father. It was Weathersby's solution to everything.

With him ever meddling during her life, it would be surprising for him to suddenly stop. Maybe Benedict Weathersby hadn't harmed her physically, but he shouldered some responsibility for her death, driving her into unsafe circumstances she would not have otherwise chosen.

But Shoemaker . . . wrapping his head around Shoemaker was more difficult. Shoe was a go-get-'em, no-nonsense reporter. Was stealing Mena away an act of revenge? Payback for the times Rudy had managed to beat him to a story? Maybe the two had met somewhere along the way, but so what? It didn't necessarily mean romance. If Mena spurned Shoe's advances—and he was sure she would have—did things tragically spin out of control? He pictured Fannie Byrne. Did she know what Shoemaker was capable of? Or was she the next victim of a sick, sick mind?

There was a rap on the door.

"Yes. A moment." In that instant his mind was made. He couldn't walk away from this. And really, where in this universe could he possibly flee and have peace of mind? No, he would take Weathersby's money and determine what happened. If Tatum Shoemaker was that butcher, Rudy would make sure he answered for his crime. And if the legal system couldn't give Mena the justice she deserved, well, then, he would handle it himself.

He wiped his face and returned to Emerson. For the first time in their acquaintance, Rudy saw emotion in the lawyer's face—not stained cheeks or tears, but a strained look as if struggling to maintain control. Rudy wondered how well he had known Mena.

"Sorry, Mr. Becker. I won't be showing them again. But I thought you should know what we are dealing with. A most deranged, enraged individual."

Rudy nodded. "How do you know that Shoemaker is your man?"

"We have documentation of their meeting on numerous occasions." Emerson went back into his rich leather briefcase. "Hotel registries, a consistent physical description. It's all here." He handed him an envelope.

Rudy folded the documentation in half and slid it into a jacket pocket. He couldn't handle more *documentation* at the moment. "So, you had someone following her?"

Emerson nodded but offered nothing else.

Well, the investigator was a stinker, Rudy thought. *He* himself and Mena had met dozens of times on the sly. Why weren't they considering him a suspect? "What necessitated the surveillance? Past suitors a problem? She stole something of a delicate nature? You wanted it back without a commotion?"

"Oh, nothing of an illegal sort. It's a personal issue that's none of your business."

"Well, you're certainly not giving much to go on . . ." One look at Emerson's tight expression told Rudy it would be fruitless to press the issue. He let it go for the moment. "What else can you tell me about the crime scene? Who's the other victim? But please, I don't think I can handle any more pictures. Any witness accounts? Reports of anything strange before or after the crime?"

"Even with sizeable assets at our disposal, the police have provided little in the way of leads. There may have been two witnesses, although they are not officially acknowledging that. The little information we have originated with one departmental source we cultivated early on. That source has dried up, spooked by something or someone. As we feared, politics have entered the picture. And politics and money make strange but powerful bedfellows. Our mole won't risk discovery by verifying anything else for us."

"What *did* they give you?"

"One witness. Muriel Fitzhugh down on the wharf. Her husband died back in the summer and she's trying to keep their business afloat. Literally. Lost her house and now lives on their fishing boat, the *Sunrise Pelican*. She initially told police she heard some scuffling and screaming. Then changed her mind and said it was just some of the religious pilgrims getting overexuberant."

Rudy jotted it down and underlined the name twice. "All right. I'll start there. And the other victim? A young male?"

"Correct. They found a bicycle and a Western Union hatband at the scene. They feel certain the second victim was a delivery boy. No name, but a townie. It shouldn't be too hard to nose around and find out who's missing a kid."

"Excellent," Rudy said, adding that information below Muriel Fitzhugh's name and putting the number *2* in a circle in front of it. "Western Union logs everything that comes in and goes out. Anything else?"

He glanced up from his writing pad. Emerson was gazing out the large conservatory windows toward the beach. If Rudy were to guess, he supposed Emerson was seeing something much more distant and different than the gray undulating waters of the Chesapeake Bay. "Anything else, Mr. Emerson?"

Emerson turned sad, thoughtful eyes on him. "Unfortunately, no."

Where can I find you if I have further questions?"

"I'll be here at the Bayside for the next week. Meet me here a week from today. If you've made significant progress before then . . ."

Rudy agreed and got up to leave. Emerson's expression had shifted to something harder, less wistful. "Sorry, did I miss something?" Rudy asked.

"When we first spoke, I was under the impression that greed was your motivation in taking the case. Yet you haven't broached the subject of payment. Don't you want to know what I'm offering in compensation? Or have I misjudged you?"

"Expensive suit, latest Italian shoes, and a valise I'd value at more than the sum total of my First National bank account. I'd venture to say that you're the agent of someone who could buy and sell you many more times over. And their motivation in solving the case is no doubt deeply personal. I'm sure the payment is more than sufficient. Would you prefer that I negotiate?" He sat again.

Emerson laughed wryly. "That would be out of the question. But I've done business long enough to know that a man's motivations are as important as what he promises to do."

"The fact that you're here talking to me tells me that you haven't been able to dig up any dirt on me, so why don't we just leave it as, my motives are pure. The satisfaction of nailing an individual so depraved will more than outweigh what you could offer me."

Emerson nodded but Rudy sensed he was still trying to figure him out. "I've given you a thousand dollars in that information packet. Twice that much more when you've brought me what I've asked for."

Rudy nodded. No amount of money could ever compensate him. Justice, that's what he yenned for. They parted with a handshake and a *good day*. It sounded hollow and inappropriate considering the circumstances, but sometimes etiquette was all one had.

As he exited the conservatory, Rudy's eyes momentarily drifted to the stairs before he snapped them away. He fled the building, pushing his way through the rich woman's entourage as they packed her belongings into her car. She sat contentedly in the rear seat of an elegant dark green touring car, blocking the passage of a line of irate drivers idling cars in the driveway.

Rudy managed to reach the street before tears began streaming down his face, puddling at the corners of his lips and continuing down around his sharp chin. His hand went to his heaving chest and found Emerson's envelope pressed there. If he found Emerson's reconnaissance to be accurate, he would nail Shoemaker's carcass to the nearest buoy.

Chapter Thirteen
Fitting in a Little Softball

Shoe eased into the *Evening Star* building from the alley. The place was eerily quiet, the printing press silent, the linotyper absent. It was as if someone or something had throttled the life out of the place and left behind a corpse. He shook away the thought as the gruesome images in Emerson's pictures flooded his brain. He gently closed the door. The last thing he needed right now was an assignment to pull him off his investigation. He headed toward the massive shelves housing the huge rolls of newsprint.

"Don't think I haven't noticed."

Shoe froze, his head slowly rotating toward Tanner's voice. Relief washed over him as he realized it was booming from the other end of the building, and it didn't seem to be moving his way.

He moved to the paper supply and stood before the huge rolls, considering how best to proceed. He didn't need a whole roll—just enough to plot out and connect his leads. He tilted one sideways and attempted to roll it away from the others, but he quickly righted it again when it almost toppled over on his foot. How on earth did Perkins move these unwieldy things? His gaze roved the nearby shelves searching for inspiration and fell on sheets of newsprint already cut and stacked. He abandoned the rolls for the stack, which upon examination he found to be pages of comic strips: *Gasoline Alley, Buster Brown,* and others. He hated to steal Perkins' work and get him fired, but then the printing error caught his eye: a thick black line running the length of the Buster Brown strip that cut bodies in half and obliterated dialogue bubbles. No way the *Star* would release a mess like this.

"Perkins!"

Holy hell. Tanner again, only this time he was coming Shoe's way and there was nowhere to hide. Shoe would look rather foolish if Tanner discovered him trying to blend in with the supplies. He came out from behind the printer and waited as Tanner approached from the front of the press room.

"Shoe!" Tanner said, all smiles. "Just the face I was hoping to see today. Wasn't quite sure how to get in touch with you now that you're back. Too bad you weren't here a minute earlier. Just finished upfront doling out plum assignments to the chosen few. Not to worry, though. I saved you a humdinger." He shoved a piece of paper at him.

Shoe read through the chicken scratching. "Calvert Cliffs? Way down on the peninsula?" He checked Tanner's expression for amusement. Surely he wouldn't play him this way.

"That's the perfect story for you," Tanner said, reading his mind. "I know you're probably chomping at the bit for something more challenging, but this story requires a little finesse. I need someone I can trust who won't go stumbling in and cause a commotion. Know what I mean? It'll be an exclusive and I'll give you the byline."

It was the crap assignment nobody else wanted. "Just so I have it right . . . you want me to go down and interview this fellow from the National Museum about the fossils in the cliffs. 'Zat right?"

"You got it!" Tanner motioned for Shoe to follow him into his office. "How much do you know about the University of Chicago's Oriental Institute?"

"Absolutely nothing. Should I?"

"No, not really," Tanner said, taking a seat at his desk. "It was founded by an archaeologist named James Henry Breasted, and he had a close associate, Nicholas Darby. Breasted eventually headed east to make a name for himself in Mesopotamia and Egypt. Interesting fellow, hobnobbed with the likes of Gertrude Bell and T.E. Lawrence. Darby stayed local—relatively speaking—and labored in relative obscurity out in the American Southwest. He's managed to attach himself to the National Museum in Washington, D.C., and they're studying marine deposits down at the cliffs. He contacted me late last week about doing a story. He was a bit circumspect about what they were finding, but adamant that it was earth-shakingly important."

"A fame whore," Shoe said, still reeling from the notion that Tanner would think he was the least bit interested in this claptrap.

"For sure. I imagine it's hard to hear about peers like Howard Carter and his impressive Egyptian discoveries in the Valley of the Kings and not covet the attention." He stopped to light a stogie. "Don't get me wrong, Shoe, I don't think this is anywhere near as exciting as King Tut's tomb, but the time is ripe for a story like this. Go down and get the basics. Spin a bunch of bones in Southern Maryland into something more glamorous than Lawrence of Arabia, and the story will get picked up all over the place. It'll be good for everybody."

"Bones, big egos, and T.E. Lawrence. Got it! I'll head out today and nail down Darby's story. Be back before nightfall." Shoe pointed out the window. "Keys still in the flivver?"

Tanner shook his head. "Hoof it down to the pier and take the mini-train up the boardwalk to the boats for hire. If you hit the ladies for hire, come back a ways. Ask for the Captain. He's berthed around warehouse 20. He'll take care of you."

As Shoe turned away, Tanner grabbed his sleeve. "Don't rush into something stupid. Nobody else's boat, hear? And don't even look at that Hanner Mackall fellow—he's the *Sea Kingdom,* and a bad one. It's a rough crowd down there on a good day, Shoe. And with that lunatic running around . . ."

Shoe left Tanner in his office humming "April Showers" and searching for an ashtray. Obviously he was more intent on hitching a ride on the coattails of a Pulitzer nominee than getting a hard-hitting news story in on a short deadline. That was okay. Tanner's assignment wasn't the albatross he thought it would be but instead might be just the softball assignment he needed and an excellent cover for snooping around. He'd stretch it out, put on a big show for Tanner. As for Mackall, as long as the cabbage wasn't coming out of Shoe's pockets, he wasn't interested in negotiating the best boat fare to the cliffs.

He swiped a stack of newsprint as he left.

Chapter Fourteen
Calvert Cliffs

Shoe wasn't whistling showtunes, but there was a spring in his step as he made for the dock. He was born to be an investigative journalist. How did he know this? By the adrenaline rush he got whenever he came out from behind the desk. Now the private-eye thing, it was okay, and it did allow him to be his own man. Well, maybe not, he thought, visualizing the dunning notices spilling out of Fannie's in-box. Oh, poppycock, if he were being totally honest, he had taken on some real crappy cases just to stay afloat. It suddenly dawned on him there might be few pros to sleuthing. He hit the waterfront seriously contemplating a career change.

The Baltimore-based *Chessie Belle* had berthed and the last of the passengers were making their way down the gangplank of the large white steamboat. He watched a steady stream of cargo begin rolling out of its stowage. There was an interesting, happy bustle in the air, and he didn't think it was just him projecting his good mood on the world. There were evergreen wreaths and bows everywhere, even the surrounding businesses adorned with red bows on their doors. It brought to mind his promise to take Fannie to her Christmas tree lighting in Washington. He rarely reneged on a promise, but so far nothing was breaking . . .

The wharf ran some five hundred feet. The amusement park tram was the easiest way to travel it. He verified that it was still running so late in the season—less frequently, but reliably, he was assured—bought a nickel ticket, and leaned up against a nearby light post to wait.

He didn't wait long, which was swell, because his dogs were getting cold and were cramping. The little red and white train— festooned with more red and green Christmas cheer—looped around the main pier and chugged his way. He waved at the conductor, who slowed down long enough for him to grab a pole and swing onto the rear bench. He tipped his hat to the family of three in the front seat and began searching for the Captain and warehouse 20.

The tram moved at a fair clip but slowly enough for him to check the multitude of piers jutting out into the dark, rolling waters. The area near the steamboat landing was all about warehouses—all numbered but maddeningly out of numerical sequence. They were nothing fancy. A metal roof and thick walls sturdy enough to withstand the occasional nor'easter sufficed. Away and south moored the commercial fishing fleet—dozens of boats bobbing to the rhythm of the bay's ancient song, sails and flags floating in the breeze. Most of the big boats were owned by oystermen and crabbers: graceful skipjacks; and white, low in the water, solidly built bugeyes and deadrises. A few others were probably owned by discreet bootleggers running something of value along the coast.

In the distance, Shoe noted the respectable businesses giving way to a stretch of what could only be described as decrepit dives of the sin-and-skin variety. Flammable wood shingles replaced sheet metal roofs, and shanty-like buildings of questionable integrity replaced the earlier solid structures. Most certainly the tram would make a flip-flop before entering there, but to be on the safe side, he pulled the yellow bell-cord early and bailed out when the tram stopped. The family must have been of like mind and followed suit.

He retraced the tram's journey, passing up the first few boats, which seemed too insignificant to be piloted by someone with the honorific *The Captain*. He wasn't a fan of water travel, but he did know that the bigger the vessel, the smoother the ride. He scanned the moored boats, chose the biggest oyster boat there, and made his way down its short pier. Even if it wasn't the Captain's, they could direct him further.

The buckeyes and the skipjacks, with their sleek lines and stately sails and rigging, were a pretty and noble sight to behold, but this vessel was neither. It was a flat-bottomed Chesapeake Bay deadrise, well designed for navigating the shallow coast, an old workhorse in dire need of a wire brushing and a new coat of paint.

When he had closed half the distance to the boat, Shoe cut a wide path around a shaggy brown dog—cuffing behind his ear with his back foot—and his apparent owner, a hard-bitten, shifty type sorting fishing tackle from another deadrise. The man had obviously been watching him, for when he drew even, the man asked without looking up, "Boat for hire?"

About as much as I need a knife in the gut and the loss of my wallet. Apparently, the seedy side of town didn't need a dark alley from which to operate. Still, Shoe hesitated. "You the Captain?"

The fisherman tipped his head toward the end of the pier. "*Parker's Bet*, last one down. I'll beat his price, though. *Sea Kingdom's* a better boat." The dog scrambled up and wagged his tail invitingly.

Sea Kingdom? Tanner's admonition came flooding back. *Well met, Hanner Mackall!* Shoe's gaze shifted to *Parker's Bet*. "Thanks, but I've already paid." He pushed on with the distinct feeling that the man was still studying him.

There was no activity on the boat. *Swell.* He wondered if the grifter knew the vessel was empty. The thought of running a gauntlet back past him needled Shoe to climb aboard. "Captain?" he called as he put a hand on the boat railing.

A voice floated up from somewhere in the boat. "Be with ya shortly." A minute later a white-haired curmudgeon popped up in the forward cabin and came aft. His face was stern like granite and looked as if the relentless sea had chiseled its features.

"Good day, sir. I'm Tate Shoemaker from the *Evening Star*. Riley Tanner said you could take me down to the cliffs. I need to talk to a man named Darby. He's conducting a dig—"

The Captain jerked a thumb toward his boat. "Yep. Get on."

Shoe scrambled in and found a secure place to stand among the baited traps, tubs, and whatnot. After several minutes of watching the Captain putter about, he asked, "Are we getting along soon?"

"Just making sure nobody else is coming."

Shoe saw Hanner still loitering at the end of the slip. He wasn't looking their way, but he seemed tense and hyperaware, like a big cat about to spring. "I'm on a tight deadline. The newspaper will pay you double to make it just me."

"You don't have to worry about him," the Captain said, pulling a loop of bull rope free of one of the pier posts and tossing it into the front of the boat. He pushed the boat free of the pier. "Hanner Mackall does plenty good. He'll catch another one soon."

Shoe shifted his gaze as Hanner turned his way. "What's the story on him?"

"Works as hard as anybody else. Been here forever. Never heard of Moll Mackall Dyer?"

"No, can't say I have. I'm not from here. Philly-born and raised."

"Like I said, he's a Mackall. Family's been here forever." The Captain was silent a moment, and then he added, "Wouldn't trust him with my ex-wife's mother-in-law. But that doesn't mean he doesn't have a place here."

Shoe supposed the early-bird and catching-the-worm thing applied to fish as well, but Mackall didn't appear too busy. "And that would be doing what, exactly?"

The Captain headed for the stern. "Best sit down. Water's rough today."

Shoe found a small wooden bench and sat down portside. The water was choppy from a stiff wind that was coming in from the east, bringing with it a cold breeze that cut straight through his jacket. He pulled out the assignment sheet Tanner had given him. It fleshed out Nicholas Darby as a rather colorful figure in what he and his journo friends referred to as the rocks-and-crocks movement. Like many of his peers, Darby was an egotistical windbag. The international hubbub over Carter's discovery of King Tut's tomb in the Valley of the Kings must have been like a harpoon to the heart.

A sudden swell sent the front end of the boat upward and Shoe slid halfway off his seat. He clutched the boat side for the next few minutes until the ride smoothed out. When the boat ceased its bouncing and smacking against the water, he relaxed his grip and put Tanner's notes away. He got the assignment: feed the ego, record a few jaw-dropping examples of what Darby was unearthing—if that was even possible with old bones—and romanticize the hell out of it. Readers would lap it up.

The once-flat, tree-lined shore gradually rose to bare, impressive cliffs. There was also a subtle change in the boat's course. For a time, the Captain had been running parallel to the shore, but now he angled his craft landward. In the distance, Shoe thought he could see the faint outline of a long pier. As they drew closer, specks that had been dark spots on the thin strip of beach became scurrying workers, tents, and all sorts and sizes of machinery. Several small boats and a sizeable barge were moored at the dock. This was no fly-by-night operation.

Shoe made the Captain promise to stay put at the dock and took off to find Darby. He needn't have worried about identifying anyone. Two steps off the pier he was intercepted by two serious fellows twice his size who desired conversation with him.

"Shoemaker, *Evening Star?*" one of them asked, looking him up and down. For a second, Shoe thought he might frisk him.

"Yes, Tatum Shoemaker." Shoe extended a hand, which was ignored. "I'm looking for Nicholas Darby."

"And so, you have found him, Mr. Shoemaker," said a third man, pushing his way between the greeting party. Dressed neatly in a khaki uniform with immaculate knee- high leather boots, he looked as if he'd momentarily stepped away from an African safari. He offered a chubby, calloused hand. Shoe shook it as he struggled to keep his eyes off the stylish khaki hat. "Nicholas Darby. I've been expecting you."

Darby's gaze was keen and his grip vise-like. In the expression was a decision and in the grip a warning: he didn't trust Shoe, and transgressors would be pursued until the heavens fell into the sea. Shoe wondered who was so deep into his business that he was able to give Darby a heads-up about his visit. And quickly at that! Certainly not Tanner. Once he gave out a story, you were on your own.

Darby was already on the move, heading toward the long tents at the base of the sheer cliff. Shoe wondered if he'd be chasing him throughout the interview. He hurried to catch up.

"I'm afraid I can only give you half an hour," Darby said over his shoulder. "We're very busy today. How about we start with me?"

Of course. Shoe flipped open his notebook and scurried after, letting the man drone on a bit about his laurels before he nudged him into the particulars of the Calvert dig. "How far do the deposits go?"

"Twelve miles north," Darby said, pointing to his right, "and about the same the other way. And if you don't want to traverse that, there's up there," he said, looking up the cliffside. "It rises a hundred feet in some places. Picture warm seas and cypress swamps covering this whole area." He waved his hand like a magic wand that could make it so. "Eventually, the seas recede, leaving Calvert Cliffs behind. Chockablock with plant, mammal, and marine fossils. This is the only section of the cliffs with a beach wide enough to support all these people and equipment. Elsewhere we would be traipsing about in waders from dawn to dusk."

Darby was off again. He ducked under a rope and approached several tents pitched right up against the cliff formation. "You can see the layers quite clearly here. The earliest sediment—on the bottom, of course— is blue clay. And then about a quarter of the way up it changes to yellow sand and clay. Whales, porpoises, even a few rhinoceros, and mastodons. Nothing complete, mind you, but the diversity and sheer volume is staggering—the largest fossil deposit on the East Coast." He let out a contented sigh.

Shoe ran his hand across the clay and immediately jerked it back. The slice running across the tip of his finger was sharp and clean. And a bleeder. He fumbled in his pocket for his handkerchief.

Darby offered no assistance in wrapping it. Instead, he presented the backs of his hands, which were covered in old scars and healing cuts. "Consider yourself one of us." He pulled a small pick out of one of his oversized coat pockets and with a few taps on the rock plucked a dark, penny–sized tooth out of the rise and dropped it into Shoe's good hand. "Shark tooth—just as damaging in death as in life."

"How old, Darby?"

"Middle Miocene, but that won't mean much to your readers. Tell 'em it's ten million years old. Keep it," he said when Shoe tried to give it back. "Nobody's going to miss a tooth. They're everywhere. Come on, and I'll show you what we won't be giving away."

Shoe slid the tooth into the same pocket as his notes. A tooth and a scar—two souvenirs in one trip. Lucky him.

Darby took him into a long green tent—postwar Army surplus, no doubt—pitched flush against the cliff. Inside, workers were nose to wall, working like dentists with small picks and other fine instruments to uncover something shoulder high on the rock wall. No common shark teeth, Shoe guessed.

"Like I said, shark teeth are plentiful," Darby said. "The locals say you can come out here after a good nor'easter and fill up a bucket. But the bigger specimens? Elusive . . . until now." He walked up behind a worker, who began to move out of his way. Darby stayed him with a hand on the shoulder. "Stay put, Bradley. Just want to show us off a bit. Take a guess, Mr. Shoemaker," he said, motioning to the area the worker had been picking.

Shoe peered over the worker's shoulder at the rock-like protrusions stretching about twenty feet from left to right. "School of porpoises?"

Darby laughed. "Not a bad guess, actually. What would you say if I told you this was a single mammal? And if it's what we think it is, that it's going to rock the scientific community?"

"Camel?" Shoe said, taking another stab at it. It would be his last. He came to ask questions, not to answer them.

Darby laughed harder, clearly enjoying his little game. "Oh, they're here, all right. The climate was much warmer in these earliest deposits. We have pieces." Darby's look became conspiratorial and he whispered, "It's a mastodon. And we think it's all here. *All* of it."

Shoe studied the fossilized bones again. "How—"

"—do we know it's whole? Experience, son—position, fossils in close proximity, its location high up on the cliff where there's less erosion. And when we prove it, all eyes are going to be on Calvert Cliffs. The name Nicholas Darby will be on the front page of every newspaper that's worth reading. Write us a nice story, son, and you can say you broke it first. Be quick about it. Even the Museum doesn't know the extent of what I've found here. All of that will change when I submit my first formal paper in two weeks. This discovery will change everything. What a spectacular way to ring in the new year."

Shoe ignored the patronizing *son* as his competitive side began to dance. "You're giving me the exclusive here?"

Darby's eyebrows arched. "Of course this is exclusive. Tanner and I have an agreement. Did you think I let every Tom, Dick, and Tanner interrupt my work? Next time bring ham sandwiches," he said, moving toward the tent flap. "We'll sit out on a blanket and watch the sun set."

Shoe scrambled after him. "Oh, no. I'm afraid we're off on the wrong foot here. I wasn't sure you were going to give me so much valuable information *today*. What with you being such an important person. Mr. Tanner made it very clear this was an exclusive." *Just like pigs can fly and their ears make excellent purses.*

In an instant, Darby was back to babbling about how wonderful his world was. Shoe tried to appear engrossed, but truth be told, he had enough information and enough of the man. It was hard to believe no one from the Museum was keeping tabs on what he was doing. Shoe could smell mismanagement in the venture all the way. He gazed out across all the activity and equipment spread out before them and tried to formulate an easy, quick question and a graceful exit.

"One last question, Darby, and then I'll get out of your way. Where's the funding come from for an initiative this size? I would image there's some fair cost. I wouldn't think the National Museum has the budget to underwrite all this."

"Heavens, no! Everything you see here, as well as other worker bees and specialists doing additional study at the Museum annex in Washington, is underwritten by a hefty grant from the Benedict Weathersby Foundation."

"Benedict Weathersby," Shoe repeated. He stopped writing midword. "As in the Newport Weathersbys?"

"None other. I take it you've met?"

Oh, if you only knew the half of it. "No, sir, but maybe one day. Does he, uh, come out here often?"

"Not to my knowledge. Occasionally I hear he's been in town, but it's after the fact. He's supposed to have deep ties to Nevis."

"Seems odd he'd throw money into the project and not come take a look."

Darby drew back and glared. "When you reach a certain eminence in your field, Mr. Shummer—"

"*Shoemaker.*"

"—They let you handle things as you see best, Mr. *Shoemaker.* Two busy men deep in their craft. Being in the newspaper business, I'm sure you've met people like that before. I suppose if he ever came down here, I could free up a little time and give him a grand tour."

Shoe nodded. All this money and no one providing oversight. It was a bit eye opening. *Waste not, want not* was a guiding credo for the Newport crowd, and Weathersby was known for his cutthroat business acumen. Then something else struck him as odd. "I don't see any kind of storage facility here. The barge . . . do you send them right to the Museum?"

"Too time consuming to do it bit by bit. We've got a warehouse on the Nevis waterfront. Number 17. When we get a sizeable load, we freight it by rail to D.C."

"I would guess some of the larger specimens could fetch a hefty sum on the black market."

Darby laughed and gestured back toward the tent they had exited. "It's not like you could hide that mastodon in your pocket and be off with it. And if you wanted to steal something smaller, you'd have to be sharp enough to know your bones. An inside man, a big boat, and lots of unsupervised time here, that's what it would take. And none of that is remotely possible with the security measures I've instituted. I've personally cleared every one of these workers, and as you experienced earlier, nobody sets foot off that pier without being challenged and sorted: authorized individuals sent this way, lookie-loos directed outside our roped-off area. No, we're a Fort Knox in miniature."

Until now, Shoe had assumed everyone was connected to the dig, but south of the pier he saw a scattering of what looked like townsfolk—pant legs rolled up as they waded through the shallow water holding buckets. Another few were positioned on the far side of the security rope quietly watching the dig. Among them? Rudy Becker. Tailing him, no doubt. If he didn't detest the man so much, Shoe would have had his own laugh. Did he really think Shoe was hot on the trail of some clue related to the Weathersby murder? Shoe watched as Rudy realized Shoe had made him. He left the rope and tried to blend in with a family saving their beach pickings in a silver bucket.

"The pier isn't yours?" Shoe asked, seeing a boat on the opposite side of the pier discharging more people with more buckets. And if Shoe wasn't mistaken, it was Hanner Mackall on the bow.

Darby looked that way. "If it was, they'd all be gone."

"Does Hanner Mackall work for you?"

"Hanner Mackall? Don't know the name." Darby clapped Shoe on the back as if they were chums and gently shook him several times. "Think you have enough?"

"Certainly, Mr. Darby. Thank you, and sorry for keeping you so long."

"Quite all right, son. You tell your Mr. Tanner I'm expecting good things." Darby began to walk away and then turned suddenly. "D-a-r-b-y, right?"

Shoe laughed. "Got it!"

And then Shoe crossed the beach to find out why Rudy had suddenly developed an interest in paleontology.

Chapter Fifteen
Mirror Image

Shoe stayed well above the high-water mark so Rudy couldn't keep track of him without looking obvious. When he had drawn close enough to touch his back, he shouted, "Rudy Becker! Were you looking for me?"

Rudy whirled around. "Shoemaker! Monkey's aunt! What brings you to the cliffs?"

"Why are you following me?" Shoe asked.

Rudy's eyebrows arched liked a drawbridge rising to let an ocean vessel sail through. "Following you? Your editor friend, Tanner, gave me something to do down here."

"He did nothing of the sort. He would have told me."

Rudy shrugged. "What can I say?"

"Start by telling me what story he gave you."

"And have you scoop me? Sorry, bud." Rudy checked the dock and said, "Want to share a ride back?" He began walking.

"Let's cut out this cat-and-mouse stuff. I know Emerson paid you a visit."

Rudy ignored him, climbed the pier, spoke a few quiet words to Hanner Mackall, and hopped into the bobbing craft. "In or out?" Rudy asked.

Shoe hesitated. The Captain had gamely stayed put while Shoe conducted his interview, and he was watching him now from the deck of his boat. How would he react to being stiffed? His services might be needed again. Mackall was also watching, as creepy as before, his expression unreadable. And then there was Rudy, hands on his hips, smiling like Louis Carroll's Cheshire cat.

Uh uh. Becker wasn't getting off so easy. Shoe thanked the Captain for his time and palmed him a silver dollar. "I'm coming," he shouted at Mackall, and put a foot into the vessel just as Mackall pushed away from the dock. With one foot on the dock and one in the boat, Shoe tottered precariously.

In two quick steps Mackall had him by the arm and yanked him into the boat. "Better watch where you step next time," he muttered, and headed starboard. He gave the ship's enormous brass bell a hard clang as he passed and continued about his business.

Shoe headed aft. His groin muscles were screaming for attention and he suspected he'd split a seam in his trousers. Mackall was at the wheel in the cabin, where he'd probably remain throughout the trip, as the Captain had. That was good, because Shoe wasn't sure whether Mackall had just admonished—somehow, the tone was all wrong—or threatened him.

Rudy had already staked out the short bench near the cabin door. It would keep him out of the wind and away from Shoe; the only other seats were on the long bench running down the portside of the craft. Shoe moved forward and latched onto the doorframe opposite Rudy's perch. "Yeah, you know, *Emerson*. Bottomless pockets. Don't play coy." As soon as the name was out of his mouth, Shoe regretted mentioning Emerson. Not because of Rudy. He was sure they were both investigating Mena's murder at the solicitor's request. No, it was the boatman's eavesdropping. Shoe shot a glance at Mackall. He seemed to be engrossed in reading gauges and logging information.

Rudy maintained an unruffled air. "Big bucks, you say? I should look him up. He in Nevis?"

"If he's retained you, you do realize you've lost half a day following me to the cliffs? I'm on assignment for Riley Tanner. If you're so tuned in, you should know that. When we dock, I don't want to see or hear you anymore. Got it?"

"That include that little chickadee been decorating your arm?"

Shoe pictured a quick knuckle sandwich in the middle of Rudy's smirking mug. It wouldn't be the first time that Rudy had horned in, nor the first time he'd rubbed it in either. A solid punch invited an overnight in the hoosegow, though, and Shoe couldn't afford the downtime. "You chasing my tail tells me you've got zip. Wise up, sucker."

"Whatever you say."

Shoe glared at him for a moment, but all he got in return was that famous Rudy Becker grin that charmed the ladies and set all their boyfriends on edge. He took a seat in the aft and watched the cliffs dwindle and the tree line build.

Apparently unable to forego vanity for even a moment, Rudy got up and began checking his reflection in a small mirror that Mackall had hung on the outside of the rear wall of the cabin, turning his head to and fro as he admired his silhouette. "Do you ever wonder why our paths seem to constantly be crossing?" he asked, still looking at himself.

Shoe had no idea where this was going. He took it at face value and laughed. "Because you're too lazy to pick up your own leads? It's much easier to follow successful people like me around and poach a little around the edges."

"While that method of business can be a very successful one, you're so far off base you need to reassess how smart you really are. Come over here," he said, talking to Shoe's reflection. He turned around when Shoe balked. "Seriously," he said.

Shoe joined him.

"Here, here, and here," Rudy said as he touched his eyes, mouth, and chin on the mirror's surface. "Doesn't ring any bells?" He was smirking.

Shoe studied the features, all handsome, and shrugged. "Just a cuckoo. Get to your point."

Rudy held up a finger, commanding him to wait. Then he reached out and touched those same features in Shoe's reflection.

Shoe's eyes flitted from one face to the other. Same bedroom eyes. Same broad mouth. Same dimpled chin.

"No wonder people confuse us. I would say 100 percent Dad, wouldn't you?"

Shoe turned and looked Rudy hard in the face. It was as if he had never *really* looked at him before and it sucked the air right out of him. "No. Can't be . . ."

"Certainly *can,* and *is. Brothers.* Welcome to the family," Rudy said, slapping him on the back. His point made, he sat back down on his bench.

Running his hand across his face, Shoe considered the horrid thought. "Uh uh. Not buying it for a minute, Becker. What's your angle?"

"No angle. I hate to be the one to tell you that your—*our*—father was a philanderer, but, well, facts are facts. I am an illegitimate son, with an official birth certificate to prove it."

Shoe should have decked him, but somehow, deep within, childhood memories were surfacing and merging. He'd always questioned whether his father was a faithful husband. Too many unexplained absences. Too many parental arguments. Although his mother never discussed her worries, she often seemed put out by her spouse. "Your mother, do I know her?"

Rudy shook his head. "And no need to draw her into this. She said she learned of your father's marital status after the fact, and I believe her. She was a lovely, saintly woman, and it—no, in answer your question."

Shoe nodded. "W-w-why? Where . . ."

Rudy shrugged. "I don't question why. The *where* is simple enough. I was born in Baltimore, and grew up in Chester, Pennsylvania, a skip and a jump from you in Philadelphia."

Shoe dropped down like a rock next to him. "Of all the people. . ."

"Yeah, kicker, isn't it?"

"Yeah, hunky dory." Rudy *S* Becker. The middle initial made sense now.

"Nothing in this life ever makes sense, Shoe."

"This changes nothing."

"Of course not," Rudy said. "I think we can agree that we won't be spending Christmases together, but I thought you should know. What you do with it is your own business." He got up and moved away.

Shoe let him, too busy noodling through Rudy's life-shattering revelation. The top of the Bayland roller coaster could now be seen rising majestically above a waterfront crowded with broad warehouses and marine activity. Thankfully, their time together could now be marked in mere minutes.

Mackall cut the engine and eased the boat back into its berth, gently bumping against the padding on the pylons. Shoe flipped him a coin and disembarked first. He could hear Rudy shuffling closely behind. The man could never seem to pick up his feet. Still fighting the inclination to deck him, Shoe increased his speed. To his chagrin, Rudy did likewise.

"Say, Rudy," Shoe said, turning suddenly. He smacked into the newsman and with an extra little shoulder move sent him tumbling into the water. He waited until Rudy bobbed back to the surface, and when he was sure the man could at least doggy paddle, he yelled, "Man overboard. We need help!"

Apparently, falling off the pier was nothing to get excited about. Hanner Mackall calmly pushed him out of the way, extended a fishing pole to Rudy as he thrashed about, and began pulling him toward several watermen who were on their hands and knees waiting to pull him out.

"Put some handrails up here," Shoe admonished. "This could have been a grand catastrophe." Actually, it couldn't have been grander— Rudy Becker, his half-brother?

The show attracted a small crowd who, by the sound of their laughter and jeers, were enjoying a dandy floundering about in a nice suit. Shoe didn't hang around to gloat but instead pushed his way through and beat tracks. He had a dedicated imbecile to shake and a story to knock out.

Chapter Sixteen
Wrong Guy

Shoe sat alone in Betty's, finishing up breakfast and his exclusive for Tanner. Fannie's mother had the touch: chicken hash, poached eggs, and fresh-baked bread lightly toasted to a delicate shade of brown. Darby, not so much. He was a pompous ass, but Shoe made him likeable for the sake of avoiding litigation. The article was standard newspaper fare and he rolled it out quickly: precocious child rises to prominence against odds that would have crushed a lesser man. Blah, blah, blah.

When he was satisfied that he had it all down, he polished off the eggs and sifted through what, if anything, he had learned from yesterday's jaunt. There was the connection between Darby and the Weathersby clan. Any other day he wouldn't have mulled it over twice. The family was known to be philanthropic. After all, how many mansions could a wealthy family build or round-the-world trips take before they had to start giving piles of money away? He supposed there was a certain satisfaction in helping others and seeing a family name emblazoned across a building of higher learning or a scientific collection. Still, did it have any significance for him and the murder? Weathersby had Nevis roots, so it made sense to throw money this way. At the moment, Shoe couldn't make any more of it than that. He decided to let it dangle a while.

And then there was Hanner Mackall. Something didn't quite measure up. In his experience, there were good eggs that scrambled up light and fluffy, disappointing ones that didn't amount to much of anything when you scooted them around in the pan, and then there were the bad ones—stank from the moment you cracked 'em open and got a good whiff. Mackall was like that. The essence of the man hit you immediately. Rotten through and through, and by far the biggest creeper on the dock. He was certain Mackall had threatened him. Still, that didn't make him a cold-hearted butcher of innocent women and children.

He caught Fannie's eye as she stood behind the diner counter, stacking Danish on a pedestal cake stand. "How much, Fannie?"

She shook her head and placed a clear domed lid back over the pastries. "You know better than that."

"Thanks. Then how about a little more coffee and I'll be out of your hair?"

She came over with the coffee pot. "Learn anything new at the cliffs?"

That he suddenly had a brother—no, *half*-brother—whom he despised more than anyone else he could think of? And a cheater for a dad? He wouldn't be able to contain the venom. "It's still one giant jigsaw," he said instead. "Do you know anything about Hanner Mackall?"

She stopped pouring. "Are you serious? Everybody knows the Mackalls. I know I've told you about Moll Mackall Dyer."

If she had, it sure hadn't stuck. Shoe hated to admit he sometimes tuned her out. "Yes, but I've forgotten the particulars."

She gave him one of those pointed looks of hers. "Oh, there isn't a kid between here and Solomons Island who doesn't know *that* story."

"I'm getting old here, Fannie."

"Moll Mackall Dyer was a colonial witch."

Shoe nodded. She was dead serious. Apparently, her bobbed hair was allowing the winter chill to freeze her brain over. "And?"

"Her self-righteous, god-fearing neighbors accused her of witchcraft. Drove her out of town. She died of exposure in the woods. Fearing a final death curse, the locals banished all the Mackalls and the Dyers. So the families fled into the forest and basically didn't come out again. They're an odd, close bunch who hate anything and anybody religious, keep to themselves, marry each other, and eschew the company of others. They own all that area south of Chaneyville—some pretty big farms and a sawmill. Totally self-sufficient. The kids don't even get schooled in town. They also own a section of the cliffs. If you're thinking of sticking your nose in their business? Don't!"

"*Eschew?*"

"Not just a pretty face, Mr. Shoemaker." She kissed him on the top of his head. "Anything else I can help you with?"

"Yeah, just one question. Did they ever make it to the docks? Own any boats?"

"Sure. Before the railroad came in, everything went by water. But the locals wouldn't fool with them. If they wanted to ship anything, the Mackalls did it themselves. They take tourists down to the cliffs, too. Out-of-towners don't know how crazy they are. Like I said, don't go poking around. They have short handles and long memories."

"No, I got it the first time. I'll leave him be. Just curious, that's all."

After she returned to the counter, Shoe left two bits next to his plate and headed for the wharf. Leads and Jack, they were one and the same, and they'd both turn up at the waterfront.

He paused at the intersection of Bayland and the boardwalk and let a hurried pack of athletic types—matching long-sleeved club shirts, shorts, and tall socks—jog past. His stopping wasn't a matter of indecision; he knew exactly where he was going. In Philly, you never stepped out into the street without looking both ways. Twice. His mother always said the wagon you didn't see was the one that was going to hit you. Anyone who ever tried to cross Chestnut Street in the middle of the afternoon could vouch for that. But what if the danger was behind him? He threw a casual glance over each shoulder, saw nothing. Yep, it was what you didn't see—a demented crazy murderer still at large, and possibly Rudy looking to even the score after his unexpected swim—that would level you. He stepped into the human flow and headed toward the seedy side.

With Fannie's warning still echoing in his ear, he wandered toward the Captain's boat. He desperately wanted another look at Mackall in his element. Best bet was that the boatman was smuggling—maybe liquor, perhaps something else. It was fairly common along the coast and when the activity was plied discreetly, a man made a tidy profit. The Coast Guard wasn't concerned. They went after the big operations. At any rate, Shoe wanted Mackall off his suspect list before he slipped up and antagonized the boatman further. He didn't relish having to watch his back.

The waterfront was a hive of activity this morning—mostly crates and unpacked merchandise coming out of warehouses. He matched the pace of, and hid behind, a large piece of furniture being carted out to one of the boats. Anything that couldn't be procured in town—finer furniture, mail-order clothes, and other necessities—initially came into Nevis by steamboat—the *Chessie Belle* or its sister ship, the *Madison Lady*—and then traveled by local boats to the smaller wharfs along the peninsula. By the looks of what was scribbled across the unfinished back of this piece, the Buckmaster family near Sollars Wharf was getting a brand-new hutch.

Whatever Jack was doing, he didn't appear to be on the dock. Rudy either—hanging out or shadowing him again. Perhaps that was the last of Mr. Becker. It gave Shoe a sense of pride to think he had intimidated him. How often was a journalist able to do that?

Shoe slipped into a narrow passageway between two of the newer warehouses—their barnwood sides still blond and unweathered—and watched Mackall working against the flow of the other workmen as he hauled a series of crates from his boat to a smaller warehouse two doors down.

It was hard to tell whether Hanner Mackall knew he was being surveilled. He stopped several times and leaned up against a lamppost to smoke for a while, but the moment was anything but one of relaxation. He was constantly alert, a wily and cautious one who completed every activity with a narrow-eyed sweep of his surroundings to see who might be watching. It was the wagon-in-the-street admonishment all over again. When Hanner Mackall's focus swept in his direction and remained there, Shoe withdrew a little deeper into the alley until all he could see was Mackall's elbow, and he stayed there until the elbow disappeared again.

Mackall crushed out his smoke underfoot, pulled his collar tighter against the cool breeze coming in off the water, and took off toward the shanties. Shoe gave him a lead and then stepped from the alley.

There was a sudden shuffling of feet behind him. "Rudy," he said, turning. Hands yanked him backwards and down he went—no match for the two men who had jumped him. That's all he saw before they threw a rough cloth bag over his head and dragged him by his arms to the rear of the alley. They seized his legs, hoisted him up in the air, and down again into a farm wagon; the stench of animals and dung was overpowering.

"Be still, Shoemaker, or I'll slice you up nice and even," whispered a voice in his ear.

He felt the pressure of a cold blade against his neck and quit struggling. The voice wasn't Mackall's, but the thought of Mackall sitting nearby with plans to carve him up like an apple was almost enough for him to lose urinary control. He should have followed Fannie's advice and steered clear. He stayed quiet and listened to the muffled conversation going on around him. He got nothing.

The wagon didn't travel far before the smooth ride turned bumpy. That was short too. As he tried to calculate how far out the Mackall farms might be from town, the wagon rolled to a halt. A swift kick of a well-placed boot brought him up quick. They manhandled him out of the wagon bed as if he were a featherbed pillow and tossed him onto the hard ground.

"Oof," he said, feeling his back crack. But then they yanked the bag off his head and that snapped his spine back nicely. He stood up in the middle of a huge field, the furrows covered in dried cornstalks left from the summer's harvest. In the distance, a flock of geese was systematically marching along the rows, gleaning any remaining corn kernels. His captors had chosen well. There wasn't a farmhouse or barn in sight. Before him stood three strapping fellows, all dressed in overalls and scowls. None was Mackall. Who were these people?

The largest of the three—although that was irrelevant considering how big the smallest one was—patted him up and down. He pulled out Shoe's wallet and rifled through it. Surprisingly, he moved past the piddling of cash and pulled out his *Washington Post* credentials.

"Tatum Shoemaker?" he asked, his eyes darting between the

identification and Shoe's face. "You got a nickname?"

"Everyone calls me *Shoe*."

"Shoe?" The behemoth frowned and handed the wallet to the others. "Well, *Shoe*. Is it *Rudy* Tatum Shoemaker?"

"Ah," Shoe said. He politely eased his credentials free from the smallest of the oafs and consulted them with a fresh eye. "I see the reason for your consternation. It's a case of mistaken identity, my friends. You have me confused with someone else. *Rudy S. Becker*. That isn't me."

The brawny trio exchanged glances. "Related?"

"Of course not," Shoe said, feeling bold enough now to take back his wallet. "I'm a *Shoemaker*. He's a *Becker*, middle name beginning with *S*. See the difference?"

Behemoth's eyes narrowed. "You know him, though. Where is he?"

Shoe stuffed his wallet back into his pocket. "Not the faintest. Now if you'd be so kind as to drop me off back in town, we can forget this whole unfortunate misunderstanding." He made a move for the cart.

The smallest abductor dumped him on his caboose. "He insulted our sister. You're obviously acquainted. Help us track him down."

"Hey, no need to get violent," Shoe said. He started to get up and then reconsidered the three serious faces staring at him. He stayed put. There would obviously need to be some sort of barter here. "Where did this alleged . . .er, insult occur?"

"Clinton."

"Ah, yes. Never been there myself, but Rudy was speaking of it just the other day. He was very upset, and very sorry for any misunderstanding. I think you can catch him at—"

Shoe put the skids on his blathering and looked at the three brawny farmhands. He detested Rudy, but could he really throw him to these wolves? Yes. Er, no. "Boys, unfortunately, he couldn't stick around to discuss *things*. Pressing business, you see. He's booked passage on the 8:45 a.m. train with connections to New York." He checked his watch. "It's 8:30 now. If you hurry, you might be able to catch him."

The three exchanged glances and sprinted for the wagon. Before Shoe could dust off his backside, they were rumbling down the field road. In seconds more, they were gone.

Shoe looked at his desolate surroundings. He'd been in worse. He set off in the same direction and hoped he'd get to the main road before the farm boys realized he had duped them. He wasn't going to worry about Rudy. A good beatdown might be just the thing to send him packing on the next *Chessie Belle* out.

Rudy slunk along the boardwalk, window-shopping as if he had an unlimited supply of money and insatiable desires. As a matter of fact, everything he owned was in his right-front pants pocket, and the only thing he coveted was revenge. Tatum Shoemaker was dead ahead, creeping along just like him—a gifted snoop but lousy at shaking a tail. The pause-and-check-over-your-shoulder routine was worthless. Had his pronouncement that they were brothers rattled him that much? Actually, Rudy wasn't so much following him as trying to get around him. It didn't matter if Shoe knew Emerson had hired him. Other than sending him for a nasty tumble into the bay, there wasn't much he could do about Rudy working the case. Right now, Rudy was more worried about the rest of his work enterprises. They were strictly off limits; he couldn't afford to lose them.

Emerson might believe Shoe killed Mena, but a far as Rudy was concerned, Shoe was innocent. When Emerson had dropped that little nugget on him, he had jumped all over it in the heat of passion. But after replaying it dozens of times in his head, he realized it wasn't possible. *He* was the only one sneaking around with her. He was the one who had foolishly forged Shoe's name at their rendezvous. Why had Emerson hired them both? Was *he* Shoe's chief murder suspect? He wondered.

He watched Shoe duck into an alleyway. It looked like he wasn't through with the cliffs, the Captain, or Mackall. Maybe all three. Shoe needed to take a hike. Rudy cast about, hoping for some sort of diversion even if he had to initiate it.

He immediately regretted it. A hot flash of fear ran through him, and he watched with horror as a tall, hefty man in overalls disappeared into the alleyway halfway between him and Shoe. He'd never forget a build like that. The Clinton boys had made their way to Nevis.

He began backing up, jiggling doorknobs as he passed each business. They were all closed. He kept going. When he came to the cannery, the last of the group, he edged his way around the corner to the alley between the two buildings.

His legs were quaking, his mind racing. He inhaled deeply and let it out in little puffs of air. There would be no dashing or panicking. That only drew attention. Option *A*: calmly reenter foot traffic on the boardwalk and walk away. Option *B*: chance the back alley. The multitude of witnesses on the boardwalk would deter any violent acts if the boys saw him, but he couldn't camp out there forever. He went with the hopefully deserted alley. He eased his head out into the space and took a peek.

They were there—three of them, and they were otherwise occupied with throwing a struggling body into the back of a wagon. What the hay? Had Arlene entertained all of Nevis? Rudy nixed the alley and took off like a shot down the boardwalk. What had he done to deserve such karma?

Chapter Seventeen
Coping

Opposable or otherwise, thumbs were marvelous creations. As soon as he hit the main road back to Nevis, Shoe used his to hitch back to town. After the rough morning he'd had, he might be a bedraggled sight, but the *T* driver didn't ask any questions, and Shoe resolutely decided it was in his best interest not to fabricate an explanation. When they hit town, he flipped the guy a nickel and went right back to the steamboat landing. Tempus *fidgeted*, and so far, he had nothing for Emerson.

His guardian angel was doing double-time. Not five minutes back on the boardwalk and he found Jack hanging out at a snack shack near the bathhouses just off First Street. Tony's Funnel Cakes was one of a surprising number of attractions still open around the amusement park. Once the cold January winds started, they'd all be shuttered until spring. If Barnum could find a sucker every minute, Tony's was picking up all the spares on a breakfast special of funnel cakes with a generous heap of bananas on top. There was already a line of chatty tourists trying to get their daily filling of grease out of the way early.

At first glance, Shoe almost missed his young protege. Where was the street urchin that had tried to hustle him at their first meeting? Gone, long gone. Shoe found instead a tall and athletically built youth—almost but not yet a man—studying him from his perch on a nearby picnic table. How had Jack sprouted several inches overnight?

"I know that look," Shoe said to him as Jack sauntered over. "How much is it going to cost me? And don't forget, I've been paying your way for the last six months, so go easy on me."

"Not one red cent."

Shoe's eyes widened. "What's wrong with you?"

"Tsk," Jack said, eyes traveling skyward. "Nothing wrong with me. Been snooping around, that's all. The murdered kid is probably Charlie Koenig. A year behind me in school . . . when we both weren't skipping. He had a job as a bicycle messenger for Western Union."

Shoe studied his serious expression. "Sorry. Did you know him?"

"Not well, but I knew who he ran with. He wasn't a bad kid. Certainly didn't deserve to get sliced up on a dock. He's got a brother, Butch, but nobody's seen 'em since the murder. His mother said he's out of town visiting relatives."

"Do you know him well enough to go pay respects?"

"Butch was in my class and we skipped a few times. Besides, it's a small town, remember? I wouldn't be hanging around downtown ten minutes before someone was asking why I wasn't in school. Too many parents."

"And you still didn't listen, did you?"

"God only gives you one set of parents," Jack said, "and I got shortchanged at that."

In all the time they'd been acquainted, it was only the second time Jack had ever alluded to his deceased father, Patrick Byrne. This Charlie Koenig death was hitting him hard, probably resurrecting all kinds of unresolved feelings. What young kid could handle the brutal murder of an acquaintance? Shoe vowed to keep a closer eye on him.

"It's all a cover-up, Shoe. Who is Donaldson?"

"Shh. Not so loud." Shoe ushered him away from Tony's. "The politician? Where'd you get that name?"

Jack rolled his eyes and waited expectantly.

"Okay, I don't need to know, but it'd better be a good source. There are two Donaldsons: Carlton and his son Theodore. Donaldson Senior is an industrialist who can buy and sell the town, and could pretty much have any political office he sets his heart on. Junior was once engaged to Wilhelmina Weathersby. Are you suggesting one of them committed the murders and the police have offered protection?"

"Maybe not the killing part. They were talking about Chief McCall being Donaldson's man and how he's keeping the rest of the police quiet about the murders because it isn't good for business."

"Who is *they*? What business?"

"The police," Jack said, becoming impatient. "I eavesdropped down at the precinct, okay? You don't get any more than that, so drop it. They never said what business—just Donaldson, the murder, and land speculation."

"What about land speculation?"

That's all I got. Jeesh! You think I'm making this up? Cause if you do, I got better things to do." He started to huff off.

"No, wait, Jack!" Shoe said, plucking at the boy's jacket. "You've done great. It's just—this is all hitting me new, and I'm not sure how to process it."

Jack studied his shoes and nodded. "They're bringing Butch Koenig into the station today to make sure he stays quiet." He looked up at Shoe and there was fear in his young eyes. "Does that mean they're going to beat him up?"

Shoe recalled his own beatdown by Chief McCall, who was no

stranger to the art of physical intimidation. "Nah," he said, trying to sound positive. "Don't let your imagination run away with you. That's just stories to keep young'uns in line. Everybody will be polite and agreeable. Any idea where Butch is?"

"They didn't say, but I think I know," Jack said, his eyes now flashing and defiant. He walked over to the bicycle propped against the side of the shack and mounted it. He shoved off without waiting for an answer.

Shoe looked at the second Schwinn. If he took it, he'd never have the nerve to show his face around here again. He glanced up the hill. Jack was already halfway up and pedaling hard from a standing position. Shoe uttered an oath, took a quick look around, and stole the other bike.

By the time Shoe caught up with him, they were at Third Street. He was out of breath and Jack was in a reflective mood, so they pedaled along in silence. As businesses dropped away and the town homes began to thin, backyard garden plots turned into expansive fields. Small white shotgun sharecropper houses began popping up next to the roadway. They were indistinguishable from one another except for the color of the horses corralled in the side yard and the clothes flapping in the breeze on the clotheslines.

The population here was still considerably German, but the enclave was not as insular as it once had been. When Shoe had first come to Nevis, the old boys at the *Evening Star* had clued him in on getting along with some of the older residents. He would get little from the Germans: a terse request to be left alone, or if he was lucky, a nod and a simple comment pointing him in a more fruitful direction.

Jack stopped in front of the house with two brown horses and an empty clothesline. At the rear of the house, laborers were carrying household goods out the back door and stowing them in a wagon. It looked like the Koenig family was pulling up stakes. It was understandable. The memories must be crushing.

Jack approached the door without hesitation and knocked hard. A matronly woman answered. The dead look in her sad brown eyes spoke of unimaginable grief.

"Jack Byrne, ma'am," he said, removing his hat. "I've—my associate, Mr. Shoemaker—we've come to pay our respects. Charlie was a classmate of mine."

Her eyes widened slightly and then began to well up, tears trickling down her cheeks. Her hands clutched at the floral apron that tied tight in the middle and made her look like two floral sacks of potatoes stacked one on another. She opened the door wider and ushered them in.

The front parlor was all but empty— a straight-back chair and lamp table along the back wall and a footstool before the fireplace. The room smelled of wet ash. Mrs. Koenig sat on the chair. Jack and Shoe remained standing near the door.

"H-h-how did you know?"

"Kids at school. I'm sorry. Charlie was a good man."

Man. Jack's attempt at consolation was sincere and commendable. Shoe offered nothing and let Jack soldier on.

Mrs. Koenig nodded. "I can't talk about it." She pulled a lace handkerchief from her housedress pocket and dabbed at her eyes.

"Butch around?"

She burst into loud blubbering and buried her face in her hands.

Jack seemed stuck in the moment. "We understand," Shoe said, gently elbowing him. "We won't keep you. We're very sorry for your loss, and if we can do anything for you . . ."

She waved the kerchief at them, too overwhelmed to speak. They let her go a minute and when her heaving stopped, she took a deep, shuddering breath and said, "The police. They won't let me. Chief McCall said it will ruin the investigation. He'll let me know when I can discuss it."

There were footsteps in the next room and a workman in dark denim stopped into the doorway. He cleared his throat but said nothing, waiting respectfully.

Shoe elbowed Jack a little harder. "Yes, ma'am. We see you're busy. We'll be going now."

Tears began to flow again. They let themselves out. When they were back on the street, Jack took one more look at the house. "Top window," he whispered, tugging on Shoe's sleeve.

Shoe looked up in time to see a moon face disappear and the curtains fall back into place. "Butch?"

"Yep. And he didn't look too happy."

Shoe checked the wagon again. They were lashing a ladderback chair and a footstool against two bedframes. That would be the last of it. When the beds went . . .

Sure enough, moments later the wagon—piled high to overflowing—eased around the side of the home. When it got to the road, it stopped briefly to allow a black tin lizzie to pass. It was a cop car and it turned onto the property and rolled right up to the front porch. Before either one of the policemen could exit the vehicle, the house door opened and a tubby youth came out.

"*Hello* Butch," Shoe mumbled.

They watched as he climbed into the back and sat down on one of the benches there. Then the Ford rumbled off.

"Jack?" Shoe asked. "What's your gut telling you?"

"What you taught me," he said as he straddled his bicycle. "Never lose a potential source. I'll take the cops. You find out where they're moving."

Shoe took off after the furniture. He hadn't been on a two-wheeler in a while and his legs were screaming, but he did his darnedest to keep up. Fortunately, the overloaded wagon took its time as it picked its way around some of the deeper ruts and holes in the road path. Shoe watched household goods slide and readjust themselves with every pothole. He slacked off a bit so he could take evasive action should anything come flying his way.

The truck headed east toward the downtown, which was somewhat puzzling. Cheap housing would be west, on the outskirts. Possibly they would hit Bayside Avenue and head up that way out of town. But when they passed that, proceeded on through Nevis proper, and took a left onto Ironwood Street, Shoe quit speculating. This was deep in the elite section of town. Two blocks past the Stroup Elementary School, the movers pulled up to a tidy white house with a neatly manicured yard behind a sturdy white picket fence. Shoe parked a few houses away and waited. A final goodbye to a friend or benefactor?

Dumbfounded, Shoe watched as the waggoneer unlashed the load, and the chair, footstool, and beds were moved inside. This wasn't a moving-*out*, it was a moving-*up*. Unless he was greatly mistaken— which wasn't often, nowadays—houses up this way were way too expensive for average folk like the Koenigs, or even for reporters like himself. Where had the windfall come from? He jotted down the house number. It was all a matter of property records.

Chapter Eighteen
Slow Cows and Fast Tails

After he picked up speed, Jack let the bicycle coast. He didn't need the smarts of Mr. Einstein to know the police car was headed back to the station house for Butch's lecture. He let it slip ahead and followed behind in the dust cloud it was kicking up.

It was a workable plan until the coppers made an unexpected left onto Birch Street—a street that could lead them right out of town. Why hadn't he anticipated that? He rose out of his seat and pumped harder, praying his feet would stay on the pedals. When he had the cops back in view, he stayed on them. It was a busy street. The police would have little curiosity about someone cycling behind them.

Just as he settled back into a steady, comfortable rhythm, the paddy wagon suddenly swerved. He found himself closing in on the rear end of a horse cart full of barrels. He jerked right and jumped the sidewalk, scattering a group of matronly biddies holding court. Screams, indignation, and quite possibly his name followed. And he was pretty sure it was Mr. Markle, the stationer, whom he chased back into the safety of his store. The rest was a godawful blur.

Miraculously, he hit nothing, and at the end of the block, he safely followed the squad car around the corner onto Atlantic Street. Another quick right put them on Bayside. His original hunch was correct. The car eased up to the police barracks and in a flash, Butch and two coppers climbed out and disappeared inside through a side door.

Maybe an hour later—enough time for Jack to get sick of flipping his Babe's baseball card—Butch emerged alone from the alleyway. Which was kinda strange, considering the lengths the cops had gone to get him there.

Butch caught sight of him right away but didn't hail him. Instead, he hesitated as if considering a run for it or at least a change in direction—which didn't seem to include a trip back indoors. He hotfooted it up Bayside.

Jack didn't cross the street after him but matched him step for step up the hill. When they were a sufficient distance from the barracks, he called out to him.

Butch checked over his shoulder, but there was no one following them. He motioned Jack further up the hill and joined him there. "What are you doing here?" he asked. "I thought you escaped this two-bit town."

"Yeah, D.C. now, but I was in the mood for a visit. I was just heading over to Mac's for a soda before I catch the train back. Want one?"

"I don't know," Butch said, glancing back down the hill. "I was getting a ride home."

Shoe still didn't see anybody. "Looks to me like you're on your own. Besides, since when were you looking forward to a ride with *them*? Are they done with ya?"

"I-I think so."

"Then come on," Jack said, pulling on his arm. "Don't you want a few minutes' peace without anyone watching everything you do?"

Butch licked his lips, contemplating. "Go, go, go," he said and shoved Jack in the direction of the depot. They ran up Bayside until they got to Seventh Street and walked the final block to Mac's Pharmacy, silently kicking a smooth pink stone between them until Butch kicked it under a flivver.

Outside Mac's sat a gray-bearded man, a thick book open in his lap and a bindle at his feet. As they drew near, he picked up the bowler next to him and shook it hard enough to bounce around the few coins inside. He moved as if every movement was painful, but his gaze was keen. "Are you prepared to enter the kingdom of your Lord and Savior?" he asked.

The boys cast their eyes away and quickened their steps into the pharmacy.

Butch's eyes went wide as they lit on the elaborately carved counter that ran the length of the back wall. As Jack had suspected, this was a first for Butch—his family was too strapped for cash to fritter it away on a luxury like ice cream. As far as Jack was concerned, this was the most beautiful building in Nevis. He hadn't been in all of them, of course. For years he had suffered through Whitey Dorsey bragging about eating baseball-sized ice cream cones inside a place that looked like King Arthur's castle. He had to wait until he was seven before he got his chance to see if Dorsey was lying. His Uncle Frank—on one of the rare occasions he came home on shore leave—treated him to two scoops of chocolate ice cream with a banana thrown in to make it all look decent. Now that was kingly! He wasn't much on fruit, but it beat out Whitey's single scoops of vanilla by a mile.

The boys slid onto chrome stools at the counter while the scowling soda jerk eyed them with suspicion. Jack didn't get any more respect here than he got at any of the other stores he had routinely *borrowed* merchandise from. He pulled a dime out of his pocket and tapped it on the counter. "Two black cows."

The jerk took the coin and bit into it. Satisfied it was legal tender, he began to dazzle them. Down into the white ceramic container his silver scoop went, and out it came again with rounded, creamy balls of frozen delight that he dropped one by one into fluted crystal glasses. He jerked silver handles and with a hiss, root beer joined the concoction, its foamy head threatening to overflow the glass. In a final flourish, the soda jerk thrust a striped paper straw into each and slid them across the counter.

It was a magical display, and as far as Jack was concerned, there was no benefit in slaving away at school when you could do this all day. He took a moment to pay homage. Butch dug in as if he hadn't eaten in weeks.

The jerk gave them a brief, smug look before turning his attention to the patron who had come in after them. "What can I get you?"

The well-dressed man put his folded newspaper on the counter. "Nothing yet. I'm expecting someone else."

It was the same man Jack had seen on the street corner down near the police station. When Jack looked his way, he nodded cordially as if they were old friends. Jack gave him a pleasant ice cream-fueled grin and wondered what he would order. Anything that suited his fancy, he decided. He just had that look.

Butch pulled out a handful of pocket change, sorted through it until he found a nickel, and slid it across the counter toward Jack. "Pay my own way," he said.

Jack cocked an eyebrow. That was some impressive dough. "Working for Western Union looks pretty good."

Butch tugged a Western Union hatband from inside of his jacket. At one end, *18b* had been added in a neat, even hand. "Twenty cents a day. Good enough money to expect us to run from one end of Nevis to the other, day or night, and they didn't think twice about sending us into the worst areas of town—places no kid should be going. Yeah, they're real good. Western Union didn't care."

His fist tightened around the band and he poked his straw up and down through his ice cream. "You know who cared?" he continued. "The whores down on the water. That's who cared. Half the money in my pocket's their tips. Something to snack on and a minute to ask what'd we'd been up to." He blushed. "Unless they was busy. And even then, they pushed us right back out again. Like, 'This ain't the place for you.'" He shook his head. "Don't let anybody tell you that what you do for a living says who you are. Nice ladies. Good money," Butch repeated with a nod. "And smart too. Always planning ahead." He fished around in his pocket change and produced a slightly larger coin and pushed it Jack's way.

In God We Trust had been replaced with the phrase: *The Fishmonger * Ten cents for a lookie * fifty cents for a doie*. It wasn't legal tender at all, but a bawdy-house coin—a man and a woman in courtly dress dancing on the obverse, and a naked Adam and Eve entwined in suggestive repose on the reverse. Jack felt his face flush. He handed it right back.

"Good for one free. 'When you're ready,' she told me." Butch returned it to his pocket.

Desperate to change the subject, Jack reached for the Western Union hatband. Butch shook his head and tucked it back inside his pocket.

"So, you're number eighteen? What's the *b* for?" Jack asked.

"Eighteen was already taken."

"Your brother?"

Butch nodded. "He knew a good thing when he saw it. Split his runs with me. They paid him the full amount and we divvied it between us." He heaved a shuddering breath.

"Was he out on a run . . ."

Butch stabbed his spoon back into the ice cream and pushed the glass away. "Can't talk about it."

"That what the cops told you? How come they were talking to you today? It wasn't the first time, was it? You told 'em everything you knew, right?"

Butch ran his hand up and down his glass.

"Were you with him, Butch?"

"Gotta go." Butch slid off his stool and patted Jack's arm before walking away. "Nice seeing ya."

"Wait! I know people, Butch."

Butch turned back and looked at him with eyes so big that Jack thought they would swallow him whole. "Yeah, me too," he whispered. "Stay away from Hanner Mackall, and if you're smart, you'll stop sticking your nose in where it doesn't belong. Go back to D.C. Thanks for the company." Three long strides and he was gone.

Jack looked at the ice cream melting in his glass and felt like puking. He left the rest. As he exited, the panhandler took another crack at him, but he didn't even look the man's way.

The door jingled a second time behind him, and the panhandler started in on that customer too. It was the newspaperman. He stopped to drop money into the beggar's hat. Evidently he had grown tired of waiting for his companion. That, or he thought a kid was too dumb to realize he was being followed. Did the guy really think Jack didn't notice him down at the precinct? Man, he hated when people underestimated him.

Jack bolted, ducking into the first alley he came to, and threw in a few more quick turns and sprints. When he was certain he had dodged his shadow, he glanced back again. Gee willikers! The man was still hot on him, hat in his hand and coat flapping as he rounded the corner after him.

Jack broke out into a full gallop. For a moment, he considered running the man ragged—just to let him know who was boss. That would have him reconsidering future pursuits. But when he eventually lost him—and he had no doubt he would—how much time would he waste worrying about where he had gone? He beat the pavement a few more blocks and then slowed to a walk. No. Playing games was pointless. Besides, his sides were pinched with pain. He needed to know who found it so important to follow a thirteen-year-old all over town. When the guy caught up with him, he would confront him directly.

He parked next to Trott's produce cart and took a breather. When several minutes had passed and the guy was still a no-show—probably still laboring down one of the alleys—Jack swiped an apple and headed toward the heart of downtown and the financial buildings. He was no stranger to finance as conducted in the hustling street life. He was barely in his teens, but before he left Nevis, back alleys and the bustling wharf were his commercial district. This fancy section of town with its bankers and lawyers? Not his forte.

Once past the bank and the courthouse, he slowed to check each storefront until he found the Western Union Telegraph and Cable office. He peered in. It was a narrow establishment, like some of the older row houses over on Tenth Street. Near the door, two women sat hunched over typewriters, and to the rear of the space, a man in a white dress shirt busied himself behind a tall wooden console. It was Mr. Cramer, the curmudgeon who had given him a disapproving eye on more than one occasion. Jack didn't see any customers. He entered to the jingle of the doorbell and clacking typewriter keys.

Mr. Cramer took off his glasses and looked up from a puzzling array of electric tubes and wires that Jack supposed was the telegraph machine. "May I help—" His friendly smile drooped into something less inviting. "Young Mr. Byrne, isn't it?" He pointed his spectacles towards the door. "Out. Go pester someone else."

Jack respectfully removed his cap. He'd been bum-rushed out of more exclusive joints than this. "Mr. Cramer," he said. "I heard you're looking for messengers. I've come to apply, sir."

Cramer arched an eyebrow and considered a moment. "How old are you?"

"Fifteen," Jack lied.

"Bicycle?"

Jack's eyes flicked to the window as he tried to recall where he had left it. "Not a problem, sir," he said.

Mr. Cramer waved him over to an empty chair opposite the typists.

Jack hesitated. He didn't know anything about typing.

"It just so happens I'm desperate for another messenger," Cramer said. "What jobs have you held before?"

It was mostly freelance stuff at the wharf, but Jack didn't think Cramer would appreciate that. "Odd ones. This and that. Here and there. I'm told I'm a reliable self-starter, sir."

Cramer stared at him as if a printed message would suddenly scroll across his forehead and proclaim him either the perfect job prospect or dismiss him as laughably unsuited. When that failed to appear, he said, "I need someone to deliver in the evening, late night if necessary, and anywhere on the wharf. You need to be quick about your delivery and not get into other people's business. You don't see anything, you don't say anything. You can handle that?"

"Sure. I can start tonight."

Cramer drew out a black notebook from a desk drawer. "Sign your name and address on line nineteen. *Nineteen*, that will be your number."

When Jack had scribbled in the space beneath the Koenig brothers at *18* and *18 b*, Cramer handed him a celluloid black-and-yellow Western Union pin. "Put this on." Then he produced a black hatband with *Western Union* plastered across it in yellow. "That goes on your cap. Write your number on it." When he was done handing out the accouterments of a messenger boy, he turned around and pointed to a chalkboard hanging next to the door. "Starting at 8 p.m., start checking that board. Once your number hits the top, you get the next message. Got it?"

"Yes, sir."

"I'll have a special package going out tonight. Come back at eight . . . and not a minute short. Clear?"

Jack nodded. The only thing left was to procure another bicycle.

Chapter Nineteen
Old Faces and Lost Places

The Nevis courthouse was right around the corner from the train depot. Made sense to Shoe. It was railroad money that really built the town. When the Chesapeake Railway Express laid tracks into the sleepy bay town in 1901, they also laid the foundation for a strong banking system and a legal arena to handle all their business, not to mention all the collateral accountants, attorneys, and crooks that big money normally attracts. Some of Shoe's best noncontroversial stories came out of here.

The courthouse and First National Bank of Nevis stood side by side. With their flights of broad stairs, ornate Corinthian columns, and chiseled pediments, they appeared as shrines to great American business acumen. Shoe supposed burnt offerings could be made around the rear of the building.

His black cap-toe oxfords echoed across the marble floor as he entered the courthouse and approached the records clerk's desk just inside the archway on the right. He crossed his fingers and silently recited for a final time his sob story about an elderly aunt getting cheated out of her homestead by a couple of con men. If that didn't get him a few sympathetic tears and access to the property records, he'd have to trot out his Pulitzer nomination and the *Do you know who I am*? card. He preferred to avoid that one. A low profile was always the best profile.

The girl behind the desk was young and cute—curly red hair, a mass of freckles that dotted her fair skin, and eyes of a startling deep blue. She looked familiar, but if their paths had crossed, he couldn't recall where.

"How may I help—" she began, and then stopped. "Newspaper, right?" She gave him a smile and a friendly tap on the back of the hand.

He relaxed a bit. "Uh, yeah. Would it be possible to check property records? I'm working on something. Can't say what right now, but it's absolutely essential to the story I'm on." Okay, a half-truth, but close enough.

"All right," she said, still smiling, "but it's *Katherine* with a *K McGinty* if you need to credit someone. *M-c-G-i-n-t-y*." She pointed behind her. "Gray file cabinets at the bottom of the stairs."

It was all too easy.

The two metal cabinets contained meticulously-kept Nevis land records dating back to the late 1700s, although the further back you went, the spottier the documents. Still, there were enough historical documents to send an historian straight to Nirvana. The older records all seemed to be copies, the originals, no doubt, now housed in the official Maryland archives in Annapolis. This would be a quick search and Shoe's mind was already jumping ahead to his next steps.

The documents were arranged by street name, then house number. He opened the third drawer—Sixteenth to Twenty-Second—and located the group for Twenty-First Street. He thumbed through the ascending house numbers. Thirty-three, thirty-four, thirty-six. Thirty-five? Nada. He checked the last of Twentieth Street. Zero. After Twenty-First? Goose egg. He started with Sixteenth Street and ran straight through all the documents in the drawer. The official records were strangely silent on 35 Twenty-First Street. He banged the metal drawer closed. When a cold stare failed to produce results, he yanked the drawer out and started all over again. Zip. Naught. Nil.

He returned to Miss *M-c-G-i-n-t-y's* desk. "I can't seem to find the property records for a house on Twenty-First Street. Is it possible that recent activity has them out somewhere for some sort of updating?"

"I'm the only one who updates," she said. "It may be on my desk. What's the address?"

"Number 35 on Twenty-First Street. I'm thinking the property might have changed hands."

She looked at him a moment as if it were too much information to process all at once. "Number 35? No, sir, I don't recall seeing anything on Twenty-First Street."

He pointed to a wooden box marked IN. "Can you check there? Maybe someone else . . ."

A scowl replaced her earlier sunny countenance. "No, sir. *Just* me. Perhaps you overlooked it. Two records stuck together? Returned to the wrong place in the drawer by another researcher?"

He shook his head. "I searched the whole drawer. There has to be something somewhere." He gestured to the box again.

She huffed once and emptied the box. "I can assure you there is nothing concerning Twenty-First Street in here. Are you sure the address actually exists?" she asked as she leafed through. "Sometimes things get renumbered."

"Oh, it's there all right. Checked this morning." He tapped impatiently on the edge of her desk, eyes roving. Was there no one of higher authority to whom he could plead his case? His eyes settled on the robust gentleman in the nice suit across the room—an upper-level bureaucrat if he ever saw one.

She followed his gaze. "No. Mr. Hunnicutt would not know anything about the day-to-day activities of property records."

Shoe took off for bigger fish. *No* and *not know* were not in a reporter's vocabulary. "Mr. Hunnicutt," he said, approaching the civil servant, who had to be tipping the scales at a good 250 pounds. "A moment of your time, sir."

Hunnicutt looked up, startled. Whatever he did here, it apparently didn't include cavorting with the locals. "How may I help you?"

"Tate Shoemaker, *Evening Star*," Shoe said, tipping his fedora. "I'm working on a story for the paper. Was hoping to get it into tomorrow's edition, but I can't seem to find the property record I need down in the archive."

"Miss McGinty should—"

"Miss McGinty was a peach, but she couldn't help me. You're her supervisor, right?"

"What's the address?" Hunnicutt said, putting aside the document he had been reading.

"Thirty-five on Twenty-First Street."

Mr. Hunnicutt might be further up the management hierarchy, but he seemed clueless. He floundered around, moving everything within reach until finally settling on a nearby folder underneath an elaborate millefiori paperweight. His review of the documents proved to be slow and aggravating. Shoe thought himself better off with Miss McWhatever.

Shoe checked to see if she was still at her post and froze mid-look. Not ten feet from her stood Prentis Gant, the very politician his Prohibition exposé had toppled from his lofty position of power and influence and sent to jail. A meeting would be most unpleasant. Shoe put his elbows on the counter and shielded his profile by massaging his temples. He stayed that way until Prentis's noisy entourage passed through to another room. How on earth was the man out of jail?

"Yes, sir," Honeycutt said, tapping a paper in his hand. "There was a transfer of ownership on that property quite recently."

"When was it sold?"

"No, sir. No money exchanged, no sale. Just the name changed on the deed. Donaldson to Koenig." He shoved it under Shoe's nose. "Here. See?"

Shoe moved it back three inches. It was a simple document transferring the deed from Carlton Donaldson to Mildred Koenig two days earlier. Donaldson again! Was this some sort of *Sorry you got involved* gift? A bribe? "May I see the rest?" he asked, indicating the folder.

"Certainly, Mr. . . . Mr. . . ."

"Schoenberger, from the *Tribune*." Shoemaker, Schoenberger, did it really matter? Not to Honeycutt. He immediately turned away and started a new conversation with another associate behind the counter.

Shoe clutched the folder to his bosom and slipped away. He was almost out the door when a thought struck him. What did the history of the original Koenig house show? He slipped back down to the basement. From there, his luck ran out and things headed south. He couldn't remember the house address or the street name. Sure, it was the Seventh Street extension, but the street changed names at some point outside town. Opossum Pike, was that it? And the house number—he could kick himself. He'd looked right at it when Jack knocked on the door. His brain was now racing like his heart, and the more he wracked his brain, the faster they galloped. He yanked out the drawer marked *M through P* and started plowing through the *O*s. One hundreds. Two hundreds. He found it in the 300s block—315, his father's birthday. He lifted the whole folder, slammed the drawer shut, and vaulted the steps two at a time, pausing only at the top to see what Honeycutt was up to and to pick up on any lurking politicians. He had worried needlessly. Prentis Gant was nowhere in sight, and the consummate bureaucrat was huddled in an animated discussion with several people. Miss *McFlinty Whatever* was nowhere in sight. He walked out as if he had stock in the place.

Chapter Twenty
New Players

Shoe scuddled straight to the *Evening Star*. He needed the lowdown on Prentis Gant before someone sneaked up behind him and meted out some retribution on the politician's behalf. Riley Tanner would know, only he wasn't in his office or anywhere else in the building, which was puzzling. Sure, evening was rapidly descending, but Tanner lived and breathed this business. Shoe searched the newsroom for another friendly face. There wouldn't be many. The senior staff had never warmed to him and his meteoric rise to fame had no doubt added to their animosity. No worry, the place was deserted—the only sign of life the chugging of the printing machine at the other side of the building.

Shoe leaned around the Chandler and Price press as it zipped out news pages and shouted at the linotyper. "Perkins!" He yelled it several times before the two made eye contact.

"Damn syndicates and their boilerplates," Perkins said, fuming. He ran his fingers across the metal plate in his hand, jiggling the type letters to check their placement. "Someday they're going to put me out of my job."

Shoe sat down on the corner of a nearby desk. "Well, if news organizations get big enough, that could be a lot of us. But not the local news. You'll always be setting type for the local stuff. Waste your ire on something else."

"Already got my replacement lined up anyway. Dubbya Arthur, have you met the young pipsqueak yet? Tanner thinks I don't know I'm training my replacement. Hell, spent all yesterday replacing his upside-down *M*s with *W*s. Hopeless," he said, shaking his head.

Asking Perkins not to complain was like asking a dog not to bark. Shoe would need to be quick about it—hit him in between beefs and then be off again. "Listen, maybe I've been working too hard, but I would swear I just saw Prentis Gant over there in the courthouse."

"No mistake," Perkins said. "Exonerated not more than four hours ago." He pulled a finished sheet from the press and shoved it a him.

It was a special edition of the *Star* and the banner headline made Shoe's knees wobble: *Criminal Charges Dropped against Mayor's Office.* "But they caught them red-handed, bootlegging down at Parkers Wharf. How the—"

Perkins' eyebrows knitted together. "If the feds are gonna let 'em go, why even have a law? Course, Volstead was crazy in the first place to think you can legislate—"

"Federal District Judge Morris Hopper in Baltimore," Shoe said, interrupting the momentum of Perkins' swelling tirade. "Lemme see, lemme see. Okay, here it is. '*Of particular interest was the dismissal of all charges against Nevis, Maryland official Prentis Gant. Although federal agents identified him as an active participant in the now-infamous raid at Parkers Wharf, Judge Morris ruled in favor of Mr. Gant, citing improperly obtained search warrants as well as other legal irregularities. For his part, Mr. Gant maintained his innocence throughout the trial, claiming he had come to the wharf to pray at St. Raphael the Archangel Catholic Church and was indiscriminately swept up in the frenzy federal officials created.*'" Shoe balled up the paper.

"Yeah, shame about Mr. Gant there," Perkins said, shaking his head.

"Right nice fella. Bought me one at Kelly's Tavern before they closed up. Can't arrest a man for practicing religious beliefs now, can you? Constitution says so. Hell, he didn't seem to have profited in any way from what was going on. Feds checked his bank account. Poor man was pretty much a pauper—just like you'd expect of a civil servant. If he was guilty, he'da had a bushel-basket load of cash tucked away. Had to have friends pay his fine. One thousand bucks!" he said, shaking his head, "and two months served. I say justice has been done."

Shoe slid off the table and handed the wadded paper back. "No way, Perkins. This is bullsh—I documented the whole shebang. Even a baby could follow . . . They fined the rest of them a thousand dollars and let them go to. I thought they'd at least get the six months' jail time." He slumped into a nearby chair.

"You really thought these uppities were gonna do serious time?"

"Well, yeah."

Perkins shook his head in disgust and picked his boilerplate back up. "Then you really don't understand Maryland politics. Prohibition is a federal dance, but the State holds the dance card. Judge Hopper knew he could only go so far without risking someone filling him full of lead out on Charles Street. What's the compromise? Everyone stands up before His Honor, says they're sorry, and promises not to do it again. Then they leave the courthouse discussing how they can be more careful about covering their behinds the next time. Men don't change. Laws and circumstances change."

Perkins sputtered on with a profanity-laced tirade about repealing the Eighteenth Amendment, but Shoe had moved on to how *he* could be more careful. He walked past the empty desk that used to be his and looked out the building's front window. A wagon loaded with split wood clattered up the hill, and a few businessmen in dark suits scurried from unknown point *a* to destination point *b*—the same activities he'd seen out the same window six months before. He didn't expect to see a lynching party approaching. Not yet, anyway, and certainly not with Prentis Gant leading it. He was much too clever a man to get caught directly again. Shoe was already certain he had one little shadow ghosting him around town. Was it a Prentis associate? And then again, he was fairly certain he hadn't put an end to the Clinton boys. Maybe they could all meet together at a prearranged place and beat the hell out of each other— the victor taking the spoils. The absurdity of it made him chuckle. He would simply keep moving.

He drifted away from Perkins and found an empty desk to spread out the documents about the house on Twenty-First Street. Apparently, both the Weathersby and Donaldson families had histories in Nevis. Donaldson's ownership of the property went back decades to a land transfer from his father, Orville. In fact, the title traced back through many Donaldsons to Benjamin Starker Donaldson, who had acquired the property for three dollars and some change in 1785. Shoe stared at the latest land transfer. Why would he gift it out of the family? He leafed through the rest of the papers but found nothing to answer that.

He moved on to the Opossum Pike records. As suspected for this working-class section of town, there was no passing of property from one generation to the next. Property ownership regularly changed hands between families. The Koenigs had been living at the residence for the previous five years. The latest sale was recorded the day before the paperwork on Twenty-First Street, the buyer a company called Calvert Unlimited. Shoe tried to recall employers in Nevis big enough to buy housing for their employees. The railroad, for sure, but those would probably be owned by the Chesapeake Railway Express and they were usually on railroad rights-of-way. Bayland Park? Possibly. Shoe found nothing else of interest in the folder. He closed it up and made a note for Fannie to hunt down Calvert Unlimited and determine if the company owned any other houses on the Pike.

He looked at Perkins' girlie calendar tacked up on the opposite wall, where Theda Bara was staring back at him with a come-hither look. What was today, the 19th? That left only five days until President Coolidge lit thousands of lights on the National Christmas tree. Holy Jerusalem! What he wouldn't give for just one bright light and a tiny bit of illumination.

As Riley Tanner took a seat across from the acting mayor, Leedon "Buddy" Bowen, he glanced at his fly to make sure it was fastened. He also took a quick tug on his tie, the only one he owned. It came out of his desk drawer maybe once or twice a year when he found it necessary to impress. Like now. In the last five years, he'd been called to this office exactly three times. His recall was precise on that because he never forgot when his rear end got chewed out. He swallowed hard and smiled politely. "Couldn't ask for nicer weather, huh, Leedon?"

He'd been friends with Buddy Bowen all his life—forty years and a few extra. They'd learned their sums and alphabet on Miss Martha's back porch back in the '80s after a lightning strike burned down the old schoolhouse. Ate corn they stole from Mr. Harper's fields and spent many a summer night swimming buck naked in the Piscataponi with the rest of the boys. But the face that looked back at him now was anything but friendly. Today, anger had a name, and it was *Leedon*. Politics was like that.

"Riley, we've known one another a long—"

"Long time," Riley agreed, nodding.

"We have a problem, you and I."

"Oh? Leedon, after all these years, I'm sure there isn't anything we can't fix. What is it?"

"Fire Tatum Shoemaker."

Prentis Gant already pulling strings again. That hadn't taken what, less than half a day? "Except that. Good man, great reporter. Anything else I can do for you?"

"Riley, be reasonable. We'll all . . . *all* be happier if he goes back to Washington. Now. Without any more ideas about sensational stories. I'm asking as a friend. Send him packing."

"'Preciate that. And as a friend of yours, my answer is *no.*" He stood up. "Anything else while we're just two friends shooting the breeze?"

"It's not me. I, uh, er. . . *Please,* Riley, see it everyone else's way for once."

"'Bad company corrupts good character.' 1 Corinthians 15:33. Have a blessed day, Leedon."

With that, Riley walked out of the office and into the twilight. He liked this time of day: smack in the middle of the light and dark. It was like being a good journalist—neutral and unbiased. He pulled out a Camel and started puffing. By the time he got back to the newspaper offices, he'd flipped it away and begun scribbling on his notepad. The *Star* was in for a rough time, but, damn, how he relished a good fight. Shoemaker's notoriety and ambition hadn't worked out so well for the young fella, but he had a job at the *Star* as long as he needed it.

Chapter Twenty-One
Brother's Keeper

Shoe's eyes popped open with the first squeak. The second had his fingers inching toward the Police Special Colt lying next to him on the patchwork quilt. He found the hard rubber grip and eased off the safety. The night was moonless, the Bayside room pitch dark. Point of entry was either the window or the door. He bet his life on the latter. He aimed the gun toward the door without rising. It would be a hell of a recoil. "Talk fast before I plug you good."

"Don't shoot! I'm not armed." The light flipped on, revealing Rudy at the door with his hands raised above his head.

"Rudy Becker!" Shoe slipped the safety back into place.

"Who else would it be?" Rudy lowered his arms and shrugged his coat back into place. "Do you make a point of shooting people before you identify them?" He clicked the door shut again.

"Only when they sneak unannounced into my room in the middle of the night. What do you want, Rudy?"

"Unannounced? I left a note." Rudy pointed to the writing table under the window.

Shoe's eyes found the sheet of stationary propped up against the brass lamp on the table. "Well next time, give me a little extra warning. I've had a very trying day. Most of it because of you." He turned his

149

attention back to Rudy. "How much clearer could I have made it on the wharf?"

"We need to have a talk."

"I'm done talking."

"Yeah, I noticed, but did you have to try to drown me? Not everyone knows how to swim."

"Yeah? Well, next time you'll hear chin music."

"That was my nicest suit."

Shoe let out a long, slow sigh. "I'm not running a flophouse, Rudy. Spill and then take a hike. Why do you find it necessary to break into my room *twice* and at such an ungodly hour?" A simple message left with the extremely accommodating concierge would have sufficed."

Rudy sat down at the bottom of the bed. "I'm in a bit of a fix."

"Here we go," Shoe mumbled. He swung his legs off the bed and waited for the new variation on a Rudy story he had heard repeated dozens of times by his newspaper buddies. "I'm sure that's an understatement. And I'm pretty sure I really don't care."

"I met this girl over in Clinton. It seems some of her family think we, uh, spent some quality time together—"

Shoe nodded thoughtfully. "Yes. Now I'm positive I don't care." He pointed to the door. "See yourself out."

"You don't understand. A couple of Arlene's outraged menfolk have tracked me to Nevis. When they find me, they're going to beat my brains out."

"Old news, Rudy. I ran into a few of your *friends* this afternoon down at the warehouses. They thought I was you, took me for a nice little ride, and nearly beat the crap out of me before I could convince them otherwise."

Rudy's jaw dropped. "That was *you?*"

"Yeah, thanks, *brother*. Apparently you diddled their younger sister."

"I most certainly did not! But it kinda looked that way. She crawled into my bed, and I politely showed her the door. The next morning, I found her asleep on my floor. Her brothers must have discovered her empty room."

Shoe shuddered at the thought of some used-up hooker offering sex and clap for the next month's rent. "Didn't you stop to think who else she might have propositioned before you?" He threw in a little applause for emphasis.

"No, I put her right out, I swear. And she wasn't like that. Young country girl."

"First time?"

Rudy gave him a disgusted look. "Shoe, you've got to help me dodge 'em." His eyes were serious and sincere. "Besides, you owe me for the shoulder off the pier the other day."

"Owe you? *Owe you?* I nearly get pummeled to death in an isolated farm field, and I owe *you*? You're full of it. By my count, you're in *my* debt. I corrected their misinformation and told them you were headed out of town. Make yourself scarce for a bit. They'll eventually wear themselves out and go back home."

Rudy flopped back on the bed. "Oh, thank you, Jesus."

"You're thanking the wrong one, but that's okay. Scram and don't come back. Go to Philly, where the Clinton farm boys can't find you."

Rudy propped himself up on his elbows. "I got it. I got it. But I can't leave yet. I'm very busy here." He seemed outwardly calmer, but the brain was still barreling ahead on all four cylinders.

"Before you go, Rudy, there is one thing I need to ask. I've been churning it over in my noggin here, and I still can't figure it out. Why did they have me and you confused? *That journalist in Nevis* might have been a reason to grab me off the street, but considering we're both recent arrivals, I don't believe that's it. No," he said, shaking his head, "they were specifically looking for *Shoemaker*. You didn't perchance fall back into old habits and give sweet, chaste Arlene my name, did you?"

Rudy's eyes went south.

Shoe rolled toward Rudy and shoved his gun into his side. "You lousy—give me one good reason why I shouldn't kill you right here. An intruder, in the dead of night, sneaking into my room to do God knows what? They'd never charge me."

Rudy grabbed the barrel of the gun and twisted Shoe's wrist counterclockwise as he rolled over to pin him on the bed. "Try taking the safety off first," he grunted.

"Love to," Shoe countered as he wrapped his free arm around Rudy's neck and began to squeeze. They grappled a moment with neither gaining an advantage before both rolled off the bed, Shoe on top. They stayed like that a moment, both panting heavily.

"Truce?" Shoe asked.

"Truce."

Shoe staggered up. As he latched onto Rudy's wrist and pulled him to his feet, his eyes fell upon a small red mark peeking out from the edge of his shirt cuff. "Fresh ink?" he asked, trying to drawing Rudy closer to get a better look. "I didn't think you were the type."

Rudy pushed him away with a *le'go*.

"No, let me see the mark. Maybe I'll get one just like it."

Rudy yanked free and assumed a boxer's stance. "I didn't come here to get into fisticuffs with you, but—"

Shoe stepped out of range. "Stop it. I just asked about the tattoo. I don't need you Dempsey-ing me onto my rear end. I'll never understand two men getting paid to pummel each other's faces."

Rudy remained in fighting position. "Because maybe you don't know what it's like to grow up having to fight your way out of your house in the morning and back in again in the afternoon."

"Can't control where my parents decided to live, Rudy." Shoe cocked his head sideways and took another stab at deciphering the tattoo. "D-E-L-L-A. Della." He did a double take. "*You're* Mena's mysterious suitor? You're Lewis Ware?" He staggered back several steps. "Well, I'll be a monkey's—. Haven't *we* moved up in the world."

Rudy stopped his posturing and pulled down his sleeve. "Pfft. I'm flattered, but I hardly fit into Weathersby's Newport set. There's not an elitist bone in my body."

"Yeah, maybe not, but from what I've heard, Mena wasn't traveling in those circles anymore. And how is it you know who I'm talking about? I didn't say anything about the Weathersbys. Come on, Rudy, what are you *really* doing in Nevis?"

Rudy looked like a squirrel in the middle of Main Street with a Model A bearing down on him. Was it going to be another lie or would he come clean?

"How did you know about the tattoo?"

"Confectionary. Everybody talks if you pay them enough. Emerson told you she's dead, right?"

Rudy sank straight down to the bed, put his head in his hands, and sobbed, "Dear God, my sweet Mena."

Shoe didn't know whether to hug or slap him. He settled for an *I'm sorry* and sat down next him.

"Rudy, you've got my head spinning. Nobody's tighter with information than Emerson. He hire you? Or are you buddied up with the cops? No wait, you're one of the dicks they hired to shadow Mena. Come on, Rudy, straighten me out. Emerson wants me to find out who killed her. A boyfriend would be a prime suspect, but your name never came up in conversation."

Rudy let out a long, slow, shuddering breath. "I didn't kill her. I loved—*love* her. We did a lot of sneaking around, ferociously protective of what we had. We often used the aliases Lewis and Della Ware. Private joke. Lewes, Delaware? A favorite place."

He gave Shoe a quick look, got no reaction, and continued. "Emerson had no clue. None of them did. Mena cut them off as much as they cut her off. She hated that vacuous life. So, so passionate about people and life," he said, shaking his head.

"You say you've changed, but an addict from the Bowery? With all due respect, where's your good judgment?"

A venomous look replaced the pain in Rudy's eyes. "Addict? Don't be absurd. You don't know anything. She was bright and funny. One of the most talented people I've ever met."

"Stop right there. I don't want to hear any specifics about your kinky sexual habits."

The anger turned to befuddlement. "Kinky sex? What in tarnation are you talking about? Mena was a painter."

"P-p-painter? Emerson said she was a hook—er, plying a trade in the Bowery's red-light area. Stage name *Mena Beebe*?"

"Filthy liar," Rudy said, looking as if his head were ready to blow off. "Let's see. The best ones I've heard are that Mena was ensconced in the Bowery suffering from opiate addiction, she was turning tricks in a bordello . . . no, wait, there was a better one. She was so talented that she had become the madame in said whorehouse." He let out a long slow hiss as he vented his rage.

"Look. I'm sorry, but all I had to go on was what Emerson told me."

"Sick, sick family. Choosing to live in the bohemian section of New

York is not on the dance card for women of her pedigree. Mena didn't sell herself or have a problem with addiction. She had a *family* problem. She hid out in the Bowery and took money from them with one purpose in mind: escaping them. I was the only man Mena was ever with or wanted. You can trust me on that."

Shoe's mind flashed back to Rudy's flirtatious encounter with Fannie. "Well, okay. If they can sink so low as to besmirch the character of their own daughter, what's to keep them from nailing your hide to the wall when they find out you were involved with her?"

"If they haven't found out by now—" Rudy's chin snapped up, his face plastered with a wide-eyed, incredulous look. "Wait! You'd rat me out?"

"Of course not. But we're probably not the only ones Emerson has approached. No telling how many more gumshoes are out there trying to earn big bucks. Every time I go out, I'm looking over my shoulder. Somebody's going to nose out your relationship. You know they will. Nevis is the last place in the universe you should be right now. Get out of town, man. I can keep you apprised. Besides, you're probably too close to be objective."

"No dice," Rudy said, shaking his head. "I promised that I'd take care of her. I owe it to her to stay. If something bad happens . . ." He shrugged. "They can plant me where they find me because I really don't care anymore."

Promises to a dead person. In Shoe's experience, most survivors often went off half-cocked with ill-considered plans, and the end results never turned out well. Maybe Rudy needed someone to stay close and keep an eye on him, but that someone wasn't Tatum Shoemaker.

"Me being close is good. You see, I've got inside information. Mena messaged me the night she died. I know exactly where she was going and why. You and I should work together."

"Where?"

"Uh uh," Rudy said. "I'm not saying anything else until we're in agreement. Do we have a deal or not? I want the sonuvabitch who destroyed my life. The Clinton crew is an unneeded sideshow. You watch my back and we split Emerson fifty-fifty. Whadda ya say, Shoe? Together?"

There were fifty thousand reasons Shoe should say no—the first three being that Rudy was a lying, philandering sneak. But hey, so was dear old Dad. Shoe didn't hold to the proverbial *blood is thicker than water*. Despite sudden family connection and hearty handshake, he believed Rudy capable of trading up on him as soon as the opportunity arose. If Rudy had insider information, then he needed to be pumped before he was out of sight. Of course, the same didn't apply to what Shoe knew. Until Rudy proved he was the least little bit trustworthy, he wasn't sharing what Jack uncovered about the young Western Union victim, his brother, or the strange goings-on with property in town. He thrust out his hand to shake on a deal he had little doubt he would come to regret.

Rudy settled himself into the upholstered chair near at the window and Shoe surmised he intended to stay the night. If Shoe didn't hit him up now, he risked falling asleep and having Rudy sneak out on him before sunrise. "So, Rudy, why did you come to Nevis? Seems a long way to rendezvous with Mena."

"Business in Nevis and I was to meet Mena."

"What was in Mena's message?"

"You go first," Rudy said, kicking off his shoes. "I've already given you something."

Shoe gave him a bewildered look. "What—"

"The tattoo," Rudy said, tapping his cuff. "I've given something.

You can't just take and give me nothing in return." He cocked an eyebrow and waited.

Shoe glanced at the clock. It was 3 a.m., and if he didn't get some shuteye soon, he would be a goner for the rest of the day. Rudy's information was valuable and the man knew it. "Okay, but then you tell me about Mena," he said. "How much do you know about Hanner Mackall?"

"Owns a boat."

Both of Shoe's eyebrows shot up. "You're wandering around that side of town and that's all you know? Christmas! He's a scum bucket like all the rest of those shifty dock characters. They don't fish, and they're not employed by the established businesses along the water. They're freelancing smugglers. You pick the cargo, offer a decent price, and they're game."

Rudy's hands went up in a "whatever" gesture.

Yep, Rudy was troublesomely fearless and half-cocked. He'd be dead by the end of the week. "Darby says he doesn't know Mackall, but I'm not buying it. The Mackall family owns the cliffs south of the dig, and Mackall's raking in the scratch escorting tourists down there to hunt fossils. There is no way they haven't met to establish boundaries. Something funny's going on and I aim to find out what it is."

"Maybe," Rudy said, "but then again, it might just be good business. Maybe Darby didn't want you including Hanner in your little piece."

"No, Darby's so full of it. He'd never consider Mackall worthy. And it's only good business until you start threatening people. When I got on Mackall's boat with you, he warned me to watch my step. His intent was clear: don't go snooping around. No," Shoe said, shaking his head. "It's as clear as my father's nose on your face. Mackall's after more than the two bits someone's throwing at him for a family bucket of sharks' teeth. Whatever he's up to, he's afraid I'll find it out."

Rudy yawned broadly. "If you think I'm going to hang around the docks all night waiting for some cutthroat ruffians to bring illicit goods offshore, think again."

"Of course not. We hit the wharf tomorrow morning about nine. Darby said his storage is in warehouse 17. We snoop around that a bit to see who's who and what's what, and then we pull back." He hopped out of bed, pulled an army duffle bag out from under it, and produced a set of binoculars. "We find some high ground and watch. Does somebody come in and take stuff out, or do they squirrel it away in storage for someone to pick up later? If nobody shows, we take a look-see inside the warehouse." He slid the bag back under the bed. "You game?"

Rudy didn't answer.

Their agreement was what, three minutes old and it was already souring? Shoe looked over at Rudy, ready to light into him. His feisty, pugilistic half-brother had been replaced by a soft body that had melted into the shape of the chair, and his chin was almost on his chest. The soft buzz of gentle snoring drained the fire right out of Shoe. The stress of loss and of being hunted like prey was taking its toll.

He walked over and bumped the toe of Rudy's boot. Rudy emitted an ugly snort and adjusted his sleeping position without waking from his deep sleep. Shoe studied his relaxed face a moment and then turned away with a shudder as he realized how much Rudy resembled their father.

Rudy might look like Shoemaker, Sr., but Shoe was certain his half-brother wasn't half the man their father was. He dragged the wooden desk chair across the carpet and tilted it backwards until it wedged under the door handle. Then he stepped back to admire his ingenuity and with a nod deemed it satisfactory. Let the little brother try to sneak past that without making a commotion.

Chapter Twenty-Two
Dependability

Shoe woke with a start, a crick in his neck and soft light streaming through the window. The wooden chair was back at the desk. Rudy had blown the place, and Shoe suspected he wasn't coming back with biscuits, coffee, and any of his secrets. He should have beaten the information out of him when he had the chance. If Rudy didn't track him down by nine, he'd know a deal with his brother—dear God, what a painful address—was as worthless as a plug nickel.

He dropped his Calvert Cliffs story at the *Evening Star*. Tanner wasn't around, which was ideal. The assignment on the Darby expedition had provided a promising lead but Shoe didn't need a second assignment. There was no way he'd get that lucky twice. He left it on the editor's desk and headed for Betty's diner. If Fannie's mother could spare her, he would grab Fannie and send her off to check on Calvert Unlimited and the ownership of the Opossum Pike houses.

At the diner door, he caught sight of Fannie conversing with someone at the counter. He stopped and watched the way her eyes sparkled when she laughed. He always liked it when she looked like that. Apparently, the young gentleman at the counter did too; Shoe could hear him laughing heartily. It suddenly dawned on him how little time he had spent with Fannie since their return to Nevis. The dame was the whole package and he had no money problems now. What was he doing? God forbid her girlfriends set her up with some guy. Maybe this guy? Was he a regular customer? Shoe pushed through the door vowing to take her out for dinner, dancing, or some other hooley-goo women enjoyed.

Jack was leaving as he was coming in. "Busy tonight?" Shoe asked. "I need some help."

Jack breezed past and started down the stairs. "Don't know. Got a job."

"Job? Does that mean you aren't interested in helping me anymore?"

Jack paused at the bottom of the steps. "I never said that. I'm fourteen. Time to stop drifting and carry my own weight."

When they first met, Jack's age was one of the first lies he tried to put over on Shoe. Jack was a solid thirteen. What was ailing the kid? "What do you mean, *drifting?*"

Jack shrugged and his shoulders stayed up next to his ears a wee bit too long before sagging back down.

"Okay, I got it. It's your friends. You come back and everybody else seems to have it all together. Might be making a little cabbage too. That's okay. When I first came to Nevis, I couldn't wait to bolt back to Philly, but then I met your sister and the feeling passed. You'll find your niche. Promise."

Jack gave him a contemptuous look. "I'm not interested in no girls."

Shoe came back down the stairs. "No, no. That's the right answer, Jack, 'cause trust me, they can turn you upside down and make your head whirl."

"My dad was already carrying water on the railroad at my age."

"Yeah, but I'm pretty sure he'd want you to get a better start than he had. All parents do."

"You got kids?"

"No, but I know enough people who do."

Jack remained quiet, but Shoe could see waves of emotion ebbing and flowing across his face. "Jack, what can I do to help?"

"Butt out."

An awkward silence followed. Shoe looking out across the street toward the small shops there, and Jack tried to kick free a stone imbedded in the dirt. Apparently neither wanted to walk away and leave things like they were.

Jack spoke up first. "Depends on when they need me. I'll find you later. Got to scoot."

"Who's *they*?"

"Western Union."

"Are you crazy?" Shoe followed him out into the street. "Late nights on the town with hookers, thieves, and a murderer running loose?"

"Been there, done that a million times before, Shoe. I know lots of *those* people. They're fine. The ladies give the biggest tips."

"*Ladies? Before* is not *now*. With somebody floating around down there . . . Don't kid yourself—yeah, that's exactly what you are, a kid. Poor judgment is clouding your thought processes . . . Bicycle, hatband, the full uniform?"

Jack gave him a guarded look. "Yeeaahh."

Shoe threw his arms up. "Jeez Maries, Jack. That just screams dough in your pocket, an easy mark for lots of unscrupulous people."

Jack glared, opened his mouth to speak, and then shut it again. He took off, matching the speed of a passing wagon, hoisted himself up into the open bed, and moved up behind the driver. "It's fine," he yelled at Shoe.

"Seven p.m.," Shoe yelled back. He got no response. Jack turned his head away and started a conversation with the driver. *Damn fool.* Why did kids think they were invincible? What did the young'un expect to find out by haunting the wharf at night? Shoe suspected he would be doing the night's reconnaissance alone.

As soon as Shoe went inside, he got the third degree from Fannie. Not verbally, but with those amazing eyes that locked on him and weren't going to turn away until he explained what was going on with her brother. "Hormones and girls," he said, bussing her cheek. "And how about you? Still my girl?" Her puzzled look told him he was trying too hard. He picked a table and parked himself. "Have to stay all day and do the waitress thing?"

She looked at Betty, who shook her head in a vigorous *no* and waved her off. Fannie sat down across from him, eyes and lips smiling broadly—the same way she looked when she brought home new shoes. "Free. What do you have in mind?"

Shoe returned the smile. Betty's diner—it was better than hooley-goo. He didn't have to plan it and it wouldn't cost him a red cent.

Shoe started to ask her about Jack and Western Union, then decided against it. Jack wouldn't have told her, so there was no use in worrying her. "The Koenigs' new house on Twenty-First Street was a gift from magnate Carlton Donaldson. The old one was bought by a company called Calvert Unlimited. All this selling and buying and moving . . . Boom. Boom. Boom. It's too convenient. My guess would be that Calvert is a shell company of Donaldson's. For what profit, I'm unsure. We need to know whether any of the other houses on Opossum Pike are owned by Calvert, or by any other company, for that matter. If they are, get names and the dates."

"Oh, I can handle that. In the courthouse, I suppose."

"Right. The land records are in metal file cabinets at the bottom of the basement stairs. If I were you, I'd waltz in with that beautiful smile and just go down there. If that makes you uncomfortable, tell Miss McGlinty at the front desk that you need to follow up on some things for me."

"Katherine *McGinty*? I know her. Consider it done."

She said it with a swagger that almost made Shoe chuckle. She was fearless, and he pitied anyone who tried to deny her access. She initiated a peck on the lips and he happily obliged. "I'm meeting Rudy Becker at the wharf. If you don't hear back from me by the day's end, send in reinforcements."

"If you don't trust him, why on earth would you—your knickers are in a knot over this fellow. Walk away. You're the better man. It will all work out."

"Ahh," Shoe said, trying to rub out an imaginary spot on the table. "It's a bit more than that." He could feel her stare trying to bore a hole through the thick protective wall he was throwing up around his thoughts and feelings. Her unspoken questions were bouncing like badly aimed arrows off its irregular stone surface. Sooner or later they would find a way through one of the arrow-slits in his carefully constructed battlement.

She reached out and tilted his chin up until they were eye to eye. "We'll both feel better if you don't shut me out."

"It seems Dad was, a, uh, good father, a really good father, but a lousy husband." With a sigh of resignation, he added, "Rudy Becker is my half-brother." He leaned back just far enough to slip out of her grasp and shifted his gaze out the window. Foot traffic on the street had picked up. Apparently no one wanted breakfast; the doorbell hadn't jingled once since he sat down.

She dropped her hand. "Well! Certainly didn't see that one coming. Does he know what's what?"

"Oh, yeah. And more. The dirty laundry's been beaten against the rocks and hung out to dry many times over the years. He grew up without a father and supposedly I never had to do without. It's no fault of either of ours, you know? But his animosity is thinly veiled. I'll never been able to make amends."

She was thoughtful a moment. "Watch your back, but don't ever stop trying. Brothers aren't all bad."

"Oh, it's not him I'm worried about. Well, yes, I do worry, but not in terms of safety. That's someone else." He sighed in frustration. "Too complicated, Fannie. Suffice it to say we have a truce. Maybe it will all work out."

He kissed her again, a kiss as deep as they could get away with in a public place. She made him feel strong and capable, but he still walked out carrying as much worry on his shoulders as he had when he walked in. What were his plans if Rudy didn't show?

Chapter Twenty-Three
The Dance

Rudy picked up two messages from the Calvert Hotel concierge and took the elevator up to his room. The first was from his employer, Calvert Unlimited, noting his failure to attend a prearranged meeting at Oscar's Restaurant. It wasn't intentional. Their crab imperial was excellent, and he had no desire to get on the wrong side of a reliable employer. He simply had too much on his plate. He'd reschedule right after he decided what to do about the dispatch from Emerson, who seemingly thought Rudy could conduct an investigation, coerce a murder confession out of Shoe, and tie up all the loose ends in a matter of days. *Not happening, Mr. Rich Man's Lackey.* Of course, he'd have to dance around that. He checked his wristwatch. Emerson wanted a nine o'clock meeting. Rudy had three hours to decide how to either waltz or tango around framing Shoe for murder and still earn a paycheck. Emerson struck him as a waltz aficionado.

At midmorning, people were packing the hotel as if they were giving away lifetime supplies of French champagne and Camel cigarettes. Bellhops trotted overflowing luggage carts from curb to elevator as rich clientele floated aimlessly through the lobby on clouds of entitlement and indifference. The eggers' Christmas Season was in high gear. Rudy threaded his way to the conservatory, where Emerson waited, chain-smoking as he watched the door.

"Mr. Emerson," Rudy said, offering a handshake.

Emerson ignored the formality and snuffed out his cigarette in a nearby ashtray. "Give me one good reason why I should continue your services, Mr. Becker. You've been all over town with Mr. Shoemaker, and yet I have received nothing from you. You should have something by now."

So it would be La Danse Apache, would it? Rudy wasn't too surprised. He sat down with no intention of following Emerson's lead. "So, you *have* had someone tailing me! Tell me, Mr. Emerson, have they fared any better than I have?"

Emerson gave him a steely look and silence.

A definitive *no* as far as Rudy was concerned. "With all due respect, while this may seem an open-and-shut case, it isn't. Shoemaker and I have bonded nicely along journalistic lines, but you can't expect him to serve up his darkest secrets in a matter of a few days. If you feel that I'm not up to it, then maybe you should go with your other man. Pay me for additional services above your initial retainer and I'll get out of your way—all confidentialities maintained, of course." Yeah, it was a bit cheeky, but if Emerson trusted the abilities of the other investigator, he never would have hired Rudy in the first place.

Emerson continued to stare as if no one had ever bucked him. Then he slipped his hand into his inside breast pocket. So that was it. Emerson was an expert in booting employees to the curb. Rudy continued watching as he pulled out a checkbook, flipped it open, and began making out a check to him. When he had signed at the bottom, he folded it once against the top of the book and detached it. No emotion, no chitchat, just a passing moment in a busy day.

"I think this is more than fair," he said, handing it to Rudy.

To maintain an air of indifference, Rudy desperately wanted to tuck it away in his jacket without peeking at the amount, but he could not. His heart skipped a beat or two. Three thousand dollars. Holy crap, *three thousand dollars.* It was the full sum Emerson had promised him the first day they met.

Emerson arched an eyebrow. "Quite frankly, I don't have time to bring someone else up to speed."

"You want me to finish and you're paying me early?"

"Not exactly. Consider that an incentive, with the final agreed-upon payment still to come."

Six thousand dollars total? "All right," Rudy said, nodding. Well, not really all right at all, but it seemed like the right response.

"With one caveat."

Ah, the rub!

"We wish you to do some additional work on another pressing issue. It seems someone may be land speculating here in town. Rumors are circulating that outrageously high bids have been made to some owners of sections of Calvert Cliffs. I don't think I need to tell you what changes in ownership could mean to the scientific endeavor there. Find out what is going on, starting with the company that's buying up the land. Dig up what you can on a Calvert Unlimited."

Rudy nodded again. Only this time it wasn't because he had nothing to say. He could say plenty about the company, but the conversation would not end well for him. He would start with his own employment at the land-sales company, and then he would finish with the man behind the shell company: Carlton Donaldson, Weathersby's arch–political rival. Donaldson was a true environmentalist, and yes, the intent of the buyout was to preserve the cliffs, make them inaccessible to excavation, and create a national park for the benefit of the American public. Weathersby would go apoplectic.

He put the check inside his jacket. "Done." *Somehow.*

"Now," Emerson said, putting his checkbook away. "Where are you with Mr. Shoemaker?"

"First things first. Shoe knows someone is shadowing him. You need to get your other investigator to back off. No, on second thought, terminate his services: he's not particularly good."

Emerson smiled slightly. "That's not your call, Mr. Becker."

"If you won't fire him, put him on something useful. There's a boat called the *Sea Kingdom* at the wharf. The owner, Hanner Mackall, is a big-time smuggler. Have your guy stake him out. He may be in cahoots with someone down at the Museum dig stealing artifacts for the black market. Some of that Weathersby sponsorship money might be benefiting a few rich individuals. Tell that to your employer."

Rudy leaned back in his chair and waited. If Emerson was truly in Weathersby's inner circle, he would know whether Weathersby was using Mackall to acquire specimens for his own private use.

Emerson said nothing. Instead, he beckoned to the waiter, whispered a few words, and sent him scurrying off again. He remained silent as he took a cigarette from a handsome silver cigarette case—without any offer for Rudy to join him—and methodically lit it. And when the waiter returned shortly with an ice bucket and an opened, unlabeled wine bottle in it, he proceeded to pour two half-glasses without comment.

Rudy took a sip of the finest wine ever to hit his palate. Without a doubt, it was the best bribe he had ever been offered. But it would take a lot more to buy him, and certainly, it would never be by this man. "Well?"

Emerson polished off his glass and said, "Mr. Weathersby's grant to the National Museum is a philanthropic gesture to the American public that will provide fruitful bounty for countless future generations. To suggest it might also be self-serving is a disgrace, Mr. Becker."

"And you pulled out his finest private stock to tell me all that?" Rudy emptied his glass and placed it next to Emerson's so that the two touched. "Check," he said. "I don't care what Weathersby does with what he skims. I do care who killed Wilhelmina Weathersby and I'm very close to discovering the particulars. When I know, you'll get that information, and I hope that there is no blood on your hands. In the meantime, you keep your people out of my way."

He walked out with his three thousand dollars and his dignity intact. Mena would have her justice no matter what.

Chapter Twenty-Four
Singing in the Key of C Note

It was 8:45 a.m.—enough time for Railway Express riders to depart the 8:30 thirty train and begin making their way to the boardwalk. Shoe melded into the crowd. They fell into four easy groups. There were suited businessmen who liked to take a quick look at the water and then hike back up to Main Street for their appointments; parents trying to entertain rambunctious children as they waited for the gates of the amusement park to open; and religious zealots looking for the site of the visitation, their noses buried in paperwork as they tried to marry up crudely drawn maps with what they found in front of them. Someone was missing a great opportunity to earn a few bucks by pointing out the way to *the way*. The fourth was a group of one: Rudy, dead ahead at the clock and watching him approach.

Shoe wondered if his brother would apologize for ducking out on him. Rudy didn't have to be forthcoming about everything he knew—and Shoe suspected it was considerably more than what he let on—but if they couldn't be honest with each other, an alliance between the two of them would be impossible. He needed to see some sort of contrition. He angled his course away from Rudy.

"Hey! Gone blind?"

Shoe kept walking and didn't even look Rudy's way. "No, deaf to your nonsense. Mind your own business." He kept walking but didn't get far before Rudy fell in beside him.

"This the way you treat all your partners? Jeepers, no wonder no one likes you."

"You have us confused. They like me just fine. I just dissolved our partnership due to nonperformance on your part. Now scram!"

"Mad about the early rise? I didn't promise to serve you breakfast in bed. Didn't you get my note? Nine o'clock where the *Chessie Belle* docks." He pointed to the clock. "The tower says you're ten minutes late and still I waited."

Rudy's expression was as solemn and angelic as an altar server's. But he was lying. Shoe had checked for a note before he left. He glanced at the clock. If it were correct, he was late. Only, it was never accurate. In the two years he'd lived in Nevis, Shoe had seen it both drag time and accelerate it. And it wasn't a tower either, but a beautifully elaborate clock case mounted on a puny black metal lamppost. It didn't chime, it didn't bong, it just kept consistently inconsistent time. Townies spoke of it with reverence and most local directions included reference to it: "go right at," "proceed past," "meet me by." It was a Nevis landmark and a strange source of civic pride. "That's never right," he said, proceeding on. "Come on. If we're going to slink around, we need to look the part."

Tanner's Mercantile—no connection to Riley Tanner—was at the end of the steamboat landing. Rudy reckoned it had been there almost as long as the ships had been sailing in. All the steamboat landings up and down the Calvert coastline had stores, although none as elaborate as this one. It had been a much-needed symbiotic relationship for an area whose lack of roads made the transportation of goods difficult.

A man here, a woman there . . . they weren't the only Tanner's shoppers. The store still turned over a good business, but its days as the only place in town with access to dry goods was over. As the downtown expanded with new stores, a variety of luxury goods, and the railroad to ship it all, the mercantile was slowing becoming an anachronism. Most of what Shoe saw here was run-of-the-mill, ungraded fabric goods. It was safe to say that the place had to either step up its game or have a fire sale. In Baltimore, he'd seen too many mom-and-pops fold the same way. It was great if you wanted the latest at competitive prices, bad if you had to find a new livelihood. Just ask his granddad.

They cruised the shelves of men's britches, bypassing the few of fine cloth and cut in favor of overalls and coveralls. As they dug through a stack of dark denim pants, a pleasantly plump employee approached.

"May I assist you?" she asked.

"Two pairs of these, and, uh, khaki work shirts. Medium size?" Shoe added hopefully.

The woman considered each of them in turn, pulled a few items, and propelled both toward a fitting room at the rear of the store. Fifteen minutes later, they emerged with a look that would blend in more thoroughly with the dock workers. Rudy spent another few minutes selecting some other things—something about a lost suitcase—and they elicited a promise from the clerk to bundle up everything and deliver it to Shoe's room at the Bayside by the end of the day.

"Okay," Shoe said, not wasting any time on picking Rudy's brain. "Spill on what you know. What was Mena doing the night of the murder?"

"Yeah, yeah, we'll get to that. But there's something more pressing. A witness."

So Rudy did know about the Koenigs. "What about him?"

"*Him?*" Rudy's expression darkened. "You have a *him*? I have a *her*." Rudy grabbed Shoe's arm and stopped him. "*I'm* the one keeping the secrets? Who's the *him*?"

Shoe shook him loose. "For the last time, tell me where Mena was and I'll tell you about the other witness."

"Very well, but this won't work unless—"

"Preaching to the choir, Rudy. *Tempus*—"

"Muriel Fitzhugh. She operates the *Sunrise Pelican*, and I dug up all the skinny yesterday. And you're right. We don't have time to argue. Hold the rest of the information until we check her out. Then, tit for tat."

"Deal. This a brothel?"

"Boat. Husband died recently and she's having a hard time making ends meet. We're paying her a visit before she sells out and moves on. There ahead," he said, pointing, "the deadrise with the green-and-yellow flag. Come on. I'm afraid she'll take the boat out and it'll be one more delay."

Shoe saw the pennant but no woman he would consider a sailor. He checked farther down the boardwalk. They were uncomfortably close to Mackall's dock. Even though his boat was out, hanging around to stake out Fitzhugh's return didn't seem like a good idea. "It's getting too cold to fish. Maybe she's done for the season."

"She's still in operation, at least for a while. Look at the boat. She hasn't weatherized. Probably wants to unload it before going through all that bother."

Shoe had no idea what he was supposed to see, and he doubted Rudy did either. "Are you sure she'll show?"

"No, but where else would she be? "Look!" Rudy said, landing an elbow. "In the yellow slicker and hat. Gotta be her. How many women sailors could there possibly be?"

Shoe would have sworn *she* was a *he*. As they drew closer, he decided gender might be immaterial, though. If God had decided to create the perfect sailor, the prototype might very well have been Muriel Fitzhugh: low-built for sure footing in rough waters, intense gaze that didn't seem to miss anything and probably questioned much, and rather largish hands that could successfully tie off a knot, haul a net, or deftly handle a fishing knife. She was almost as intimidating as Hanner Mackall.

When Rudy told her they wanted a word, she looked them over a moment and then motioned to follow her off the pier and up to the overhang of warehouse 19. "If you don't need a boat, I don't have time." The whole time they talked, she played with a length of rope and her eyes never stopped roving.

"For your trouble," Rudy said, offering her a double sawbuck.

"If it's trouble, you can keep it," she said, refusing to take it. "What do you want?"

"We're not police, but we're investigating the—"

Shoe saw her eyes dart toward Mackall's boat.

"Not interested," she said, and began to walk away.

He pulled out a C note. "More interesting?"

She put it in her pocket. "Didn't see anything." She gave him a defiant look.

"I was going to marry her," Rudy said. "Losing someone you love . . . it's unbearable."

Her hands stopped and for a split second her look softened. "'And no other thought than to love and be loved by'—" The sound of a revving boat engine cut her off. "It's done. Move on." She turned her back on them and headed back toward the *Sunrise Pelican*.

"Well, we tried," Rudy said, watching her go. "Tough nuts down here. Think she knows?"

Shoe was too busying watching the next pier to comment. Mackall's boat, the *Sea Kingdom*, was back, bumping its way along the dock as it eased it into its slip. "Oh, she knows. But we're not going to get anything from her or anybody else. Nobody's going to rat out a neighbor without expecting a knife in the belly or the back."

Curiously, the pilot wasn't Mackall. Shoe watched as the stranger threw a bull rope around a mooring, tied it off, and hurried down to the end of the pier. He entered warehouse 20, but he wasn't there long. Moments later, Shoe felt a rush of adrenalin as he emerged, accompanied by Hanner Mackall. There was an ongoing conversation between the two, but other than a string of profanity, Shoe couldn't catch it. Mackall locked the warehouse's double doors and they both returned to his boat and pushed off immediately. "Where's the fire?" Shoe mumbled.

Rudy shifted his gaze. "Don't like him either. Let's go."

They fell in with stevedores rolling enormous barrels towards the steamboat landing. Neither spoke—Shoe still worrying about Mackall's fire and Rudy looking as if he were drowning in runaway emotions. Sooner or later, the dam was going to burst on those feelings. Although there would be no right time, Shoe just hoped the timing would not be so inopportune as to wash them both away.

He hated to admit Rudy was ever right, but his assessment of Hanner Mackall was a bullseye. There was an undeniable malevolence about the man. What was he so heated about and what was in his warehouse?

Chapter Twenty-Five
T. Winks and Dead Marty's

Rattled and defeated, Shoe and Rudy found themselves once more at the town clock. It was as if they were circling on a carousel without gold rings or prizes. "Well, that went well. Any ideas, Rudy?"

"Not a one," Rudy said. He let out a burdened sigh. "Maybe we're in the wrong job, Shoe, because I'm coming up zeros. The murderer is right here in front of us somewhere and we can't identify him. I can almost hear the taunting laughter." He pointed at a hook and bait shop with fishing creels in the front window. "Is he there? Or there?" he said, gesturing toward the shop next door. "Or maybe it's this one." He pointed to Ripley's Hock Shop, right behind them. "Go—*what?*" He emitted a sound somewhere between a hiss and a whistle.

Three strides had Rudy at Ripley's door. He yanked it open with enough force to bounce it off the front of the building, went straight to the window, and pulled something from the display. "Where did you get this?" he asked, wheeling around on the proprietor cowering at the register. He put a delicate emerald necklace with an intricate cross pendant down on the counter.

A look of fear swept across Mr. Ripley's face. He looked from the jewelry to Rudy and shrugged with false bravado. "Same way I get everything else in here. Fair trade. Money for precious family items."

176

He picked it up. "Gave a good price for it too. Interested? I can contact you if they don't come back for it."

Rudy pulled it out of his hand. "They *who*?" He said over his shoulder to Shoe, "This is Mena's."

Ripley peered around Rudy to look at Shoe. "Don't know, sir. It came in a day I wasn't here. Mr. Marty dealt with the other party."

"Let me talk to Marty."

"Can't. He died yesterday."

"Yesterday," Rudy repeated, giving Shoe the side-eye. "Rather convenient, wasn't it?"

"Fell off the pier and drowned. Terrible thing," Ripley said, shaking his head.

Rudy's face colored a deep red and his fists clenched. Shoe latched onto his arm, which was quivering with anger that had only one other place to go. "A word outside, Rudy." Rudy remained rooted in a staring contest with the proprietor. Shoe leaned over and whispered, "A stretch in the can will solve nothing."

Rudy emitted a low growl. "Let's go," he said, shaking free, and he took off.

Ripley tore around the counter after him. "Hey, you can't leave with my stuff. I'm calling the cops."

Rudy turned around and seem to grow three inches taller. Shoe had never seen anything like that from a Shoemaker. Rudy's chutzpah had to come from his mother's side.

"Listen, pal," Rudy said, holding the jewelry up just out of Ripley's reach. "You've been had. This merchandise is hot. Evidence in a murder case. Someone will be by later to take a statement from you. Or, if that doesn't suit you, we can take you down to the *clubhouse* and address things now."

All defiance drained from Ripley's face. He nodded meekly.

"Make a note in your books, and reference," Rudy said. "*T. Winks.* Got it?"

Ripley had a beanpole build and wiry little hands. He got it, but as he returned behind the counter, he mumbled a few expletives and said, "I'm making a note in my book. This *T. Winks* better cough up some reparation. I don't run no charity kitchen."

"Excellent." Rudy slid Mena's jewelry into a pocket and returned to the counter. "While you're in there, tell me who Marty listed as bringing in the necklace."

Ripley's blank look told Shoe the proprietor wasn't fast enough to talk his way out of the corner he'd put himself in. Hostility began rolling off him like lava running down Mt. Vesuvius. Shoe never met a store owner who didn't pack a heater or at least stow one within easy reach of his cash register. This one was gonna blow. As Ripley's hands disappeared beneath the counter, Shoe grabbed Rudy by the back of the jacket and yanked.

Rudy staggered backwards. Ripley backed away from the counter, both hands clutching his leather-bound ledger. Rudy delivered a well-aimed elbow to Shoe's rib cage and he let him go.

"If you'll please show us the ledger," Shoe said, massaging his side, "we'll be on our way."

Ripley put the ledger down and with shaking hands flipped to the last page. But before he could read it, Rudy had swung the oversized notebook around and begun running a finger down the page.

Ripley, now a ghostly shade of pale, grabbed the book back and hugged it to his chest. "Sir, your behavior is completely unacceptable. Get out!" There was a warble in his voice that diluted any authority he might have commanded.

The next few events occurred so quickly that Shoe would be hard-pressed later to remember exactly what transpired. As near as he could recall, Rudy's hands went for the book, Ripley's dove for the cash register, and Shoe's threw something big and heavy at Ripley's head. The Keystone Cops couldn't have choreographed it better.

Ripley's first shot went wide but his aim was much improved by the second, and glass shattered behind them just as they cleared the doorway. Rudy passed him in three strides, arms and legs pumping like a well-oiled engine.

"Where?" he said as he passed Shoe.

"Left," Shoe said, directing him between the first two buildings. Bad choice. A high wooden fence blocked their way at the end of the alley.

Rudy bent double, clutching at his knees as he struggled to catch his breath. "Now what?"

Shoe breezed past him and leaped at the fence. His foot hit somewhere in the middle, his hands grabbed the top, and he was up and over. As he landed in tall weeds on the other side, he heard his name included in several colorful pejoratives and Rudy's oxfords scraping the boards on the other side.

Rudy hit hard and they were off again, hopping through trash and briar behind the buildings as they raced toward the main dock. Rudy continued his diatribe, but as Shoe pulled away it faded into babble.

When he reached the main thoroughfare, Shoe halted at the entrance to the alleyway and took a gander. He saw no cops barreling his way, that way, or any way. No enraged gun-wielding store clerk. No commotion at all—just a steady stream of peaceful strollers taking in the cool December air and views. He and Rudy could disappear in this and walk at a clip fast enough to get them off the wharf but not so fast as to draw unwanted attention.

"Looking good, Rudy," he said over his shoulder. Nothing. No heavy breathing, no slapping of Rudy's enormous feet, no shove to keep him moving along. In fact, Rudy was still halfway down the alley, a hand to the side of one of the building as he gimped along. Shoe sprinted back down the alley. He didn't see any blood, but Rudy was limping badly. "What happened?"

"Bum knee. No more fences." Rudy's voice was tight as he grimaced through the pain.

Shoe put a shoulder under his arm and helped him hobble past the last of the warehouses. When they reached Main Street, they stopped for a breather—more for Shoe's benefit than Rudy's. Rudy was going to hurt regardless.

"*T. Winks?*" Shoe asked. "Did we really need another moving part in this?"

"Tiddly Winks. Great game. Ever play?"

"You moron. We're gonna get time for impersonating the police."

"I never said I was police. I can't help what that palooka inferred. Half of his business is under the table. He won't report us." He tried to take a step and grimaced in pain, his hand shooting out to the warehouse for support. "Did you, uh, buy that on *Marty?*"

"Haven't you ever been in a hock shop before? *Marty* is code for *none of your business.*"

"Birthdays and Christmases, *brother*. I was the red-headed stepchild, remember? Never had anything worth hocking."

Just one more Rudy Becker story. The man was in the wrong profession, a fiction writer all the way. *Ass.* Their father wasn't that kind of man. Guilt quickly tossed his annoyance aside as he recalled the look on Rudy's face as he held the necklace. Rudy was a jerk, but he was also toting a wagonful of baggage. *Half-*assed, then.

"We've poked the underbelly, Rudy. We've got to go. If it gets around that we're peepers, our lives are going to go swirling down the crapper. If Ripley has an enforcer, we can't show our faces around here anymore. If he tells Mackall, we should hop the next freight out."

He gazed up the avenue as it climbed away from the water on its way out of town. "Can you make it up there?" he asked. And then he said, "Sorry, Rudy, that wasn't a good question. We've got nowhere else to go. We'll stop somewhere along the trip, but we can't stay here." He seized on Trott's produce stand, halfway up. "Trott's, okay?" He started pulling Rudy forward again as pain began rippling through his shoulder under Rudy's weight.

"Shoe, when we make it up there, we hop the next train out and sort where we are."

Shoe liked the fact he was talking *when* and not *if,* but he wasn't so sure about leaving town. He felt as if they were about to make a breakthrough, and he couldn't just up and leave Fannie and Jack. They'd just have to be stealthier. "Sounds like a plan, Rudy."

They were stopping every fifteen feet now. Rudy was sheet-white, his jaw set into a slow grind. Shoe's shoulder was keeping rhythm like a musician's foot. He checked behind them. There was no parting of the crowds as a posse headed after them and no sign of any coppers. If Ripley had called out the cavalry, they were heading in the opposite direction. Rudy was probably right. Ripley might be playing it close to the vest. That thought was even more frightening. The theft wouldn't be forgotten, just dealt with in some dark alley some night.

Nobody approached them, not even to offer assistance. In fact, Shoe saw more than a couple of *decent* folks cross the street to avoid them. He guessed he didn't blame them. The best way to keep out of trouble was to mind one's own business.

Then Rudy shifted more of his weight to Shoe and that was it. They weren't going to make the summit. To their left: Roper's Blacksmith. To the right: Seymour Attman's Delicatessen and Keller Brothers Cigars. With no place to sit, Shoe would have to dump Rudy onto the floor. That wouldn't be so bad, but the odds of getting him up again were one-in-a-no–way. Shoe's eyes darted. With adrenaline pumping thoughts of flight through his head, he couldn't get them to stop long enough to pick a place.

Rudy sagged another few inches. "Come on, Rudy, not here on the sidewalk." *How about a wagon, too?* he silently begged whoever conjured up those sorts of things.

And lo, as if someone had heard his plea, he perceived the sound of a wagon creaking up the hill behind them. As it drew abreast, he noted the empty bed. Before he could hail the driver, the wagon halted a few feet ahead of them, and the driver jumped down and took a few steps toward them. "Ride?"

"Yes, sir," Shoe said. "Top of the hill, if you don't mind." He tried pulling Rudy along at a quicker pace lest the offer be rescinded once the driver had a better look at them. The attempt was futile; Rudy was spent.

They had to look an awful fright with beggar's-lice and what-naught stuck to their clothes from their alley flight, but the waggoneer must have seen worse. He caught Rudy under the other arm and somehow they got him up into the wagon bed. Shoe tried to explain the knee, but apparently the driver's good-heartedness didn't extend to small talk and exchange of pleasantries. Other than a grunt and a groan, Rudy said nothing.

In the end, it didn't matter. There was enough goodness afloat to get them all the way to Betty's diner. However, when they staggered in, Fannie's expression shot that down like a clay pigeon.

Chapter Twenty-Six
I Do and You Can't

After the initial shock and a look of *we're going to have a serious discussion later*, Fannie managed to get Rudy comfortable in a chair with a bag of ice on his leg. The knee had swelled and colored up nicely in a manly shade of angry pink. Rudy looked considerably better and the color in his face had returned. The women of Betty's pronounced it a mild sprain and suggested he stay off it. Rudy blamed it on a trick knee and assured everyone he'd be all right shortly. He was seemed to be of the mind that he and Shoe would successfully figure things out if they stayed away from the water a while and just put their noggins together. By that logic, Shoe figured they were going to somehow strike it rich in the next twenty-four, and a smartly dressed stranger was going to deliver an elegantly wrapped box containing all the evidence they needed to find and convict Mena's murderer. Shoe saw it as wishing in one hand and—

"Coffee?" Fannie called out, interrupting Shoe's thoughts. She poured two without waiting for an answer.

"Giggle water?" he whispered, miming a drinker.

She nodded and added a splash of dark liquid from a bottle they kept under the counter. He took the bottle from her and added that much more again.

"Don't see your mother. Are you here by yourself all day?" he asked.

"Yeah. I gave her a much-needed day off."

"So you haven't gotten a chance to check the land records. That's okay. I'll work it in."

"No, actually, I did. Someone else opened for me and I checked first thing this morning."

"Any trouble?"

"Cakewalk. Like I said, Katie and I go way back. Half a dozen or so of the properties scattered along that road are owned by Calvert Unlimited. And they've all been purchased in the last year. Guess who the signatory was."

Shoe shook his head.

"Him," she said, pointing at Rudy. "I don't want to know what happened this morning. But if he didn't already tell you about Calvert, you can't trust him, and I am going to ask—no, *plead*—I'm going to *plead* with you to go back to Washington. As soon as Mom is well enough, I'll follow."

"Don't let that imagination run away with you," Shoe said, stirring vigorously as he dumped sugar into the coffee. "He did. Everything's under control. Rudy's just clumsy. He tripped in the dark. End of story."

He started away and Fannie began to protest. He shushed her and set the coffee back down. "You have anyone else helping you here?"

She shut up and nodded, but Shoe could tell that he'd used his one and only pass when he shushed her. He dug down into his pants pocket and pulled out a portrait of one of the presidents, or maybe it was some other statesman. Didn't matter. Timing was everything. "Before I forget. Great shoes in the windows on Seventh Street. Go buy a pair you like and I'll take you dancing over at the pavilion." He tucked the bill into her lightly curled fist and walked away. For an instant, he considered keeping the spiked drink for himself, but he overcame the temptation when he saw Rudy grimacing in pain.

"Calvert Unlimited," he said, setting down the drinks. It's a land speculation company. Why didn't you tell me you were working for Carlton Donaldson?"

"Because it's a short-term thing, and it's none of your business."

"It is when I waste time running around trying to figure out who's buying off the Koenig family with a nice house. You just can't come clean, can you?"

Rudy's eyes narrowed. "*Me?* Who, pray tell, are the Koenigs?"

Jiminy! Shoe couldn't keep his *p*s and *q*s straight. "I, uh . . . didn't I tell you that part?" Reluctantly, Shoe filled Rudy in on everything he knew about the Koenig family.

When he was through, Rudy gave him a put-out look. "You realize this means I don't fully trust you anymore. Holding out on anything else?"

Shoe bit his lip and shook his head. No, that was his last bargaining chip. If knowledge was power, he now had little sway over his brother. "I swear. Things have been moving so fast . . . You still owe me anyway, Rudy. Where was Mena the night she was murdered?"

"Down at the water waiting on me to return to Nevis."

Shoe's jaw dropped. "The bad side of town . . .in the middle of the night? Are you loco?"

"*Non compos mentis*," he said softly. His gaze drifted away and there was a look in his eyes suggesting something profound and leveling. "They should lock me up. Toss the key. Oh, how I failed her."

Shoe looked at him thoughtfully. There it was again: a whole lot of grief bottled, corked, and no place to go. It wasn't possible to carry that much grief around and not have it erupt somehow: hysterics, complete emotional shutdown, or the desire to follow Mena into the afterlife in a blaze of glory. "Don't get lost in crazy thinking like that. You know she loved you."

Rudy blew across the top of his drink and gingerly sucked at the liquid. A slight smile crossed his lips as the taste of liquor hit him. He took a second, longer drink before setting it down. "Don't ever get married, Shoe. It'll break your heart."

Shoe raised an eyebrow. "Married? Are you telling me—"

"One month, tomorrow." He turned suffering eyes on Shoe. "I can still celebrate, right?"

"Er, sure. Was this, um, one of those midnight promises, um, to have and to hold forever, or did you actually, you know, get around to official paperwork?"

Rudy's eyes bristled with fire.

"Not that it all wasn't lovely and real and permanent in your eyes," Shoe quickly added. "Um, congratulations?"

"Official," Rudy said. His eyes dimmed and he took another sip of liquor. "A license, City Hall, the works. Official and legal."

"I wish you had told me this sooner, Rudy. It kinda changes things."

Rudy looked at him as if *he'd* lost *his* marbles. "*Everything.*"

Shoe nodded. "I don't think you understand the magnitude of what you just told me. Did Mena have any money in her own right?"

Rudy's cup stopped midway to his lips. "Are you insinuating I married her for her money?"

"Nothing of the sort. I've no doubt you married her for love's sake. But if Mena had a trust fund, you might be the legal beneficiary. You could be sitting on a fortune!"

"I don't care. I'd never spend a penny of it."

Shoe watched him down the rest of his coffee. "Maybe you don't, but it creates a motive for murder. Who else knows?"

"The officiant. Two witnesses. We weren't stupid."

"And you think you pulled off a secret wedding?"

"We found our ways. Everybody's got to sleep sometime," Rudy added. "We slipped out at an odd hour of the night and disappeared until the Hall opened. Nobody was the wiser."

"I'm sorry," said a voice behind them.

Shoe whirled around to see Fannie and a customer in the middle of an awkward dance: she trying to balance a tray of food and he struggling to keep from plowing her over. Shoe had been vaguely aware of the gentleman arriving after he and Rudy had hobbled in, but had paid him no further mind. Now that he had a second look, he realized the man looked familiar. But it wasn't the face he recognized. There was nothing outstanding about his mug; it would blend into any crowd. No, it was the shoes—maybe a small detail to someone else, but not to this journalist, who had wasted half a day writing a feature on the latest men's footwear. They weren't flashy two-toned oxfords or nubuck brown, but Converse tennis shoes in dark brown. Given the man's nicely cut suit, they were a most unusual fashion choice.

"Sorry," the man said again. He stepped around Fannie and quickly exited.

A sick feeling sank like a lead fishing weight in Shoe's stomach as he watched the gentleman bound down the diner steps and sprint toward the train station.

Rudy, do you have a copy of that marriage license?"

"Lock box off Lexington in Baltimore. Why?"

"I don't think your marriage will be a secret for long."

"Him?" Rudy said, nodding out the window at the retreating figure. "Emerson's man?"

"My guess. I had the feeling we weren't the only ones working this mess. He heard everything we said. Dammit, I should have been more careful. Trouble's going to come of that one. Mark my words."

Shoe continued watching until the eavesdropper disappeared from view. "Oh well, can't be helped now. And I think you've got it right about laying low for a while, Rudy. Fannie can arrange a ride for you back to the Bayside. Stay there and rest up. I'll need you later. As soon as it gets dark, I'm going back to Ripley's. One less loose end. We need a crack at his bookkeeping."

Rudy cocked an eyebrow. "Nice try, but you can save it for Sweeney." He set the ice pack aside. "You're not running off without me. It's too dangerous. Besides, I'm not sure you'll be forthwith when you return. Our partnership seems one-sided." He stood up and attempted to put weight on his leg. With a caterwaul, he quickly dropped back into his seat. "Just need to walk it off," he mumbled.

"Yeah, *nice try.*" Shoe picked up the ice pack and settled it back on the knee. "Now you're on the trolley! Don't worry. It'll be jake. I'll tell you everything." It wasn't enough. Rudy's face was full of doubt and mistrust. It was a new experience and it hurt a little. "On Dad's grave," Shoe said, making a quick sign of the cross over his heart. That was as solemn as it got for him.

As he left, Shoe stopped at the counter for a quiet moment with Fannie. "Jack coming back by here today?"

"He promised later today. Why?"

"Oh, nothing in particular. Keeping an eye out for him, that's all. He said he'd help me later today. I'll be hanging around the Ferris wheel. Can you send him that way? It's important."

Fannie didn't buy his nonchalance. She gave him a long, concerned look before agreeing. "Him too?" she asked, indicating Rudy.

Shoe shook his head. "Keep him *happy* for a while, then bundle him off to the hotel." Then he scooted out the door before Rudy could muster up a second wind.

There was no way Ripley recognized who they were, but sooner or later, with enough questions and snooping, somebody would make them. Nevis was too small a town to hide . . . unless you sliced and diced a couple down on the wharf. Then it was a boundless piece of real estate warrened with hidey holes. No, if he and Rudy were living on borrowed time, they needed to get cracking before Ripley and crew had a chance to noodle things through.

Chapter Twenty-Seven
If Initials Were Birds

The top of the Ferris wheel made a perfect observation point for observing the comings and goings on the wharf, but at this time of evening, Shoe could only guess on which warehouse belonged to whom. A sense of relief washed over him when he picked up Jack's approach. With dark circles under his eyes and rumpled hair, the boy looked as if he had just rolled out of bed. There was nobody else on the Ferris wheel. Shoe gave the operator a fiver with instructions to ride them until it ran out. That would be plenty of time to get what he needed from his young protege. They climbed into a bucket, and Shoe handed him a hot dog dripping with yellow mustard and sauerkraut.

"*Esskay* hotdog," he said. "Coney Island's Nathan's can't touch 'em."

Jack didn't stop to consider. He downed half the bribe in a single bite.

"Anything new?" Shoe asked, watching him chew.

Jack grunted. Nothing else, just the grunt. Shoe looked him over. The fast-talking, cover-all-your-bases street urchin had grown into a lanky youth of few words and plenty of attitude. Not that he hadn't any attitude before. Back then, it was all about the hustle. Now it was solely *none of your business*. Only it *was* his business. Important business.

The only thing harder than getting Jack to speak more than two words was getting him to sit still long enough to talk at all. Shoe's game plan was short, to-the-point questions. "Ripley's," he said, pointing down toward the wharf. "Got anything on that? Friends, enemies, illegal activities?"

"Uh huh."

"Come on, Jack. Specifics. I need to visit tonight and check a few things out. Background would be nice."

"Are you meeting just him?"

Shoe gave him a sour look.

"Shhh . . ." Jack mumbled. "Now who's not helpful?" He shifted his feet until his knees bumped up against the front wall of the cart and his pant legs rode up even higher on his socks. "That's an easy lock. Meet me at the clock tower at eight sharp." He took another big bite of the wiener.

Shoe gave him a quick look. "You don't steal, do you, Jack?"

Another growl suggested he was pushing it.

"Eight, then. It'll be quick, Jack. And we won't be lifting anything," he swiftly added.

With the hotdog almost gone, Shoe had a couple more questions at best. He pointed toward the bay again. "Those warehouses . . . is there any rhyme or reason for the way they're numbered? Doesn't make sense to number them but have the numbers nonconsecutive."

Jack turned his gaze on Shoe and studied him thoughtfully as chewed. "Fire took out the low numbers," he said, apparently placated and energized by his meal. "When they rebuilt them, they gave them new numbers. Which one are you interested in?"

"Uh, none in particular. Just curious. Like, how about that tall one in the middle of the other two tall ones right there on the water? About twenty or so down from the old glassworks? Just for instance? Would that be 20?"

"Mackall's? Twenty. Gonna rob that too?"

Shoe started to stand in mock indignation and then remembered where they were. He sat back down as the cart bounced and swayed precariously. "I'm not robbing anyone! What's wrong with you?"

Jack smirked. "You're breaking into businesses and I'm the one with the problem?" As they passed the ride operator, he motioned to get off. "Stop next time around," he yelled at him.

They both crossed their arms across their chests and looked in opposite directions. When the ride slowed to a stop, Jack stormed off and disappeared in the flow of visitors drifting past.

At precisely eight o'clock, Shoe stepped out of the shadows and approached the clock tower. Except for the scrawny yellow tabby weaving in and out of his legs, the wharf was deserted—dark and silent except for the steady wash of the water against the shore and a rumbling of thunder in the distance. It was an illusion, of course. The deeply religious were keeping vigil all day and late into the night at the place on the pier where the Blessed Virgin was said to have appeared. Apparently they had run out of hymns and were currently in deep personal prayer.

Shoe heard Jack's footfall on the sandy boardwalk long before he saw him. The kid was a lot of things: cocky, indifferent to rules, and befuddlingly misdirected at times. Unreliable he was not.

Jack passed him by as if they were strangers. Shoe let him go, then followed at a respectable distance. Right before he reached the hock shop, Jack flicked his hand toward the alleyway that ran between

Ripley's and the shop next door.

At least, Shoe thought he saw that. He turned into the alley and hoped to Hades that Jack would duck into the next alley and meet him on the backside of the building. The alley was relatively clean for the docks area, no doubt due to its proximity to the steamboat landing. By the time one reached the brothels, all bets were off for passing between buildings. Given the potential for being rolled or beaten up by opportunists or inebriated wanderers, you wouldn't want to do that anyway. Shoe moved quickly to the alley's end and peered around the edge of the building. Jack was already on his knees working hard at the back-door lock. A moment later he pushed the door open.

The shop was all one room. By the soft glow of lamplight filtering in through the broad front window, Shoe eased past cabinets and tables filled with the excesses of the financially secure and the broken dreams of the down-and-out. As he inched by, machines, jewelry, and musical instruments crowded him with silent pleas to be rescued and taken home.

"We've got about five minutes," Jack whispered, following behind him. "Since the murder, cops been patrolling this section of beach. Anywhere the *good* folk might walk. Tell me what you want. I'll help you find it."

"Don't touch anything. I got it," Shoe said as he slid behind the checkout counter. He stared into the cubbyhole beneath it until his eyes adjusted to the light. "Here," he said, pulling out the ledger. He put it on the floor and flipped to the back.

"Light?" Jack asked.

Shoe sat back on his haunches. "Didn't want to risk it. You?"

"Nope. Your party. Try the street lamp at the window?"

Shoe didn't like it. It was a bit like waving *here I am* to the local flatfoots. The front door would have offered better protection, but it was boarded up where Ripley had shot out the glass. He looked around the dim room, searching for inspiration. Ripley had a lantern on the shelf behind them. Shoe nixed that. It would be even riskier than a quick shot at the window.

"Okay, window," he said at last, "but it's going to be quick. I need the name of the person who hocked an emerald necklace. It should be one of the last entries."

As Shoe got up, Jack stayed him with a hand. "Wait. I have a better idea. I'll go outside and keep a watch. If you hear this"—he whistled softly like a redbird— "you beat it. Okay?"

His finesse was worrisome. Before Shoe could respond, he was gone.

By the time the back door clicked, Shoe was at the window and Jack was already chirping like a bird. Shoe ran a trembling finger down the latest ledger entries. *Yesterday. Yesterday. Yesterday.* Shoe broke out into a cold sweat. He could hear Jack talking to someone outside.

Finally! "O.S.," he read aloud. What did it stand for? He double-checked the entry again. *Gold necklace and pendant, green "emerald" stones . . . O.S.* "Mother . . ." he mumbled, and slammed the book shut. He made his way across the floor and shoved the book back into the cubby. Then, stooping low, he scooted toward the back door. The store filled with the bright light of a lantern as he pulled it quietly closed behind him.

He lingered at the door a moment. Could Jack handle the police? He was a shrewd operator, and when he wanted to be, an excellent talker—clever, and innocent enough for the coppers to give him the once-over and let him go. But at some point, everybody's luck ran out. He strained to hear any conversation, but the waterfront had become troublingly silent.

Beyond the alleyway on the landward came the soft coo of a turtledove. The boy knew his birds. Maybe initials too. Shoe fled. By the time he emerged from the alleyway onto Bayside Avenue, Jack was waiting for him.

"Didn't find it?" Jack asked, eying his empty hands. "Are we going down to 20 now? Mackall's boat is out."

"Like I told you—" Shoe was wasting his breath. Jack apparently thought stealing was a justifiable means to an end. "Got what I wanted without doing that. The initials O.S. mean anything to you?"

"Nope."

"Come on, Jack. You know everybody in town. Give it another go. Someone brazen enough to hock the jewelry of a dead woman within days of the murder and right under the noses of the police. Something? *Anything?*"

Jack was quiet for a while, hopefully going through a slow, methodical, street-by-street inventory of everyone he knew in Nevis. "Nothing. Out-of-towner? Maybe somebody who didn't even know where it came from."

"Good thought, but I sure hope not. That would leave us dead in the water."

Jack shrugged. "All I got." He made a sudden right hook and sauntered off into the dark. "If I think of anything else, I'll let you know."

"Where are you going?"

"Later."

Shoe sure hoped so. If Jack didn't know, he couldn't imagine who would. The sound of a hoot owl sent him hurrying off to the security of the Bayside Hotel.

Chapter Twenty-Eight
Behind Locked Doors

Shoe and Rudy spent the next day lying low, squirreled away at the Bayside, ordering room service and watching the swelling on Rudy's knee go down. His knees were butt ugly, but at least they were a matched pair again.

As he stood at the window watching the last of the light slip away, Shoe concentrated on the whitewashed building at the edge of the property. In warm weather, a Bayside employee stayed busy pulling and returning deck chairs and striped umbrellas from it all day long. In December, the attendants were brought inside to polish and shine and hammer out all the imperfections summer heat and crowds could create. Still, Shoe wondered who else might be out there creeping and watching.

The only problem with removing oneself from the flow of things was that the mind jumped into the void and created all sorts of troubling scenarios: the Clinton Boys were now brazenly parked out on the main drive waiting for them, while Mackall's henchmen lurked in the darker corners and alleyways closer to town. It would only be a matter of time before someone stole a room key and paid them a serious visit.

Rudy passed behind him, taking his hundredth test walk between the bed and his chair. "See? Perfectly fine. Trick knee, just like I told you. If we want to cross Mackall off our list of suspects, it's imperative we know what he's up to now. He's hiding something in 20. And if we don't go tonight, it may be gone tomorrow. An irretrievable loose end, Shoe."

With Rudy chomping at the bit and threatening to strike out on his own, Shoe had taken one brief excursion to get the lay of the land, so to speak. He went as far as the train depot and made it back without molestation or any significant sightings. That was an hour ago. Other than an uneasy feeling, he had run out of excuses for staying put.

"Good as new, Rudy," Shoe said without turning around. "Let's beat tracks."

Ten minutes later, they were heading to the wharf. Except for one smitten couple strolling romantically through the flowerless, leafless hotel garden, they passed no one. They did engage a mongrel dog who adopted them at the clock and trotted contentedly along with them.

"Shoo!" Shoe said, fluttering hands at him.

The dog danced away, tail wagging.

"Leave him be," Rudy said. "We're buddies." He pulled the dog over and scratched his back end right above the tail. "Good boy. Your name Wags? Huh, your name Wags?"

"It's Mackall's dog. He probably sent him to find us. Run him off, Rudy."

"Pfft, not anymore. Fixate on something else. He's coming." He offered the dog something from his pocket. Wags gave it a sniff and a lick and then galloped off into the darkness.

Shoe chuckled. "I think you've been weighed and found wanting. Come on, let's go. We'll indulge your childhood fantasies later."

Rudy sniffed the treat. "Phew, I wouldn't eat that either." He hurled it out into the bay.

Conditions were ideal for keeping people tucked away at home: late, dark, and a nip in the air that would work an achy cold into your fingertips and toes and stay there. The never-ending lap of the water, a couple of lean tabbies hunting rats, and the distant conversation between two great horned owls were all they saw or heard. Given a choice, Shoe would never reconnoiter at night, but when he had to, he again took to heart a variation on his sweet mother's admonition: "It's the fist you don't see that's going to deck you." He might not be good at sneaking around, but he had brought along his pocket pistol to even the score. Likewise Rudy. His Colt was at the ready under his unbuttoned coat, so that maternal nugget of wisdom might have come from the father they shared. Regardless, like greenhorns to a stampede, they sallied forth.

They moved quickly past warehouses, looking for number 20. It was on the more respectable end of the dock, not far from where the Captain and Mackall berthed their boats. Shoe stood watch as Rudy checked the large cargo doors, which unsurprisingly were still chained and double locked. They weren't crazy or desperate enough to expect to enter through the front anyway, just testing old Lady Luck. They melted into the shadow of the building and inched their way around to the rear, each step carefully placed lest they walk off a short plank and tumble into God knew what below. Rudy's labored breathing drowned out the sound of lapping water.

Shoe walked ahead, steadying himself with a hand on the rear wall, inching over and around scattered bricks, lumber, and other discarded trash. Every so many steps, he stopped and tapped his foot along the bottom of the building. These old warehouses had no need for a back door, but they often hinged a small opening in the wall to sweep refuse through—something like an ash-dump door in a fireplace.

"There," he said, stopping to tap a section a second time. "Hear the wobble?" The door wasn't latched and it pulled open easily. Getting through such a small opening was doable, but it would be close.

"Anything that low is not a door," Rudy whispered as he eased down, still favoring his knee. He ran his hand along the wall until he found the opening. "Really? I haven't been that small since elementary school."

"It's not that hard. Mind over body. You think small and somehow you can wiggle through it. It's just science. Go with it."

"Fine," Rudy said, "but you're going first."

Shoe went through head-first on his back with his arms extended above his head. Once his armpits cleared the hole, he leveraged against the wall with his hands and pushed himself into the dark warehouse.

"Light," he whispered, and Rudy slid their Coleman lantern through the opening. He lit and raised it, sending pale, ghostly shadows bouncing off tall walls and driving rats and other vermin scurrying for dark corners. Shoe's initial reaction was disappointment. Big tarp-covered pallets sat just inside the large cargo doors on the bay side. And to the rear, a few crates were stacked in a corner. That was it. Freeze some water on the floor and Jack could ice-skate.

Shoe waited while Rudy wiggled through the opening. Halfway through, Rudy grumbled something and reversed his course.

"Stop. You're ditching me?" Shoe asked, grabbing at his extended hands.

"Shut up. My pockets are full and I'm hung up." Rudy disappeared for a moment. "Pull," he said at last, shoving his arms back through again. Shoe grabbed his wrists and helped him wiggle the rest of the way.

Rudy remained on his back a while, studying the opening just past his shoes. "I'm not sure about doing that again." He got up and followed Shoe, who had begun circling the pallets, which were parked so close to the door that a man could barely squeeze between the two.

"Looks like they dumped and ran," Rudy said. "Whatever it is, it's merely here for storage. The space is too tight to do any work in here." He gave the closest pallet a shove. "Damn heavy too."

Shoe gave it a go. "Yeah. Explains not moving them any farther inside than this." He lifted an edge of a tarp and moved the light closer. The light played off the craggy edges of solid rock. "Well, I'll be, Rudy. Fossils."

Rudy leaned in and let out a low whistle. "God, I'd hate to be eaten by anything that big! Tusks? Ribs? What is that thing?"

"Dunno, but they aren't your common sharks' teeth."

Rudy flipped a couple more tarps back. "All these. What a wasted trip. Darby's fossils in a warehouse just like they're supposed to be. Now what?" He sat down on the floor and stretched out his bum leg.

Shoe poked around in some of the other pallets. They all seemed to be large specimens—he couldn't put a specific name on any—all still partially encased in rock. He joined Rudy on the floor and doused the light. "Darby said they were using warehouse 17. So, what's this stuff doing in 20?"

"Because he didn't trust you enough to tell you where he really had them stored."

"Nah. The man was out of his mind with inflated thoughts of glory. Falling all over himself over a set of bones they're digging out now. Why would he lie? He told me it was rare to find big specimens. And lo and behold, we've got a warehouse full of them. Why would he leave these up here alone and unguarded? Out of character. He should have shipped them off for safekeeping at the National Museum and a showy press release."

"Beats me," Rudy said. "Pompous asses never were my bailiwick."

Shoe was pretty sure Rudy was an expert on the subject, but now wasn't the time. "So, you got nothing, I got nothing. Muriel Fitzhugh got nothing."

"Not so fast, Shoe. Been thinking about something Muriel Fitzhugh said."

"Besides nothing?"

"What was the name of Mackall's boat?"

"She didn't say anything about Mackall's boat."

"No, not that. It's the *Sea something*?"

"*Sea Kingdom.*"

"Yeah, that's it. *Sea Kingdom.* Kingdom by the Sea."

"No," Shoe said, shaking his head. "It was *Sea Kingdom.* I distinctly remember looking at it and thinking it was a too highbrow for that scum."

Rudy chuckled. "Maybe. 'And this maiden she lived with no other thought / Than to love and be loved by me. *She* was a child and *I* was a child / In this kingdom by the sea . . .' I take it you're not a Poe fan?"

"*Annabel Lee?* I may not have been born in Baltimore like you, but everybody who knows anything knows that one. An old salt who quotes poetry . . . Point?"

"In between taking our money and saying *nothing*, old Muriel gave us *everything*. She's so terrified of Mackall that all she could do was talk around what he did. The line she threw at us: 'And no other thought than to love and be loved by me.' It was a reference to his boat. He killed Mena. He took the necklace. He ruined my life. He took my Annabel Lee." Rudy stood up.

The light was dim, but even so, Shoe watched Rudy pull his gun from his jacket. "Whoa now, wait, Rudy," he said, springing to his feet.

He locked his hand around the barrel. "Who you gonna shoot? Nobody here but you and me. Put that thing away. Then we get the goods on Mackall and put *him* away. Mena doesn't want you to shoot anybody. She wants you to be happy. No happy from a jail cell. Rudy?"

Rudy yanked the firearm away.

Shoe put up his hands and began backing up, inching in the direction of the refuse door. "Rudy! We're wasting time in a bad place. The hatch, okay?" The farther he drew away, the less he could see of Rudy's expression in the dim light, but the firearm was still in his extended hand. He watched the arm lower and let out a relieved sigh.

They were halfway to the hatch when a scraping sound—like boots grinding sand beneath them—froze them in place. The warehouse doors rattled and low voices began murmuring just on the other side.

Shoe was on the floor and partially out their escape hatch when they heard the clink of the heavy chain securing the door. They'd never get out without being seen. He started back inside.

"What in God's name?" Rudy whispered. "Go. I'll hide."

As far as Shoe was concerned, it was a good plan, but he didn't need Rudy shooting anybody. He pulled out of the hole, did a roll, and darted for the crates in the corner with Rudy right behind him. As they cleared the crates, the warehouse doors squeaked open on their big hinges and the interior space was illuminated with low light.

"Over there. Be quick." It wasn't Mackall but someone else barking orders in a husky smoker's voice. The strong smell of tobacco smoke wafted their way.

The next few minutes were filled with grunts and groans, the shuffling of feet, and vocabulary only a sailor could appreciate. Shoe raised his head to get a better look and immediately felt an elbow in the ribs. He dropped back down. By his quick count, there were at least six figures illuminated by the light.

Their hideaway suddenly brightened. Shoe watched the play of light on the opposite wall. It swung back and forth like a pendulum, as if someone were swinging a lantern side to side as they walked. Despite the cool weather, sweat popped out on his forehead. He held his breath and followed the sound of heavy shoes as they approached. Just when he thought they'd been made, the feet stopped. The light changed course. Then more profanity, and the light dimmed. Dear God, the postern door was still open! The beads of sweat began to journey down Shoe's face as he listened to the squeaking of the little door. Back and forth, back and forth, back and forth, followed by a grunt and the grinding of metal on metal.

The lantern hoisted high again, bathing their corner in light once more. Then the corner darkened and the footsteps retreated.

The husky voice from a distance: "T.B., were you posted tonight?"

"Yes, sir."

"The back hatch was open. Make sure it stays locked." The directive was followed by scuffling and a cry of pain.

"Everybody out."

With a whoosh, the doors of the warehouse closed and the warehouse plunged into darkness once more. The heavy chains rattled against the door and the voices faded. Silence.

They crept along the back wall to the hatch.

"*Criminy's sakes*," Rudy muttered, fumbling with the door. "He bent the hinges to shit."

Shoe dropped down beside him and did his own jiggling. "The only way we're getting out of here is to rip it off."

"I have no problems with that," Rudy said, elbowing him aside.

Shoe sat back on his haunches, and as he waited, a cold chill inched over him. This could take all night. They were in a pickle, all right: locked in a warehouse by smugglers who might return any minute, and if Rudy was carrying the necklace—and it was a good guess he was—with stolen property from the local hock shop. Oh, the flatfoots would love that one. He'd already been roughed up by Chief McCall in an alleyway. What in the hell could he expect in the police station behind closed doors?

"Is it a no-go, Rudy?" he asked, getting to his feet. "Because that noise will get us nothing but trouble. I'd much rather spend the night on one of those crates over there than have the coppers pull us out of here in bracelets."

"You give up too easily," Rudy said between grunts. He flipped onto his back and gave the portal a swift kick with his good leg.

Shoe's shirt was now drenched in cold sweat, and he shuddered in the cool night air. No, that wasn't it. That wasn't it at all.

Chapter Twenty-Nine
The Nunnery

Jack sat back on his bike seat and looked down the deserted street, its shops dark and closed up for the night. He wasn't scared. Fear was for Dermott and the rest of his friends. It meant you were unprepared, hadn't considered all the possibilities. He'd been sneaking out at night for years. It didn't hurt nobody. He climbed back in his window before daylight and got on with his business. When he wasn't sure what was what, he took a piece of pipe with him. People found easier pickings than tangling with a crazy kid swinging for the fences.

The door to the Western Union office swung open and the nighttime manager, Mr. Martinelli, stuck out his bald head. "Hey, you, Byrne! I thought you'd be back by now. Scram or I'll get someone else."

Jack's boss was loopy if he thought there were others willing to pedal down to a murder scene in the dead of night. The whores would get their messages, but Jack would do it his way. His safest bet was to follow Bayside to the boardwalk, follow it as far as he could, and then cut across to the wharf and the sleezy end of town. He made the sign of the cross and pushed off. It would all be easy as pie.

There wasn't much light along the water. It creeped him out, but that didn't count as being chicken. He guessed people didn't need to see much down here, as they knew where they were going. He chuckled as he recalled something he'd heard once from Walter Fanwith and a dozen other times from the old wharf drunks. "Never went to bed with an ugly woman," he'd said. "But I sure have woken up with a few." With poor light like this, it all made sense now.

Unlike the large numbers painted on the top of the warehouses, if there were any addresses in the whore section, he wasn't seeing any in the dim red lights illuminating each door. He hopped off his bike and began a slower, more meticulous search. When he had it, Number 12 above a place named *The Nunnery*, he approached and attempted to peer through the curtain in one of the two sidelites framing the door.

Out in the dark, something rustled. Jack scrambled away from the door.

"Your mama ain't here," a disembodied voice said. "Get on home before I take a stick to you."

"Y-y-yes, sir!" Jack whispered. "Western Union message for Miss Shakespeare?"

There was a grunt, or maybe a painful groan. Jack stood his ground but kept a tight grip on his bicycle should he need to bolt. "Number 12?"

"I'll take it."

"No, sir. Has to go direct."

Another noise, this time a definite growl. "There," the man said, pointing to the door in front of them. "But you better not be here when I get back."

Jack watched for a moment as the drunk staggered over to the bayside and fumbled with his pants. As the man began peeing to some undecipherable ditty, Jack hotfooted to the door and banged loudly.

"*Jasus*, I'm coming," a woman's voice called. He heard something else about waiting for an invitation and keeping his pants on.

"Well, come on in, hon," the woman said when she opened the door. "Who you here to see?"

Jack thrust the envelope at her. "Western Union, ma'am. Miss Ophelia Shakespeare?" He double checked over his shoulder to see where new his friend was.

"That'd be me," she said, taking the telegram. She looked past him and yelled, "Go home, Butler. And learn some manners." She pulled Jack inside. "Ignore him. Can't teach couth to some people."

She closed the door. "Western Union, you say? I haven't seen you before," she said, giving him the once-over. "What's your name? You taking Charlie's route? Haven't seen him around since . . ."

"Guess so. I'm Jack, ma'am."

Her eyes lit up at the *ma'am*. She studied him a moment before she reached out and wiped something from his cheek with a lacey white handkerchief. "Just like Charlie."

Jack pulled away. "Y-yes, ma'am."

"You haven't got nothing better to do than wander around the docks at night?"

"N-no, ma'am."

"Well, then, be careful out there, *Jack*." There was a cough from the room at the end of the hall. She quickly pulled several coins out of her pocket and said, "Spend it up on the other end of the boardwalk. Now, git."

She opened the door. Butler hadn't made it home yet but was staggering in the general direction of town. "He ain't got no legs," she said, and pushed Jack out. "Fly, boy!"

Jack hopped on his bike and blew past Butler fast enough to spin him around in a circle. He needed Shoe *now*, the memory of the pink monogram on the madam's handkerchief spurring him forward. Ophelia Shakespeare had hocked the necklace.

Ophelia closed the door and returned to the back bedroom and the man in the bed.

"Who?"

She let her robe hit the floor and snuggled in next to him. "Just a little nobody delivering something."

He rolled over on top of her. "I said, *who*?"

"Just a little one from Western Union. I think he said *Jack*. But he couldn't see anything."

He gave her a rough kiss and got out of bed.

"Leave him be, okay?" She ran her fingers up her arm where it throbbed. She'd be black and blue by morning, but her sleeve would cover it.

"Sorry."

"It's okay," she said. But not really. *Sorry* only worked the first time. She pulled the sheet up around her and tried to make herself insignificant. There was no use antagonizing him further.

She heard him pull on his clothes, and the clatter of money landing on the nightstand as he left. She wondered if he really cared who little Jack was or if he was just growing tired of her.

She lit a cigarette. Damn typhoid! That one took her first husband, Albert. And damn the streetcar that had run over her stumbling drunk Paul. But most of all, damn Hanner Mackall, who had an uncontrollable temper, and thought the world owed him everything. She snuffed out the fag and pulled the covers over her head. Next time he came, he'd have to throw cash at somebody else.

Chapter Thirty
Smuggling and Snuggling

Jack got as far as warehouse 23. Dead ahead, dark shapes crisscrossed between the water and one of the storehouses. He veered left to the safety of an alley and got off his bike. He couldn't tell if they were loading or unloading. No matter, it was too late for legitimate business. They were smugglers.

He crept behind 23, but he found the alleyway between it and 22 too tight to navigate. He continued on behind 22 to building 21 and hesitated. The alleyway was wider, but did he want to be this close to whatever was going on? He told himself to get over it, took a deep centering breath, and began inching his way forward, hugging the wall. He couldn't make himself peek out. There was a line between courage and foolhardiness. With all the feet-shuffling and murmured oaths, whatever they were moving, it was big and heavy. He considered a moment, then dropped on all fours and slowly leaned forward, just far enough to see around the building corner. He caught the tail end of the dirge-like procession disappearing into 20, Mackall's warehouse. The cargo was going in and not out.

He retreated back down the alley and hid in the weeds behind the building. He wasn't there long before he heard the creaking of the big wooden warehouse doors on their massive hinges, the *whump* as they closed, and the rattle of heavy chains as they were locked securely. He hunkered down further and waited.

When the sound of whispering and boots had retreated, he crept out again. The figures had moved from land to boat and were already some distance from the pier. Moving by paddle, he decided. He listened until the splash of the paddles faded and the ghostly image of the ship disappeared into the night. So this was what Shoe was interested in.

He returned to the warehouse. The doors were secured in heavy chain and a lock that even he would have trouble picking. He scanned the front façade of the building. Some of the buildings had windows and loft doors, but not this one. He walked between buildings and checked the side. No luck there either.

The tittering of a woman's voice sent him up against the wooden siding yet again. Two voices, a woman and a man, and they were pitching woo as if the continuation of mankind relied on their making it a night to remember. God help me, Jack thought. He'd never get past them and off the pier! He worked his way to the rear of the building and slid around the corner. He would follow the back alley until it ended or the rats and water snakes chased him out.

He put a hand on the wall and edged along it, picking his way through the trash. Halfway across the building, he stopped a moment and listened again for the two out front. It sounded like they were still a pint or so away from the bango tango. As he moved forward, he noticed a hatch at the base of wall, open and small enough to wiggle through. He dropped to his knees.

"Back up or I'll hurt you!"

Jack froze. "Shoe?"

"Jack?"

Rudy lowered the jagged rock in his hand. "Who?"

Shoe pushed him out of the way and stuck his face in the opening. "Jack, the door's jammed up. Can you find something to pry it open? Be quick. Mackall and his buddies have been in here once already."

"Probably. Hold on a minute." He was gone for less than that. "Back up. Coming through."

Shoe scrambled away on all fours and Rudy backed away as Jack wedged a section of pipe between the door and the hatch. The iron hinges groaned, and with a sudden crack, the wooden door split from its hinges in a shower of wood fragments.

Jack stuck his head through the opening, a quizzical look on his face. "There's a watcher talking up a lady of the night out front. Won't be long before he's making the rounds again. Give me your hands and I'll pull you out."

With Jack pulling, they wiggled out faster than they went in. Then they bolted for Bayside Avenue.

At that point, Shoe grabbed Jack's arm to slow him down. "How did you know where we were?"

Jack gave Rudy the once-over. "Who's he?"

"Friend. Rudy Becker, meet Jack Byrne."

Jack grunted and tipped his head toward the red-light district. "I didn't. I was delivering a telegram to one of the ladies when I saw smugglers unloading a boat. They took it into the warehouse. You're just plain lucky I had to wait on them. They took the boat back out again, and I'm pretty sure they're coming back. What's in the warehouse?"

"These," Rudy said. He reached inside his coat and pulled out the rock he had been banging against the hinges. "Only a hundred times bigger."

Jack rolled it around in his hands. "Smuggling rocks? Why?"

"*Fossils*," Rudy said. "Mackall's skimming specimens from the big dig. Big dough on the antiquities black mar—"

He suddenly grabbed the chunk of stone back and shoved it under his jacket. "Shh, company."

A figure appeared higher uphill, working his way down the avenue. They watched the heavily bundled man alternate between light and dark as he walked through the cones of illumination created by each street lamp. His pace was rapid and directed toward them.

"See you guys back at the Bayside?" Shoe whispered, expecting a run for it. More like a hobble from Rudy who was limping again.

Probably thinking the same thing, Rudy mumbled something profane.

The figure seemed to pick up on them at that moment, veering left and crossing the street without changing pace. Shoe increased his speed, and both parties pushed past one another with heads down. In spite of Rudy's hobbling, they maintained their pace until they reached the train depot.

Rudy sat down on one of the benches. "I need a drink. Where to now?"

"Bayside," Shoe said, "but no drink."

"Really? That would have been a much easier shot if we had turned left about two hundred feet back."

"Yeah, well that's what happens when you wing it." Shoe turned to Jack. "Still with us?"

"You two sound like nervous virgins on your wedding night."

Rudy chuckled. "Son, I doubt if you've—"

"Shut up, Rudy," Shoe said. "Wish you'd give that up," he said to Jack, pointing at his Western Union cap.

"Doing my part," Jack said. He gave Rudy the stink eye.

"Yeah, well, you can't do your part if you're not fully informed.

Follow us back to the Bayside and we'll fill you in."

"It just so happens you're the one who needs filling in. I found out something tonight."

Rudy chortled. "And what would that be?"

Jack turned his back on him, lowered his voice, and spoke directly to Shoe. "The initials *O.S.,* I know what they stand for. It's Ophelia Shakespeare. I delivered a message to her tonight. She's the madame at The Nunnery and she's Mackall's girl."

Rudy exploded in laughter. "Son, a whore isn't anyone's girl."

Shoe gave him a shove that sent him staggering on his bum knee, and he wasn't sorry about it. "I don't see you making any contributions here. *Can* it." He turned back to Jack, who seemed to be ten seconds away from decking Rudy. It was a nice healthy reaction, if ill-conceived. Rudy was twice his size. Shoe put his palm on the middle of Jack's chest and walked him back a few feet. "Be bigger," he whispered. "How do you know they're connected?"

Jack gave Rudy another brief, heated glance before answering. "I could see through to the back room. Not inside. The door was closed. But his dog was curled up right there, sleeping."

"He never caught your face."

"Nope."

"Good. That's good." Shoe reached out and patted his shoulder, more to reassure himself. "It's all good, Jack. Maybe we're getting somewhere now. O.S. was probably just the middle man, er, woman. And we now we know why Hanner wasn't at the warehouse."

"There's something else too." Jack pulled out the money the whore had given him and handed one of the coins to Shoe.

Shoe ran his finger across the bawdy-house token. "That's what they're tipping now. God Almighty!"

"I don't think she meant to. She seemed in a hurry. Butch had one just like it and she asked if I was taking Charlie's place. The Koenigs have been there."

"Stay out of there," Shoe said, pocketing the token. "Come back to the hotel with us. We need to look at what we've got."

"I have to check back in, but I'll be off in a couple hours. I'll catch up with you then." He pushed off into the dark.

"Street smart," Rudy said. "Let him go. You and I, on the other hand . . ."

"Yeah, and you're a smartass. A real confidence builder, you know that? Come on before I deck you myself."

Hanner stepped back into the shadow of the clock and let 'em go; three against one wasn't smart play. He knew enough, recognized all three—the newsman and the land speculator from the cliffs, and the young messenger. He already knew all about the speculator—once a snoopy journalist, always a sharp-eyed problem. Darby could shed light on the newsman. And the third, the boy . . . well, he could get at the boy anytime he wanted.

What he couldn't figure out was why anyone was actively seeking to solve the murder of a woman who couldn't be identified and a young'un who ran the streets all night long. He wasn't sure why anyone would care. This was all too complicated and everybody a problem. Time to make it less so, starting with Miss Shakespeare. Hocking the necklace when she had strict instructions to keep it, the whore had double-crossed him. Ripley? Didn't respond well to pressure.

Chapter Thirty-One
Always About the Bones

Shoe sat across from Rudy, sipping a cup of piping-hot joe and fingering the fine silver cutlery before him. Things seemed safer within the glass walls of the Bayside Hotel's conservatory, but it was just one more illusion. They were in the midst of a swirling storm of clues they were unable to connect, and no idea where that funnel cloud was going to touch down next.

He seriously doubted Mackall was unaware of who visited his girl. And if he suspected Jack had seen any activities at the warehouse, it wouldn't be difficult to find him and dice him up like the Koenig kid. They needed to get him back to Washington, or at the very least, in the hotel behind a double-bolted door.

Rudy was lost in his own thoughts, sipping strong Turkish coffee, gazing thoughtfully out one of the windows. Shoe could see him fitting in with the rich and bored. There was an air about him. Their father had been a good man but working class all the way. It had to be the maternal side.

"Mackall, Ophelia Shakespeare, the necklace, and the murders are all connected," Shoe said. "Then there's Darby—in cahoots with Mackall, or innocent, obnoxious bystander? Whad'ya think, Rudy? Two heads are better than one."

215

Rudy put down his cup. "Here's the thing. And maybe it's the difference in what makes us tick, *brother*. You spend all your time chasing a literary prize that you will probably never get—not that you aren't really good at what you do. You look at every assignment as a steppingstone to something else. The big picture, if you will. Now me, when I signed on to all of this, before I realized it was going to be personal, it was all about the money. Without Emerson's advance, I can't rub two bits together. What if it's like that for Darby? What if it isn't fame he's looking for? What if it's about *the bones*?" He picked up his rock, which he had placed on his linen napkin. "The big specimens must be worth a fortune on the black market."

Shoe considered his recent money problems. It was *always* about the bones. He nodded. "Howard Carter's good fortune in Egypt has permanently eclipsed anything Darby could ever discover."

Rudy chuckled. "I guess I'm Darby to your Carter. Touché."

Shoe let the remark pass. "Darby did say nobody gets off that pier that his security doesn't check. But that's *his* side of the pier. Mackall owns the other half. As long as he doesn't duck or jump the perimeter ropes, he can come and go as he pleases on his own property. Darby can't control everything. He's probably willing to let poachers get away with some small stuff."

"Count on it. Mackall grew up around those cliffs, he's probably scavenged—"

"—or stolen—"

"—plenty of fossils."

"Yeah," Shoe, said, nodding. "That's the other interesting thing Darby said. There are plenty of fossils in the surf down there. But they're so plentiful, they aren't worth a red cent." Shoe reached over and picked up the chunk of rock and ran a fingernail across the seashell shapes imbedded in its face. Even if he had picked it up in the street, he would have known it was a fossil. "But here's the kicker. He said if you wanted to smuggle out something of value, you'd have to know what to look for. Who better than Mackall?"

"Mackall's stealing from Darby? Maybe you got it half-right. Maybe it's Mackall and Darby working together. Darby knows better than anyone." Rudy took the fossil back, and using it as a prop, moved it around the table as he illustrated his theory. "Darby extracts it and Mackall brings it up here under cover of darkness and stores it. Then when they deem the time right, they move it out. Railroad? Wagon?" He finished by placing the rock on his napkin and pulling it out into the center of the table.

"Guess you could move it any which way so long as it doesn't draw too much inspection," Shoe said.

Rudy nodded.

"If these are worth a fortune, that limits the buyer's market considerably. Only a wealthy person—"

"—with cash to burn."

"Correct. Someone exceedingly rich, with a place to squirrel it all away for their private enjoyment."

"Weathersby," they both said in unison.

China clinked and silverware rattled. Shoe's eyes darted to the waiter, who was busying himself with the sorting and stacking of cutlery and serving pieces. How much of that had he overheard?

"Too many ears," he whispered to Rudy, motioning him closer. "Running with your little scenario . . . most of the bones go to the Museum for study and public consumption, with a select few settling in for a nice long stay at a private museum. Darby and Mackall walk away rich men. Money soothes bruised egos and evil men."

"Too much wealth is immoral," Rudy said. "Mena knew that firsthand. The necklace is the only possession I ever saw that suggested she came from monied people. It was stodgy old jewelry, so different from her own bold and innovative artwork. I was never sure whether it was a reminder of how far she'd come or the inability to completely let go."

He reached into his pocket, appeared to change his mind, and switched pockets. "Where did I—" The color drained from his face. "Mena's necklace. I've lost it."

"You've missed it. Check again."

Rudy patted down all his pockets and shook his head. "I took it out when I was trying to squeeze through the hatch." He bolted out of his seat. "Dear God, It's on the ground outside the warehouse."

"Don't panic," Shoe said, rising too. "And don't even think about going back out there at this time of night. Nobody else is going to find it in the dark. We'll get it at first light. We've been lucky so far, but at some point, that's going to run out." He gestured for Rudy to sit.

Rudy sat again, but his expression was unsettling. The look in his eyes wasn't so much one of agreement as pacification. He was going to return to get the necklace and there was nothing short of hogtying him that Shoe could do about it. Sooner or later, their luck was going to run out. If Mackall found out they were the ones who had been in the hock shop and warehouse, he could find them easily enough. It was time to tie up the loose narrative.

"There's only one other puzzle piece, Rudy. Emerson said that the family knew Mena was in Nevis. Someone followed her onto the train. My guess would be, it's the same gentleman who overheard us at the diner."

Rudy's attention had returned to the world outside the window.

"Someone bird-dogged her all the time. If only I had gotten back sooner . . ."

Shoe tapped on the table. "Rudy, stay with me here! Emerson mentioned one other person she came into contact with, a man who assisted her down the steps at the depot: older, well-made dark suit—possibly Brooks Brothers—spotless oxfords. Emerson said he had a limp—"

Rudy looked at him with a crazy half-smile. "*Me.* I thought for sure the limp would have given me away by now," he said, massaging his knee. "It goes out at the most inopportune moments."

Shoe's eyes narrowed into slits. "You were here, with her, *in* Nevis, and you've never said word one about it? Rudy, Rudy." Shoe sighed and searched the ceiling for the patience he knew he wouldn't find there.

"No. I didn't actually *stay* with her. I saw her off, and then stepped aboard the train for my trip to Washington. That's the God-honest truth," he said, placing his hand over his heart. "Honest."

Shoe had to acknowledge that his brother's profession seemed on the level. "Okay. It would seem you and I are square now, information-wise. I'll take him off my suspects list." He took a drink of his coffee, which was now cold. "More," he mouthed, motioning to the waiter. "That only leaves Darby and Mackall. I say we go hard at Darby tomorrow, scare him within an inch of his life, and get him to confess about Mackall and save himself. Pleading coercion by Mackall just might save the narcissist's career."

Rudy didn't respond but instead developed a sudden fascination with the way the silverware was arranged before him.

"Rudy? Like I said—"

Rudy cleared his throat. "I haven't exactly been forthcoming with you. There's something else you should know."

Shoe took a deep, centering breath. "I'm not going to like this, am I?"

"Ever been to Poughkeepsie?"

Shoe shook his head.

"Well, it seems I'm not the only one who is a prime suspect for Mena's murder."

"What are you talking about?"

"Emerson. He seems to think you're good for it, and he hired me to prove it."

Shoe choked on his java. "I-I-I never even met the woman."

"Seems you may have stayed in the same hotel as Mena on a few occasions."

"I've stayed in lots of places in New York. So what if Mena stayed there too?"

Rudy nodded vigorously. "Absolutely. I rejected the notion right away. See, the thing is, whenever we had a rendezvous, I needed an alias. It seems I signed your name a few times on hotel registries. You know, your byline in a dumpy place. It was funny at the time, a running joke with my buddies at the paper. The great Tatum Shoemaker covering stories *everywhere*."

Shoe wasn't laughing. He put his cup down, missing the saucer and sending black liquid rolling across the crisp white linen. "How many is *a few*?"

Rudy shifted in his chair and pushed back slightly from the table, looking as if he was ready to scram. "Well, maybe more than a few. Probably every time I was with Mena. We kept to the less *popular* places to stay a step ahead of her dad."

Shoe popped out of his seat, nearly tipping his chair over as he rose. At this late hour, with the exception of the discreetly hovering server, they were alone in the conservatory. The penguin-dressed staffer started toward them to offer assistance, but Shoe motioned him away and turned on Rudy, who was up and gripping the back of his chair. He appeared ready to swing it. "Excuse us, please," Shoe said to the waiter.

The waiter bowed slightly and left immediately, closing the double doors behind him.

"All this time," Shoe growled, turning his fury on Rudy. "All this time, Emerson's had me looking for this mystery man and it's been me. He knew all along Mena was seeing someone named Shoemaker. Only it's not me, it's *you!* Are you out of your damn mind? You've framed me for murder, you son of a bitch!"

Rudy didn't move. Maybe he thought the murderous mood would blow over. Maybe he couldn't explain his dumb antics either. As usual, his judgment was poor. Shoe lunged for him and started shaking him by the lapels. "You're going to come clean to Emerson. Right? I'm not going to fry for your stupid antics."

Rudy wrapped him in a bear hug and began squeezing. They were of equal height, but Rudy had him by a good twenty pounds. Shoe couldn't catch his breath and he couldn't pry himself free.

"Causing a scene in here will only add to the situation," Rudy whispered in his ear. "Please sit back down so we can discuss this discreetly like gentlemen."

Shoe put his thumbs on Rudy's Adam's apple and began squeezing. As Rudy's hands went to his throat, Shoe shoved him hard, propelling him backward into his seat.

"This . . . well . . . I'm not going down for you, Rudy. Not even for a *full* brother." Shoe sat down hard, put a hand to his brow, and tried to compose himself.

There was a polite rapping on the door as the waiter peered through the glass, his other hand on the door handle as he prepared to rush to someone, anyone's rescue.

Rudy gave the waiter a pleasant nod as if to say everything was peachy and sat too. "I'm not asking you to. Emerson thinks you're good for the murder. I've been stringing him along while we find out who really did it. If I argue or quit on him, he's going to hire someone else to nail you. An unscrupulous go-getter might even frame you just to collect the biggest payday of their life. You need me to keep his suspicions unsubstantiated."

Shoe pictured Rudy sprawled on the floor, knocked out cold. It would solve little. He shifted his gaze from the floor to his brother's face. His brown eyes were intense and his eyebrows knitted tightly over them with deep concern. Shoe had seen the same expression on his father's face many times. Sincerity. But then his intuition was haranguing him with something much different. *Don't trust Rudy. Don't trust Rudy. Don't trust Rudy.*

Who then could Shoe trust with this convoluted mess? He shook his head. *No one.* "Don't quit Emerson," he finally said. "Keep feeding him bits and pieces that don't lead anywhere but keep him satisfied. Change his mind about the supposed evidence that implicates me. Because if you don't and things getting messy, I will."

"Deal," Rudy said.

"And after we put all the pieces together, we're done. Separate ways. Never the twain shall intersect again. Got it?"

Rudy nodded. "Yes. But I've changed. You'll look back and see."

Shoe signaled the waiter that they were through. "Come on, Rudy. Sleep here tonight. You can have the bed, and I'll take the chair by the door. We're out of here early tomorrow."

"I can take the chair."

Shoe dropped a sizeable tip on the table—one that would guarantee the waiter's undivided loyalty and discretion. "Sorry, bud. I'm not falling for that again."

Chapter Thirty-Two
A Dead-End

They were up at first light. After a minute or two of watching the elevator remain stationed on the fifth floor, Rudy's patience evaporated. They took the stairs. The first change in business for Rudy was that he was done with waiting. There would be no more sitting around a conservatory sipping beverages and thinking. He didn't need Shoe or his cautious approach to everything. God, how refreshing the thought! He hated to acknowledge it, but his brother was an insufferable control freak. Shoe thought their good fortune was soon to end, but he was wrong. Rudy still felt lucky. Or maybe it was Mena watching over him. Yeah, that had to be it. With her watching over him, he could do anything.

When he reached the first floor, Rudy put one foot in the lobby and promptly recoiled. The Clinton Boys stood dead ahead at the elevator, the UP button glowing ominously. He began backing up, driving Shoe back toward the stairs. "Shh," he hissed. "Clintons."

Shoe tried to peer around him. "All three?"

Rudy held up a hand to wait. He wasn't sure, and poking a head out in the open didn't seem wise. And so they waited, and stressed, and waited. The elevator was definitely locked off on the top floor. They could be here all day. Or worse yet, the boys might decide to use the stairs.

Shoe must have been thinking the same. He plucked at Rudy's sleeve and jerked his thumb upward.

Rudy shook his head. If they returned to the room, they might end up trapped there all day. There was a squeak of the metal elevator gate. Rudy peeked out and watched the three boys disappear into the elevator. He and Shoe waited several seconds after the door closed and then they fled.

Activity on the wharf was light and strictly day-laborers. The morning was crisp, the light low, the sky gray—not at all conducive to a leisurely stroll by any vacationers. Things would pick up when the steamboat came in some time after ten.

The brothers' plan was simple: procure passage to the cliffs with the Captain, where they would put the squeeze on Darby, and then return for the necklace and hopefully enough information to make Emerson a happy, generous man. Rudy wasn't keen on leaving the necklace until last, but Shoe argued that the more active the wharf, the safer the retrieval would be. Rudy begrudgingly acknowledged the wisdom in it.

Both the Captain's and Mackall's boats were still berthed, but Rudy didn't see anyone on the pier. "And you think seeing both of us heading back to the dig isn't going to arouse Mackall's suspicions?" he asked.

"If you see another way to the cliffs, I'm game," Shoe said. "I'm not sure it's wise to spread our business all over the place. He'll find out and it'll make him even more suspicious. No, once Darby spills his guts, it won't matter what Hanner Mackall thinks."

The Captain emerged from the cabin of his vessel. His movements fore and aft were quick and methodical, as if he were preparing to shove off. They were out of luck if he had taken on another charter.

Shoe picked up his pace. "Now or never, Rudy. Come on."

The Captain didn't seem happy to see them, but then again, Rudy couldn't imagine what *happy* would have looked like on the old salt's face.

"Captain," Shoe said, on the upbeat. "We need to get to the cliffs."

The Captain continued stowing gear in one of the lockers in the aft. "For Mr. Tanner?"

"Right. A few more questions for Darby about the dig."

"Who's paying?"

Who had time for this nonsense? "I have payment," Rudy said, coming aboard. He pulled a wad of cash out of his pocket and peeled off three twenties. An eyebrow went up. It was enough to put a crack in the old man's stony visage. He took the cash and they promptly pushed off.

When the boat picked up speed, the crisp December air turned biting and a fine mist added to their discomfort. They pulled their coat collars up, kept their heads down, and plastered themselves against the outside wall of the boat cabin. Once they returned to Nevis, Rudy vowed to never set foot on a boat again. It would be the comfort of trains forevermore.

By the time *Parker's Bet* reached Calvert Cliffs, the rain was pounding and driving hard from the west. There were no tourists at the cliffs, and likewise, Darby's dig seemed deserted. Rudy pulled another bill from his pocket and asked the Captain to wait.

Upon closer inspection, Shoe saw men working, albeit under tents pitched against the base of the cliff, the wind rippling and whipping the canvas, the sand, and everything else not tacked down. Two men intercepted Rudy and Shoe as soon as they stepped off the dock.

"Shoemaker from the *Evening Star*. Mr. Becker, *Nevis Gazette*," Shoe said, gesturing to Rudy. "We need to do a follow-up with Mr. Darby. Would you please point us in the correct direction?"

The first guard was seemingly unable to approve anything without strict prior instructions. He consulted the second, who raised his half-collapsed umbrella long enough to give them a quick once-over. There seemed to be some recognition when he and Shoe locked eyes. He nodded and pointed them toward a makeshift wooden building.

"*Nevis Gazette*?" Rudy asked, when they were out of earshot.

"It sounded better than your 'T. Winks,'" Shoe said.

The cabin-like structure was set apart from the rest of the dig, to the south, and just on the opposite side of the ropes establishing the dig boundaries—Mackall's land.

"A profitable lease arrangement?" Rudy asked.

Shoe threw his arms up in the air and kept moving. "Mackall's boat is still in port, so no worries there."

Their knocks on the door went unheeded. Maybe the guards had lost track of his whereabouts. Without any windows, there was no way to tell who was inside. Shoe jiggled the door latch, and he might have given it a slight twist. The door cracked open and he gave it an extra push.

The room was spartan—a bunk, a seaman's chest on one side, and a simple wooden desk on the other. Darby sat at the desk, hunched over an open book. He made no move to rebuke them as they entered.

"Mr. Darby?"

The stillness in the room, the odd posture, the red on Darby's hands.

As soon as Shoe touched him, he stirred and moaned. "Tanner," he whispered, looking at Shoe with dull, confused eyes.

"Shoemaker," Shoe said, correcting him. There was a large bloodstain covering Darby's shirt front, a knife wound by the look of his shredded clothes. Shoe was surprised he was still alive. "Who? Who did this?" he asked in a rush.

"Hann—" Darby wheezed and choked. He shuddered. "Son . . . a bitc—" He closed his eyes; his breathing was jagged.

Rudy put his lips to Darby's ear.

"Don't touch anything, Rudy."

Rudy fisted his hands and balanced himself against the desk with his hip. "Mackall's stealing from the dig?" Rudy asked.

"Ye—"

"For who? Weathersby, you, himself?"

There was a groan that might have been a yes.

"Why?" Darby mumbled. ". . .plenty." He made a gurgling sound and his breaths came in labored short bursts. "Bayside . . . Gi-gi-de—" He shuddered and went completely limp.

"Gid? Gideon? Come on, Darby!"

"Stop, Rudy. He's gone." Shoe eased his grip on the paleontologist's shoulder and Darby sagged onto the desk face first. "And we need to be, too."

"Are you crazy? Just leave him? What about the guards?"

"We certainly can't help him now, and I don't need a quick trip to police central, do you? We need to search his room before Mackall does."

They left everything as they found it, waved acknowledgement to security as they boarded *Parkers Bet*, and returned to Nevis. They discussed nothing further, but by silent agreement they had just added a potential murder charge to their previous theft and breaking-and-entering infractions. If Darby's Gideon bible didn't contain something more damning than a chocolate wrapper, they were looking at life . . . if they were lucky.

Chapter Thirty-Three
One Big Party

As soon as the first loop of rope encircled the piling, Shoe jumped from boat to dock with Rudy close behind. Mackall's boat was still berthed. If Mackall had attacked Darby—and there was no reason to doubt the words of a dying man—how had he managed to get there and back and so fast, without moving his boat? Shoe did a quick visual sweep of the surrounding wharf area. Who else was involved and where had they gone?

"Get your necklace, Rudy," he said. "Low profile and be quick about it. I'll make myself scarce around here."

He peeled away toward a nearby booze house called the Scuttlebutt. Unlike most of the surrounding dives, the Scuttlebutt's door was fastened on straight and the shutters were painted. Nevertheless, a hearty debate raged within him about the wisdom of standing outside. Right now, anywhere on the dock was too close to Mackall. Inside might be better, but bending elbows with a sweaty, swearing room full of fishermen and stevedores wasn't appealing, and the notion of a keg-busting reporter sitting down for bootlegged whiskey in a waterside dive was absurd. Still, good gumshoes went where the story pushed them.

The appearance of Mackall in the company of two other men,

approaching from the direction of town, suddenly changed all that. They were moving fast. Had they made him? Shoe pushed through the door and entered the Scuttlebutt.

The bar didn't fit the dark, dirty, and crowded image he expected. It was worse. The moment he cleared the door sill, the overpowering smell of musk, vomit, and urine washed over and christened him as its own. He kept his gaze unfocused and shouldered his way through the small enclave of moral turpitude to the end of the bar, where he shouldered in and claimed twelve inches of space as his own.

The barkeep gave him an inquiring look—which was okay because it could have been an *I don't recognize you so get out* look. By the looks of the crowd, ordering anything less than neat would be considered weakness. He ordered two fingers of whiskey. It didn't matter. He was going to nurse it anyway.

The men on either side of him left almost immediately, but they were replaced just as quickly by two others. They were grungy and a sweaty smell wafted off both. Neither ordered and Shoe could feel their eyes on him.

"I'm pretty good with faces. Weren't you in here the other day?" It was the brute on the right. He fixed Shoe with a stare that would have invited a quick dust-up with any of the liquor-fueled, hot-tempered brawlers lounging around the rest of the place.

"Never been here before," Shoe replied. He took a pull on his drink. No fine liquor for this place; it was as awful as he had suspected.

"You're sure?" His new friend's gaze threatened to bore a hole in him. "Because I'd never forget a nose like that." He motioned to the bartender. "This one's on me."

"Obliged," Shoe said, trying not to stare too hard at the dagger tattoo on his benefactor's neck.

"Nah, I got this one," said the new arrival on the left side.

This guy was equally inked, although Shoe wasn't sure whether the scar running through the man's eyebrow was the real deal or lifelike ink. He nodded politely and focused on his drink. "I think he's got it, but thanks."

"Well then, drink," the first one prompted.

Shoe took a swallow and nodded. "Thanks." His stomach lurched.

"It ain't tea. *Drink!*" Mr. Dagger slapped him on the back for emphasis.

Shoe chugged it. It burned going down, and it was a sure thing it would do so coming back up. He slammed his empty glass down and wiped his mouth on his sleeve. A mouthful of shirt would stem his gag reflex. "Thanks," he said again, wondering how much of the rot-gut it would take to kill him.

"Now it's my turn," said Scarface. He ordered another round.

Shoe turned to tell him that having a magical male-bonding experience wasn't necessary, but somehow his head felt as if it wasn't connected to his body. It had sailed out into the room somewhere and was having trouble with the return trip. And his bottom lip was sliding off his face. He looked at his glass—which had suddenly become two blurry ones—and the multiple extra fingers he had suddenly grown. How in tarnation had they gotten to him so fast? "I think I need some air," he said, and as he tried to stand his legs oozed like liquid onto the wide-planked floorboards. He clutched at the bar as all swirled into blackness.

Rudy ducked off the main walk and veered left into the first alleyway. It was stacked head-high with barrels stinking like dead fish. He squeezed by and found his way to the hatch. This would be quick. He could picture in his head exactly where he had put down the emerald: to the right of the hatch, snuggled against the foundation.

He couldn't find it. After patting the ground left and right of the little door, he dropped to his knees and frantically searched the dirt pathway between the building and the high fence that separated the waterside from the grounds on the far side of the amusement park. He popped his head through the little hinged door too and was left wanting. He mentally retraced his steps: getting stuck, backing out, emptying pockets, *carefully wedging the necklace between a sizeable rock and the building*. The rock was still there, but not the jewelry.

"Help you find something?" It was Hanner Mackall, standing not more than twenty feet behind him. "Go ahead, take it." He tossed the green necklace to Rudy.

Rudy snagged the jewelry and took off in the opposite direction. He got about twenty feet before two other rough ones rounded the corner and cut off his escape. He put his hands up. "Look. I have a money clip in my pocket. Not a lot, but you can have all of it. No questions asked. H-h-here's my watch." He fumbled with his watchband.

"Big mistake," Mackall said. He was closer now, several feet away.

Rudy's hands shot back up in the air again. "Sorry. What else can I do for you gentlemen? I'm afraid I can't stay and chat. I have an appointment."

Mackall was right next to him now. "Reschedule." His eyes were dark and calm, but beneath the cool exterior seethed something revolting.

"Sure, I can do that," Rudy said, nodding agreeably. "What can I do for you?"

"Absolutely nothing. Just tying up loose ends."

A switchblade appeared out of nowhere. Rudy flinched as Mackall lunged. The steel got him on the hand.

"Help! Fire! Fire!" Rudy yelled as he bobbed and weaved. It was like Luis Furpo playing chicken with Jack Dempsey, only he wasn't going to get up again if he went down. He bopped left and so did Mackall. The smuggler got him a second slice—deeper this time—through his sleeve and into his arm.

Mackall was chuckling now. "Where's Shoemaker?"

"Who?" Rudy took another step back, trying to keep all three of his assailants in view. The other two were hanging back, either enjoying the sport or knowing better than to interfere.

"Hey! You! Rudy Becker!"

Everyone pivoted right towards the newcomers. *God Almighty!* The bumpkin Clinton boys had found him at last—two creeping up on him from behind and the third hanging back to watch the alleyway! Rudy could have wept for joy. "I know. I'm late," he said, throwing them a quick glance. "Got to go," he said, refocusing on Mackall. He began easing away. *Up to you, chump. Three more witnesses?*

"Shove off," Mackall said to the brothers.

"No, you shove off," said the biggest. "You can take it up later. Our business can't wait."

There was fire in the big hulk's eyes and each of the brothers was carrying a walking stick. Rudy doubted there would be a second round with anybody. If Mackall was as smart as he and Shoe supposed, he'd let the Clintonites do his dirty work for him.

"Coppers!" yelled one of the Clinton boys.

The switchblade disappeared, the boys backed off, and Mackall's group retreated a few paces in the opposite direction, leaving Rudy in a sort of no man's land between them.

The tension in Mackall's face eased and he assumed a slightly more civil look. Something upspoken passed between him and his followers. He tipped his flat cap to the boys as if to wish them a good day and walked away. "Later," he whispered to Rudy as he brushed past.

Rudy's legs were shaking too hard to attempt a second dash for freedom. He whispered a silent prayer to Mena and gave in to fate. "So," he said, walking toward the trio. It wasn't so much bravado as the realization that the closer he was to the alley, the more likely someone would hear his screams for help. And God bless everyone, there would be many. "This is a big misunderstanding. I've never met your sister, and I have no wish to quarrel with you."

"Save it," said the tallest. He grabbed Rudy by the upper arm and they forced him out into the alley.

It didn't make a whole lot of sense. A public beatdown? Rudy picked up the pace, and when they reached the open wharf, he began struggling wildly. He'd save the screaming until he was sure they wouldn't stick a blade in him.

The biggest rube yanked him to a halt and pulled him up on his tiptoes and close to his face. "I don't understand you people. As I see it, you got two choices, city fella. Either you come back to Clinton with us and marry our pregnant sister or we let that Jack the Ripper take a few chunks out of you." He set him back down on his feet. "I'll give you a minute."

"P-p-pregnant?"

"I don't suppose you've ever known the heartache of watching your dear, sweet, unmarried sister grow fatter every day, have you? But that's all right. You can do the stand-up thing. You can fix it today." He began yanking him forward again. "Come on."

Rudy's thoughts skipped back to the angel with the dumpling figure. Had the clever little vixen created her own escape from the two-bit crossroads? "Wait!" he said, trying to free himself. "I swear I didn't behave improperly with your sister. She did sneak into my room and sleep on the floor, but honestly, that was it. Besides, how could what you're saying possibly be true? I was in Clinton less than a week ago. Women don't show that fast. Who else might she have spent time with?"

The first blink might have been a coincidence. The second and third indicated that all unessential body energy had been diverted to support the Big Boys' limited brain functions as they addressed the contradiction. There was a throat-clearing, and then the brother released Rudy's arm. "There may be a misunderstanding on our part," he finally said. "Our most humble apologies, sir." He made an awkward attempt at straightening Rudy's cockeyed jacket.

The other two likewise mumbled something of an apology. *That little tramp* was the last thing Rudy heard before they disappeared.

The area was full of flatfoots boarding a deadrise. It looked as if the whole Nevis police force had been mobilized. "Raid?" Rudy asked the workman next to him, who had set down his bushel of oysters to watch.

"Nah, dead body down at the cliffs," the man said, too engrossed to look away. "Take care of what 'cha got to do. They'll be back soon enough." He suddenly turned and squinted up at Rudy. "Need some oysters? Cheap."

Rudy looked at the man's bucket and shook his head. He'd pass on the questionable oysters. Yeah, they'd be back soon enough, and looking for two fellas that bore a striking resemblance to yours truly.

Mackall and crew had wisely made themselves scarce, although Rudy suspected they were hiding nearby, raring to have a second go at him. He melted into the crowd and scooted toward the Scuttlebutt, scanning faces as he darted in and out of clusters of workmen and fisherman. Mackall wouldn't dare attack him here, but they could force him into any number of dark places and alleys. In spite of a steadily increasing limp, he picked up his speed, knocking down a man carrying a crate and attracting a brown mongrel dog who matched him step-for-step as he tore at his coat sleeve. Maybe the more chaos, the better. Would Mackall really carve him up in such a public space? Rudy pushed harder.

Shoe wasn't where he said he'd be. Had the fool actually ventured inside the Scuttlebutt? Ahead, Rudy spotted someone who looked a lot like Shoe, but he was staggering in the opposite direction and he was not alone. Two men had ahold of him on either side as they half assisted, half dragged him deeper into the bowels of the roughest section of town.

Rudy let out a loud shrill whistle. "Hey! You there!" he yelled in his best Irish cop voice. "What you boys be up to?"

The men let go of the drunk. He dropped like a rag doll and they bolted.

Sure enough, it was Shoe heaped in the middle of the walkway. Rudy pulled him up by the front of his coat into a sitting position and shook him. Shoe moaned and his head lolled to one side. The safety of the Captain's boat was a mere forty feet away, but they'd have to pass Mackall's. Seeing no other option, Rudy grabbed Shoe under his arms and yanked. Shoe remained firmly rooted to the ground, hopeless dead weight, and the cuts Mackall had inflicted on Rudy were dribbling blood. This was useless.

"Sir, a helping hand," he called out to the workmen passing by. They ignored his entreaties, kept their heads down, and navigated a wide berth.

"Come on, options are limited here," Rudy whispered, patting Shoe's face to wake him up. Shoe didn't respond. Rudy yanked on him a second time and failed again. And when he released him, Shoe hit the ground hard and cracked his head.

Criminy. I'm going to kill him. Mena, he thought, if you're out there . . . And suddenly, his guardian angel heard his plea, or they just plain got lucky. He had caught a curious eye. "Wait," he said, before the waterman could look away. "My friend here seems to have fainted. Can you help me get him out of the way before he gets run over?"

There was a subtle nod and the waterman grabbed Shoe by the arm. "Where to?" he asked in a soft Scottish brogue.

"To the Captain," Rudy said, gesturing over his shoulder. He saw sudden movement to his free side. It was as if he had broken through a barrier of mistrust into acceptance. Before he could turn to acknowledge his second benefactor, a blow to the back of his head sent him staggering. His knees hit the ground and he watched helplessly as the stick came around a second time.

Chapter Thirty-Four
An Innocent Blunder

Shoe ran a cold, wet hand across his face and sat up with a start, icy water swirling around his dangling legs. His mouth felt like cotton, his head throbbed, and he smelled of vomit. It was too dark to see much, but he felt closed in, a roof above and walls to the right and left of him. He'd not dreamed this one before. The water receded, tugging on him, and then came at him again, rising up higher over his legs. Tidal water! This was no dream. He scrambled backward, clambering up onto one of the wood beams supporting the roof of this dark place.

And then details began trickling back: Scuttlebutt, awful whiskey, two new "friends". He reckoned he should consider himself lucky. He could have taken a leisurely, tragic *saunter* off one of the piers. Why hadn't they killed him outright? He felt for his wallet and found it missing. They had robbed him, but if they had expected a big score, they didn't get much. He wasn't foolish enough to carry a lot—just enough to flash around.

As his eyes grew accustomed to the darkness, he took stock. He was indeed in a small room that was dimly lit by light filtering in from some sort of overhead hatch. At his feet, a water channel wide enough to store a rowboat had been cut into the deck floor, splitting the room in half. He surmised there were doors at the far end that allowed passage out to the bay. Various bobbers, floats, and netting hung from one of the two walls that ran parallel to the channel. Tarps, wooden fish baskets, and crates sat stacked against the other one—most likely contraband liquor, by the looks of the heavy crates.

And then he saw Rudy, supine on the floor near the water's edge, looking as if the slightest movement would send him tumbling into the deep. Fear rolled over Shoe like a flash of fire. He launched himself off the beam and pulled Rudy's cold, wet body away from the water. "Rudy! Wake up, Rudy," he said. He slapped Rudy's face a couple of times.

Rudy's eyes fluttered open and he immediately propelled Shoe tumbling backwards into the crates. He scrambled to his feet and backed away, fists raised in a defiant stance.

"Sh-Shoe?" he asked, peering through the dark light. He dropped his fists and offered his brother a hand up. "Where . . .?"

"Dunno. Beneath the boardwalk, I guess. You all right?"

Rudy's hand went to the back of his head. "Yes and no. You? I thought you were smart enough not to have a drink down here. You don't fool with Mickey Finn."

"Yeah, well, the liquor was rotten, too," Shoe said. "The only relevant question now is: how do we get out of here? See stairs or a ladder?" He moved to the wall behind Rudy—no doubt west and landward—where a small ledge connected the two sides of the room. He began walking the perimeter of their prison, feeling his way along the wall. When he got to the doors at the bay side, he slid into the water, tested its depth, and found he could stand on his tiptoes. The double doors were iron, the latch on the outside. He pulled himself out of the water on the other side and continued his reconnaissance. He found nothing useful.

"That only leaves *up*," Rudy said, staring at the trap door in the ceiling. "We could stack crates." He looked back and forth between the door and the crates, shivering in his wet clothes in the cool December air. "Three or four would probably do it."

The ceiling suddenly creaked and the shafts of light above their heads shifted. They scrambled to opposite corners. Rudy picked up a paddle from the floor and Shoe slid a lid off one of the crates as the door opened and daylight lit their space.

"Shoemaker?" It was a woman's voice, hoarse and whispery, but oh, the lovely sound of it. "Shoemaker? Can you hear me? They're gone, but not for long. We have a rope. Be quick."

A thick line of bull rope bounced and jangled through the opening. Rudy motioned Shoe up first. Hand over fist, Shoe worked his way up the knotted line, teetering a moment on his stomach against the hatch frame before heaving himself out. Two women pulled him to his feet and a third threw a blanket over his shoulders.

So they had been in the cellar of a house, he thought, taking in the simple bed, nightstand, and wardrobe. The only remarkable feature in the room was the classical painting above the bed, depicting a naked man and woman in the midst of coital delight. Correction, the cellar of a *whore* house.

He assessed the women in a new light. The tallest and most forward was a bit haggard and hard-looking—a night worker if he ever saw one and no doubt the madame. The others could have been any of Fannie's friends.

"Is this your place, Miss . . ." he asked, his teeth now chattering in spite of the blanket.

"Ophelia Shakespeare," she said, "but Ophelia will do."

By the glint in her eyes, Shoe reckoned she had read quite a bit of the Bard. He took an immediate liking to her. "Saying thank you isn't enough. How did you know we were down there?"

"We don't miss much. Contrary to what you might think of me, I like a good chat and I love a good story, but this isn't the place or time. I've already done more than I should have. Upstairs with you. Pull out dry clothes from the wardrobe. Don't want 'em back. And don't want to see either of you again. 'Parting is such sweet sorrow' doesn't apply here. Up you go."

"Mackall coming right back?" It was a shot in the dark, but Ophelia's startled look told him it was a bull's-eye.

She ignored the question and turned back to the cellar hatch. "Upstairs."

The others swept him out the door and up a set of narrow winding stairs to yet another bedroom. Once there, one thrust a mug of hot coffee into his hands while another drew clothes out of the chifforobe and threw them on the bed.

It was then he realized Rudy wasn't behind him. "Where's my brother?" he asked, trying to give the cup back.

"He's coming. Stay here." They were gone in a rush, leaving the door open behind them.

He took a sip of the joe. It was heavily fortified and felt like heaven as heat coursed out into his cold extremities. The furnishings here were much more elaborate than the downstairs bedroom. Frilly white dressed the bed and window, and close by, a writing table sat tidily with a blotter and a handsome gold-capped pen resting on an ornate brass inkwell. No working girl's bedroom, it was the madam's personal domain. He saw nothing that he could use as a weapon if things got precarious.

A minute later, Ophelia stepped into the room—several of her girls crowding the door behind her—and produced a small black pistol from the folds of her skirt. "Just so no one makes a mistake, give me your full name," she demanded.

Shoe eased his hands up. Even if she was a terrible shot, the odds were not in his favor at this distance. "Tatum Shoemaker, reporter for the *Evening Star*," he said, slowly rising. "Where's my brother?"

"His name?"

"Rudy Becker, freelance journalist. And my brother. Where have you tak—" He stopped, his attention suddenly drawn to a diminutive woman in a head shawl hanging back in the doorway. He tried to make eye contact with her, but she looked away and cast her eyes down.

"Go get Mr. Becker," Ophelia said over her shoulder.

Shoe took a tentative step forward. If she was going to put them in the same room together, she wasn't going to shoot anybody. "I think you can come out now, Miss Weathersby," he said, addressing the shrouded woman.

"Mena?" It was Rudy, slightly blue but apparently unharmed. He spun the woman around, a look of joy on his face, which was immediately followed by one of confusion. "You're not Mena." He let her go. "What's going on here?" he asked, creating a unified front in the middle of the room with Shoe.

The woman slid the covering from her head. ""My name is Charlotte Sewell. Please get me out of here, Mr. Shoemaker." She burst into tears.

Ophelia slipped her gun back into a hidden pocket and wrapped her arms around the sobbing woman. "Sorry for the gun, but I had to be certain who you were. We've been hiding Charlotte since . . . since the unfortunate events on the wharf."

"What's your association with Wilhelmina Weathersby?" Shoe asked.

"I was her travelling companion," Charlotte whispered.

Shoe's gaze shifted to Rudy, who shrugged. "I had no idea Mena had someone with her. Honest."

Shoe nodded. "Your companion was brutally murdered and you didn't come forward to talk to the police? Didn't it concern you that they were unable to identify your friend?"

When she spoke again, she had regained some of her composure. Her voice was quiet, the voice of someone who naturally took to introversion and solitude. Shoe craned forward to better hear her.

"It was all so fast, but I looked right into his eyes and I'll never forget that face. I'm a loose end, Mr. Shoemaker, and whoever did this is searching for me. If it weren't for Ophelia's . . . *ladies*, I'd be dead by now. They're a tightknit group and they understand what desperation is." Charlotte buried her face in her hands and burst into tears again.

Shoe immediately regretted his brusqueness. "I'm sorry. I didn't mean to sound so unsympathetic. I'm sure you've experienced a most horrible ordeal."

"Most horrible," Rudy said, nodding. Shoe could almost hear the poor man's heart pounding out of his chest. "As soon as we can get out of here, we have work to do. This is far from over. Sit here in the chair, take a step back, and tell us what led you here to Nevis with Mena."

"No, no time," Ophelia said. "You need to change your clothes and get out."

"Uh uh," Rudy said, shaking his head. "And have her bolt as soon as she thinks she can? 'Fraid not, sister. We're not going anywhere until I know what happened to Mena."

Ophelia gave him an exasperated look. "All right, but make it quick, Charlotte. They'll be back soon. Stand right here and make it quick."

Charlotte pulled a lace handkerchief from a sleeve, and after she had patted her eyes dry, she began her tale.

"I met Mena in New York—a runaway of sorts, just like her. Not the same kind of problems—I had an intolerable husband—but circumstances that I could only change by removing myself from the situation. I never would have made it in the Bowery without her. The sharks there were already circling. They're good, Mr. Shoemaker, at finding the weak and exploiting them. Especially women," she said with a shudder.

Rudy shook his head and muttered something. She gave him a solicitous look and continued.

"When Mena decided to leave the Bowery, she said she couldn't leave me alone to *that*. She was determined that I come too. A new start, that's all either one of us asked for. I was excited and she was so, so happy. She promised to help me get established where my husband could never find me. I stayed with her at the Bayside Hotel."

She turned again to Rudy. "But don't think for a minute, Mr. Becker, that I attached myself to her because I wanted more. Mercy, we were fast friends before I learned she came from a wealthy background. How would I know?" She looked at him for some sort of affirmation.

"You wouldn't have," he said, shaking his head. He turned to Shoe. "I didn't know anything about Charlotte. Mena was to take a train and meet me at Washington Union Station. She never arrived at our prearranged time. Thinking she might have taken a later train, I waited long past the time she was expected. When it was obvious that she wasn't coming, I went back to my lodging and found word she would be waiting on the dock for me. That was okay. Things didn't have to run smoothly. They just had to run. I was on my way back to Nevis when Emerson intercepted me."

Charlotte let out a deep sigh. "All she ever needed from me was friendship and I failed her."

Rudy's eyes flicked to Shoe and back to Charlotte again. "Our final plans were all set: time, mode of transportation, final destination. Why wasn't she on that train, Charlotte?" His tone was flat, was neither accusatory nor forgiving.

"It was Emerson. Mena saw him standing outside the Bayside that afternoon. I don't know how they found us, but we knew it was just a matter of time before he was knocking on our door. She sent you a telegram, and then we grabbed some things from our suitcases and fled. Spent the remainder of the day trying to look inconspicuous down in this section of the wharf, trying to blend in with the pilgrims interested in seeing another vision. I shared a seat with one on the train ride down. As it grew later, and you didn't show up—"

"Didn't you receive my post?" Rudy asked.

She shook her head. "When you didn't appear, we considered taking a boat somewhere else. Not the steamboat, that would be too obvious. Something smaller. I inquired with several of the boat captains. There was a woman captain, and she agreed to take us to see Father McGee of St Raphael's church at Parkers Wharf."

"Muriel Fitzhugh?" Shoe asked. You booked passage on the *Sunrise Pelican*?"

She nodded. "I think that was it."

"They did," Ophelia interjected. "Muriel is my sister."

Two hardscrabble women who spouted Shakespeare? Shoe didn't doubt their relationship for a minute.

"When we arrived at the appointed time," Charlotte continued, "she and the boat were out of port, and nobody could tell us when she was due back. If we had known what a rowdy section we were venturing into, I'm sure we would have reconsidered. But everything was in motion. We figured we could soldier through any inconvenience and unpleasantness if that's what it took to shake the men Mena's father had tailing us." A look of strain and struggle pulled her face into a tight expression. "*Men!* Mena and I, not so different after all."

Rudy looked like a broken man—head hung so low that Shoe wondered how he kept from tumbling out of his chair. Looking at the two of them seemed an intrusion. He walked over to his desk and seized upon the first object he saw—a millefiori paperweight sitting next to the pen set. He picked it up and ran a finger across its smooth surface. "I know it's hard, but, did Hanner Mackall—uh, what exactly happened?"

"It was so fast," she whispered. She paused a moment, twisting her entwined fingers. "The wharf was dark now. With the exception of the two young boys delivering telegrams and a boat unloading, there didn't seem to be anyone else about. Even the religious pilgrims who we thought would stay all night had returned to town. We were at wits' end. If we went back to town, Emerson would have us. So Mena decided to trade her necklace for passage on the boat unloading on the pier."

"Smugglers," Shoe mumbled.

Her eyes darted to him and then she continued. "I volunteered to go, but Mena was single minded. She got us into the situation and she vowed to get us out. I heard her talking to one of the boys right before . . . just before . . ."

"Did you see Hanner Mackall?" Rudy asked, his jaw set tight and fingers turning white where he clenched them.

"I . . . heard, uh, there were screams and scuffling. So fast," she said, shaking her head. "Next thing I knew, Ophelia was dragging me out of the doorway, insisting I come with her. I didn't protest." And then she said, in a voice so quiet Shoe could barely make it out, "I heard they found Mena and a messenger the next morning on the boardwalk."

Shoe looked at Ophelia. "But you saw, didn't you? It was Hanner Mackall, wasn't it?"

"As God is my witness, I was nearby and I'm not going lie to you. Hanner Mackall murdered them both—the woman and the boy. Miss Weathersby blundered into the middle of Hanner unloading contraband. Wrong place, wrong time. Nobody interferes with business. And as soon as he saw the flash of that green cross, I knew it would end badly. The women's association with the pilgrims sealed your lady's fate. Hanner Mackall, just like the rest of his family, hates all things religious. It's a grudge that goes back hundreds of years, Mr. Shoemaker. Call it crazy, if you like, but he's through and through a descendant of Moll Mackall Dyer."

"But you still pawned the necklace for him, didn't you? O.S. *Ophelia Shakespeare*."

"Mr. Shoemaker, I would be the last to say I'm proud of things I've done. It's hard to understand the level of rage Mackall is capable of unless you've seen it."

"You despicable whore," Rudy said. He launched himself at the madame.

Shoe slid in between them, shielding her with his body. "Stop! It's done. And this doesn't get us out of here. Ophelia, what's the best way to get out of here without causing a stir?"

"There's a car in a garage on the land side. You can climb the slope behind the house and head out that way. It's a barter, but it'll get you somewhere else." She detached a key from a ring of them and gave it to him. "For the lock. Now get out of here."

She led them back down the narrow stairs and out a rear door. "That way," she said, pointing up the hill. She hugged Charlotte and then hurried back up the house steps.

"Come with us," Shoe called after her. "When he finds out—"

She didn't answer, but continued into the house and closed the door.

Shoe started back after her.

"Her choice, Shoe," Rudy said. "Let her go."

It was. They grabbed Charlotte and they fled.

Chapter Thirty-Five
Making Hal Roach Proud

Over the rise of the hill, they found a tiny garage sitting beside a narrow lane that seemed to run parallel to the wharf and back toward town.

"Train?" Shoe asked as he popped the padlock and swung the door open.

Rudy stopped halfway through the door. "You tell me."

Before them sat a stripped-down flivver: an engine, a chassis, and nowhere to sit but a pitiful plank seat over the gas tank.

Shoe pushed past him. "Criminy! Do you think it will even start?"

"Oh, it'll start," Rudy said. "And I bet it can fly. You drive, right? Climb up there. Flip the spark lever up. Push the throttle lever down. Turn that switch key."

"You drive, right?" Shoe mumbled, mimicking Rudy's swagger as he climbed behind the wheel. The key was still in the coil box. "Flip, push, turn," he called out as he performed the simple tasks.

Rudy cranked the heap up. It shuddered to life and then abruptly conked out. They tried again. Same result.

Raised voices were now floating over the hill from the direction of Ophelia's. Shoe pulled the key out, flipped everything off, and slid down off his perch. "We can get farther on foot. Leave it, Rudy. Unless they have another key, they'll be on foot too."

Rudy pointed him back to the car. "One more time. It'll catch. I can hear it."

"Perhaps you're not hearing what's over *there*," Shoe said, hearing the distinct bang of a door and scuffling feet.

In a flash, Charlotte snatched the key out of his hand, scooted past him, hiked up her skirt, and planted herself on the fuel tank. "Flip, push, turn," she said, repeating the steps.

This time the beast sputtered to life and kept right on chugging.

"Move over," Rudy said to her, springing up into the vehicle. Then with the finesse of an Indianapolis Motor Speedway driver, he mashed the left floor pedal down—Shoe still scrambling aboard—and eased the car through the narrow doorway. Shoe swung up beside Charlotte as three pursuers cleared the rise.

Rudy eased up on the left pedal and sent the car barreling in a wide circle around them as he aimed for the country lane. Two of the men launched themselves at the lizzie, attaching like hitchhikers to the skeleton of the car—one to Shoe's side and the other to the rear. The Model T fishtailed and sprayed loose gravel as it gained the unpaved lane, sending any other pursuit ducking for cover.

Shoe dispatched his adversary with a well-placed kick to the chest, while Charlotte screamed and struggled with the second one trying to pull her over. Shoe grabbed a handful of his clothing and yanked him sideways and off balance. The man released Charlotte and head-butted Shoe. The two men teetered back and forth on the chassis rails, trying to dislodge one another from their perch.

"Slow down!" Shoe shouted at Rudy. His brother, in typical Rudy fashion, ignored the request. Instead, he slid forward and curled himself around the steering wheel like Tommy Milton trying to set a Daytona land-speed record.

Charlotte cut loose with a bloodcurdling scream. Both men glanced her way and she sprayed the attacker's face with an atomizer she had apparently pulled from her purse. With an equally powerful scream, his hands went to his eyes. He wobbled once and then toppled off the back of the car.

Shoe vowed to never question the resourcefulness of women again. "Thanks," he said, heaving as he sat down and ran the back of his hand across his forehead, checking for blood. He found none, but he had one heck of a pounding headache.

Rudy kept the pedal high and they rocketed forward through a tunnel of tall cedars lining and overhanging the lane. The bucket of bolts let out a death rattle every time it hit a rut in the road. Shoe watched helplessly as they headed straight into a flock of chickens blocking the road. Most scattered, one smacked the radiator grill, and another landed in Shoe's lap. Shoe tossed him back out, reached past Charlotte, and flicked the side of Rudy's head.

"Ouch!"

"You've got to slow down, goof! There's no more room and we've nothing to hang onto."

"See anybody else?"

"Nobody."

Rudy eased off a bit.

The tree line abruptly ended and the car flew out onto Bayside Avenue, narrowly missing Strathmore's Milk Wagon and a truck full of logs. Rudy struggled a moment with the wheel but finally managed to swing it around to the correct side of the road. The only trouble was, well, trouble was right behind them—coming fast in another flivver. And another one behind that one too.

Shoe locked eyes with Mackall in the front car and then turned to

Rudy and said, "Can you make this go any faster? Otherwise, we're all dead."

Rudy coaxed every bit of power out of the heap—or maybe they rode on angel wings—and they somehow managed to outpace Mackall. By the time they reached the depot, their ride was shaking apart at the seams and howling like a coyote.

Chickens, Shoe thought as Rudy sent an elderly couple scurrying out of his way. Then he appeared to set the car on a collision course with the departing Chesapeake Express train, and it became something entirely different.

"Uh, Rudy," Shoe said, rising. "Only fools play chicken with trains." Charlotte, who had been a trouper up until now, turned away. Shaking and whimpering, she buried her face in his pants leg.

At the last possible moment, Rudy swerved behind the Express and moved up on the left side, even with the caboose. Shoe fell back in his seat and Charlotte's whimpering escalated into panicked screaming.

Rudy eased ahead of the slow-moving caboose and guided the jalopy in perilously close—so close you could almost reach out and touch the accelerating train. "Jump it. Go on, jump it." He gave Charlotte a shove. "Her first."

"No! No, no, no, no, no, no," she said. But before she could reach for her atomizer, Shoe launched her out of the car, arms and legs flailing. She landed in a heap on the rear platform of the caboose.

"Now you," Rudy said.

"And leave you? Hell, no."

"Jump, dammit. I'll be right behind you."

The great steel wheels of the train were clicking an allegro beat as the Express picked up steam. Ahead, the track curved and the right-of-way narrowed considerably with deep woods on either side. Shoe looked over his shoulder. Mackall's car was right on their tail, with Mackall's thug crawling across the car hood like Harold Lloyd. Even if Shoe didn't jump, old Harold certainly would. It was jump now or not at all. "Promise?"

Rudy nodded.

Shoe jumped.

The rest unfolded in seconds. The thug jumped and landed squarely on the rear frame of their car. But Rudy jumped too. He let go of the steering wheel and in two quick steps launched himself, arms flying, at the caboose. His flight was short. He teetered on the edge of the platform a moment before Charlotte and Shoe yanked him to safety.

"Thanks," Rudy said, looking both surprised and relieved.

"Yeah, you owe me," Shoe told him.

They watched their jalopy veer left away from the tracks and head for the tree line, Mackall's goon climbing over the seatback in a desperate bid to gain control of the car. Nobody needed to watch that. They hurried inside the train, walked through the first passenger car—which was nearly empty—and took seats in the fuller second.

Shoe leaned over the seat and said to the gentleman seated in front of them, "We might have hopped the wrong train. We're headed to . . .?"

"Solomons," he responded without lifting his head from his newspaper.

It was not at all in the direction of Washington, but they could work with it. "Excellent," Shoe said, and then he glanced back through the train and saw Mackall entering the last car from the caboose, moving nonchalantly but forward nonetheless. "Problem, Rudy. Everybody jumped it." He dragged Charlotte from her seat and the three of them started backing away.

"Sidearm would be good, Rudy," Shoe hissed. "You don't have to shoot him. Just wave it around."

"Uh, good plan, poor execution," Rudy said. "It's in my suitcase."

"Holy Father, help us," Shoe muttered.

Mackall moved across the train couplers and entered the second car, a gun pressed discreetly against his leg, eyes locked on the brothers.

"There you are," he said, coming forward, his eyes settling on Charlotte. He tipped his head toward the rear of the train.

Shoe glanced out the window at the woodland whizzing by. There was no way he could shoot them and get off the train. He shook his head. They would all have to keep company here.

The gun barrel raised slightly and Mackall crooked a finger at Charlotte. "I've been looking all over for you, dear. Come back to your seat."

Charlotte took a step forward. Rudy put up an arm to block her way, but Mackall managed to grab her wrist. He hurried her toward him with a yank and wrapped an arm around her. Her eyes were wide and she trembled.

The door between the cars opened again and a rotund, bald-headed man in denim work clothes entered, politely excusing himself as he tried to squeeze past Mackall and Charlotte.

Mackall stepped aside to let him pass, pulling Charlotte with him. The tubby man grimaced, attempted to suck his overhanging belly in, and probably thought tiny thoughts too, but the space was simply too tight for the three.

He smiled sheepishly at Mackall. "Terribly sorry. If you could move slightly that way," he said, nudging Mackall back toward the door.

Mackall's eyes flashed with anger. He threw a warning glance at Shoe and complied with the request.

"And you this way . . ." the man continued as he repositioned Charlotte in the other direction. "I think we'll have it."

Before Mackall could protest, the man turned on him. "Pinkerton, sir. Put your hands up. You're under arrest."

Mackall's gun barely cleared his leg before there was a quick *bang, bang, bang*. He staggered back against the door and slid to the floor, writhing in pain. Charlotte threw herself into Rudy's arms as screaming and all sorts of commotion cut loose in the rest of the car.

Shoe sagged down into the nearest empty seat. "How . . . how . . . how . . .?" He raised questioning hands.

"Must have been the angels," the railway dick said, waxing philosophical as he slapped a pair of bracelets on Mackall. "Been tracking you people all over town. The Koenig boy broke down and gave us a full account. He saw it all. Tough little nut to crack, that one. We've been looking for *this* one for hours. It was over as soon as he hopped that railing." He pulled Mackall to his feet—none too gently— and motioned to Shoe to open the door. "Do you mind? We don't want to turn this into a circus."

Shoe was pretty sure that elephant was already out of the tent, but he complied, catching a burning look from Mackall as he did. Even wounded and in handcuffs, Mackall was not a man to take lightly.

The train was nonstop, straight to Solomons, and when they arrived in station, several police officers met them and quickly bundled Mackall into a waiting vehicle and took off—back to Nevis, no doubt. Charlotte, as a material witness to the murder, followed in a separate car. The railroad dick, Paulie Fahey, re-boarded for the return trip and strongly suggested Shoe and Rudy do the same.

By the end of the day, Shoe decided being a court reporter had much more to offer than being grilled in any criminal proceedings. The Nevis cops worked him and Rudy over separately, politely but firmly, in their quest to guarantee Mackall and his cohorts never tweaked their arrogant noses at them again. Embarrassing Benedict Weathersby, whom they hated, was an added bonus. Shoe wondered how much trouble the industrialist might have been spared had he showered more interest and scratch on the welfare of the local constabulary.

When the police finished with them, he and Rudy walked out of the police barracks strings-free, unless you counted an expected court appearance somewhere down the line. They headed for Oscar's Restaurant on the upscale side of town, where Shoe ordered enough oysters and Klondike Fizz to make any unpleasant experience slip below the horizon with the last crimson rays of the setting sun.

The first thing out of Shoe's mouth before the oysters went in: "You mention Darby?"

Rudy shook his head, going for the oysters rather than talk.

"No, me either. You think they have witnesses?"

Rudy shrugged. "Don't care. They're dumping everything on Mackall regardless."

Shoe stared at him a moment. "You have attitude. Why the attitude?"

Rudy put down his fork. "Butch Koenig. Why didn't you tell me there was another witness?"

"After all this, you're going to hold on to that? Jeesh, Rudy. At the time, it seemed right. You weren't exactly the epitome of trustworthiness, and I didn't know how things were going to fit together. Somebody is buying up land, the Koenigs suddenly move up in society, Donaldson is buying up property. What could I have said?"

"All of that. And I could have saved you a lot of legwork. I knew Donaldson wasn't involved. I've been working with him for months.

Calvert Unlimited is a shell company of his. He aims to preserve the cliffs, buy up as much buffer land as he can and sell Congress on the notion of a national park like Yellowstone. Only, he can't purchase the land directly. Land prices would skyrocket. He's negotiating indirectly through the ghost company. That company hired me to acquire as much property as possible from here to the cliffs."

"And the Koenigs?"

"Donaldson courted Mrs. Koenig when they were young. Apparently there is a soft spot inside that calculating business mind of his. The new house, the movers . . . he took care of her. See how helpful I could have been?"

Shoe nodded. "I'm sorry, Rudy. I was wrong, and if I could do it all over again, I would tell you. How about we start over with a clean slate?" He extended a hand across the table.

Rudy studied the hand over the rim of his glass. "Okay," he said. He put down an empty glass and shook hands. "Clean."

"Right. But not finished. There's still Emerson. He owes us each a bundle."

"First thing tomorrow. Then I never want to hear another word from that disgrace of a family."

"Mr. Shoemaker? Mr. Becker?" It was the waiter. "Another gentleman has already covered your expenses." He set a tray in the center of the table. "He also instructed me to deliver these."

Rudy picked up an envelope addressed to him. "Lousy, chicken son of—"

"Ladies," Shoe said, reminding him of the group at the next table. He sliced his envelope open with his table knife and found a crisp pile of greenbacks inside.

"Didn't even have the decency to finish things up with us," Rudy continued, tossing the envelope back on the tray. "Just hired help. No wonder Mena hated the lot of them."

"You're taking it, right?"

"Darn tooting, but I don't need to make love to it! And then, that's the end of them."

Chapter Thirty-Six
A Final Token

The very next morning, Rudy caught Shoe and Fannie outside the Bayside. Rudy looked as if he hadn't bathed or slept in days, and more troubling, he didn't appear to care. Shoe had never seen him so subdued.

"I have an appointment," Rudy said. "Ten o'clock this morning at the bank. It seems I am to be drawn into the settlement of Mena's estate."

"She had an estate?" Shoe asked.

"Apparently so. It seems the Weathersby family has found me out. As much as I'd like to forget the lot of them, I can't. I'd like you to accompany me."

Shoe glanced at his watch. Ever the planner, Rudy had five minutes to hoof it down the street. Still, Shoe hesitated to give him an answer. There was no chance they would ever be brotherly—even friendly might be pushing it—but in either case, mixing in money was bad practice. If his suspicions were correct, Rudy would enter First National a struggling journalist and walk out a very wealthy man. Surely there was someone else he could lean on.

"Please. I can't do this by myself."

Please. Had Rudy ever begged for anything? The look in his eyes suggested he was closer to jumping off a pier than heading for potential riches and a life of security. "Yes, of course. Be back shortly," he said to Fannie, who was standing quietly behind him.

"No. I'd like her, uh, you too, Fannie. Please, I need you both."

Upon entering First National, a familiar face set upon them—or more precisely, memorable *shoes*. Mena's solicitor, Millard Hinson, greeted them at the door wearing a familiar set of Converse tennis shoes.

"Betty's diner," Shoe said, shaking his hand. "How is it you knew so early on of Miss Weathersby's passing?"

"Right this way," Mr. Hinson said, ignoring the question. He led them into the vault and directed them to sit at the rectangular table while he pulled a metal drawer from the bank of safety-deposit boxes lining the walls.

"I wasn't ignoring you, Mr. Shoemaker, but some things are better said in private." He turned to Rudy. "May I speak frankly, Mr. Becker?"

"Certainly. Consider Mr. Shoemaker my proxy."

Hinson nodded. "The Weathersby family tends closely to its financial assets, and straightaway Mr. Weathersby personally asked me to settle his daughter's affairs. He was most thorough in his discussion with me, and the information he provided led me to you, Mr. Shoemaker. Only, it appears I had the wrong person," he said, addressing Rudy.

"But . . . but . . . but . . ." Rudy said. "She was living in the slums without anything. What could she possible have . . ."?

Hinson set the drawer on the table before Rudy. "It's all here. Should you need any assistance, I'll be right outside." He left them alone without elaborating on the contents of the box.

Rudy made no move to open it. The three of them sat and stared at the box for so long that Shoe began to question whether Rudy was going to open it at all. Of course, *not* opening it wasn't going to change a thing. What was done was done. He had either been left a piddling sum or could buy a mansion on the Newport cliffs.

"Rudy?"

Rudy hesitated. "I don't know. It's blood money."

"Nothing wrong with blood connections, *brother*. Mena would want you to be happy. Put her in a special, wonderful, protected place in your heart and move forward. Someday you'll see her again and she'll be so proud."

Shoe immediately regretted his last remark. Not because it was wrong, but because Rudy's eyes were beginning to glisten. Shoe watched him nod and waited as he took it all in.

"Right," Rudy said. It came out in a whoosh as if he were a heartbeat away from leaping off a murderously high cliff. He pulled the box close, flipped up the lid, and pulled out the contents. Inside was a small gold heart on a delicate chain that Rudy said he'd given her, and a single typewritten page. He read the document through several times, his face revealing nothing of what was written there or how he felt about it. And when, finally, he seemed clear as to the contents, he handed it to Shoe and moved away from the table.

The document was a summary written in layman's terms of the legal disposition of the estate of the late Wilhelmina Barton Weathersby. It seemed "*close acquaintance, Rudy Becker*" was the sole beneficiary of her personal effects, with specific mention of the ten paintings in her studio, a Siamese cat named Elmer Valentino, and one thousand dollars currently held in trust by the Bowery Savings Bank in New York. There would be no magnificent cliffside mansion overlooking the spectacular Rhode Island Sound.

"There's no mention of *spouse*. I suppose this was done before your ceremony."

"Doesn't matter. It's really better this way. Our secret, untainted by other people's opinions."

Shoe handed the letter to Fannie. "This is nice, Rudy. Her personal things. I wonder where the cat is now. Did you know she had a cat?"

Rudy nodded but remained with his back to them, staring at the bank of deposit boxes. "Nice cat. Met Elmer before I met her. We were going to return for him after we were settled."

Shoe thought he could hear an *aww* from Fannie as she folded the letter back into its envelope.

"How did you and Mena meet?" she asked.

"I was on assignment for the *Philadelphia Inquirer*, writing a story on Gertrude Vanderbilt Whitney's Studio Club in Greenwich Village. Shoe, you're from Philly . . . the Ashcan school of art? The Studio promoted the devil out of them and other avant-garde artists who couldn't find a stage to promote their innovative work. Mena's paintings were there . . . and that cat. Elmer took a shine at first sight." He chuckled. "I guess Mena and I did too."

He paused a moment and when he began again, he perked up a bit. It was as if he were seeing it all anew. "You could see her soul in those paintings. It was her calling. But she was swimming against a swift current. What rich old bastard wants his daughter out on the street sketching the smelly, dirty lower class?" He shook his head in disgust. "From the moment she entered the world, her path had been chosen for her: afternoons of bridge and mah-jongg, a debut at The Marble with the Vanderbilt daughter, and eventually one more cold mansion along the cliffs. Cubism? How could one hang *that* on the wall of a private study?"

"But all these stories about your liaisons—"

"All a façade. Just stories. There was no one but Mena. And

anything bad Emerson told you about Mena is just more lies designed to manipulate you into helping him."

Fannie handed the summary back to Shoe and turned away as she pulled out a handkerchief.

Shoe returned the document to the box. "Did you have any questions for Mr. Hinson? I can call him back in."

Rudy shook his head. "I need to think it all through first. Let's go."

Chapter Thirty-Seven
A New Beginning

Christmas Eve morning and there was no indication that the weather would sweep in a white Christmas. What it would bring, however, was clear, if brisk, weather for the lighting of Mr. Coolidge's Christmas tree, and a bright smile to Fannie Byrne's face. And so, Shoe found himself standing in the middle of his room at the Bayside with exactly one hour to shine himself up to her very particular specifications—dark gray suit and polished black oxfords—and catch the 9 o'clock Railway Express train to Washington. What he didn't need at the moment was an unexpected call from his brother.

"Of course I have time for you, Rudy," he said, giving his clock a furtive glance. He ushered him in and directed him to sit, but Rudy declined. He walked in a few paces and remained close to the door, fidgeting with something in a pants pocket. Hardly to be believed, the poor guy looked even more bedraggled and rock-bottomed than the previous day.

He threw a copy of the *Evening Star* on the bed. "Dirty clean-up down at the wharf. No explanation for Ridley's murder or the whore's. Looks like Mackall will get away with both of those."

Shoe stopped to look at the front page. "If only she'd come with us . . ."

"Just another choice, Shoe." Rudy sat down awkwardly in the chair near the window. "Listen, that, uh, introduction at the *Evening Star*?" he asked. "Were you serious? Calvert Unlimited has shut down. When everything comes out in the papers, there will be too much poking around in Nevis for them to do anything on the sly. They'll go away quietly for a while before giving it another go. I've decided to take the money that Mena left me, and there's Emerson's payment, but I'm looking for something to keep me busy."

"Sure. But I don't think you'd ever be happy here, Rudy. Not enough action. Why would you give up Washington for this two-bit place?"

Rudy was strangely silent.

"You don't have anything going on in D.C., do you?"

"Uh, it seems I'm, uh, in between . . ."

His voice trailed off into something unintelligible. Shoe wasn't surprised at his lack of journalistic employment. It wasn't that Rudy was slow witted—his tongue was keen and his pen keener. No, Rudy was a blowhard who never seemed content with what he had. His goal always seemed to be to acquire what everyone around him possessed. He spread discontent wherever he worked.

"Rudy," Shoe said, proceeding with caution, "is it possible, and I'm not saying you are . . . maybe you're in the wrong field? Maybe news-hounding isn't your bailiwick. Calvert Unlimited was a good first step, but there are new opportunities everywhere, every day. Why don't you take some time off and use the money Emerson paid you to figure things out?"

"I need something *now*, okay? And of course I'm in the right field," Rudy said with a huff. "The money from Calvert Unlimited was quick money. Mena and I had no intentions of staying in Nevis where her father could get at us. The job was just to get me solid again, and then I'd be back to reporting." He shook his head. "No, journalism is right, it's the subject that's all wrong!"

Shoe struggled with his tie. Staring intently into a mirror seemed rude and uncaring. "Somehow I don't see you writing pulp pieces for *Writers Digest*."

"Pfft." Rudy dismissed the notion with a wave of his hand. "Entertainment." He walked over and knotted the tie in several quick, practiced moves.

"An actor?" The man was clearly delusional. Shoe had seen Rudy's clumsy attempts at subterfuge and he'd heard him caterwaul too.

"*Critic*," Rudy said in a tone more offended than angry. "Maybe radio. We're on the cusp of something great, Shoe. Hand RCA thirty-five bucks and they'll give you a radio that can give you all sorts of news and opinions. Everybody wants one, whether they agree or just need somebody to argue with. It's *the* thing. I'm taking my career to New York. Live in the Bowery—be around all the places and things that Mena loved."

"The Bowery? Big mistake, Rudy. You can't live in the past. The memories will break your heart every day. It won't be the same without her. Why don't you do it here? Washington is the center of the world, man. Do it *here*. They're licensing a new radio station in the spring. Call letters *WRC*. I know people. Let me get you in on the ground floor."

Rudy shrugged. "Maybe you're right. I just don't know anymore. I'd hate to impose . . ."

"Nonsense. I'll make the call as soon as we get past Christmas." Shoe checked the time again. Forty-five minutes. He could give his brother half. "Better yet, let's take a walk down to see Riley Tanner right now and get things rolling. See if we can set up a time to brainstorm a position that you'd like and he'd be happy to add until the radio station happens. He may be a hardnosed news man, but he's sensitive enough to recognize that you have to adapt to survive in this business. The man knows his onions."

Rudy sat motionless a while, trying to sift through all the possibilities, and Shoe began to regret throwing so many things at him. Maybe he just needed to step back and grieve a bit before making any career changes.

"Or not," Shoe added.

Rudy pointed a finger at Shoe. "Let's do it! But if I'm going to ingratiate myself, I need to see what's important in his world today. We need the morning paper." And then he added with a devilish wink, "I heard the lead story is a journalistic delight."

As they left the Bayside, they hailed a young newsie in knickers and flat cap hawking the *Evening Star* to departing guests. Shoe gave him three Indians and flipped the paper to the front page.

"Benedict Weathersby Dead at 62. Daughter Wilhelmina to Inherit Vast Fortune."

Rudy jerked the newspaper out of his hands. ". . .dropped dead of an apparent heart attack on Park Avenue after confrontation with shipping magnate and neighbor Carlton Donaldson. Mr. Weathersby predeceased in death by socialite Margaret 'Peggy' Anderson Weathersby. According to well-placed, anonymous source in the millionaire's close circle, the couple's only surviving child, Wilhelmina 'Mena' Weathersby . . ."

He stopped reading and slapped the paper into Shoe's chest and walked away.

". . . stands to inherit the bulk of her father's estate in excess of $30 million." Shoe looked at Rudy standing at the bottom of the stairs leading up to the main porch of the Bayside, a death grip on the gray banister. He walked down and put a reassuring hand on his brother's shoulder. "Where did you say your wedding certificate was?"

"Safe where they can't touch it," he said softly.

"Come on. We should retrieve it immediately."

Rudy shook his head. "Are you crazy? That truly is blood money. Not to mention that I'll throw away every last cent of it. How much do you want, Shoe?"

"Half?"

"Seriously, Shoe. Money corrupts. I'll give it all away. Whatever you want is yours."

Shoe found himself patting Rudy's shoulder. It felt strange. He continued anyway. "I'm joking. I don't want any of it. Mena would want you to have it, enjoy it, but yes, spend it wisely. Don't let your mind go racing too far ahead. Decide what to do after they square away the will, and I'll support you with whatever you decide. But you'll need an accountant. I could never manage that kind of money."

"Oh, they'll drag it through the courts forever. I'll never see a penny of it."

"No, they won't. They'll make you a sweet deal just to make it all go away. And if you don't want the headache, you'll take it. And then you'll turn around and buy WRC or some small-town paper and run it like you want."

When Rudy spoke again his voice was husky. "How would you feel about me taking my father's name? Is the world big enough for two Shoemakers?"

Shoe pulled his hand off Rudy's shoulder. "Hell no."

Rudy's eyes went wide. "Really?"

"That would have been the answer if you had asked me a month ago. I'll admit it. If someone had asked me the last person on earth I'd want to be related to, it would have been you. Dad fell off a tall pedestal when you told me who you really were. But here's the thing. He's your pop too, and you're entitled no matter what I think."

"Honest?" For a second, Shoe saw a spark of life in Rudy's flat, dull expression.

Shoe nodded. "Really. But that isn't saying I'm going to leave you anything in my will," he quickly added.

"Oh, hell. I have people who despised my type leaving me all kinds of money." Hope lit a broad smile on Rudy's face. "Our own company. We could strike out on our own like that, you know? You can handle investigations and I'll do freelance entertainment reviews. We can travel everywhere . . . see everything . . . do what we want. Tell everything else to scram, take a hike. We—"

"Whoa! A little too fast, Rudy. Get the money and then we'll see." Shoe checked how he was doing timewise. To his chagrin, ten more minutes had slipped by. "If you want me to introduce you to Riley Tanner, we need to go now. Fannie and I are catching the train—"

Rudy pulled away. "I'm sorry, Shoe. It seems I'm all about me— blathering and whining. You two go on. We can take care of it when you get back. When you move back to D.C., Tanner will need somebody."

"Oh, I'm not leaving permanently. I'll be back the day after Christmas. Then we'll tackle the Weathersbys."

Rudy's looked past Shoe and smiled—not a sly, gotcha kind of smile, but one of genuine happiness. "Gonna make her your missus?"

Shoe turned to see Fannie waiting at the end of the walkway—her cute button nose, her delightful curves, and the smart pair of black buckled shoes that she was admiring so intently. He was sure he hadn't seen them before. He'd know. He noticed everything about Fannie Byrne. She was that type of gal. "Don't get ahead of yourself on that one either."

"*Shoe and Shoe, Inc.*," Rudy said. "Nice ring. Roll it around awhile."

"Okay," Shoe said, "but I have to warn you, I'm a slow thinker."

"Fair enough. We've all got boundaries. I'm going to take life as it comes. A day at a time and just live each moment for what it gives. It will get better."

Shoe gave him a side glance. A new Rudy. This might work. It just might work. "Someday, pal, someday. You'll see."

Chapter Thirty-Eight
Big Trees, Little Towns, Forever Moments

It was a fine thing to board the Railway Express and not worry about who got on after you. Shoe offered Fannie a window seat and sat down next to her for a pleasant, uneventful ride to Washington and the much-anticipated presidential Christmas tree. The trip was nonstop, but he took in as much as he could of the Clinton depot as they barreled past. It was just as he imagined and true to Rudy's description: dead fields and nothing else as far as he could see. He could almost picture the injured John Wilkes Booth on horseback blazing through to some prearranged rendezvous to the south. One would certainly never think of tarrying.

When they reached Union Station, he hailed a cab and soon they stood with a crowd of others in the center of the Ellipse, staring at what the ceremony program called the National Christmas Tree—all forty-eight feet and two thousand lights of it. Local journalists busied themselves interviewing bystanders while an official photographer and other journalists set up cameras for a striking shot of dignitaries gathered before the tree with an eye-catching backdrop of the Washington Monument pointing to the heavens.

Fannie considered the unlit tree and breathlessly pronounced it spectacular. "You know, the presidential tree has never been outside before. I heard Mrs. Harding didn't want it on the White House lawn. You know, this is the best place; it's the people's tree." She was nonstop chitchat until President and Mrs. Coolidge stepped up to the speaking platform. The crowd hushed and remained so until Coolidge finished his brief comments. When he flipped the switch, the tree burst into red, white, and green points of light, and murmurs of approval and clapping rolled across the group like an ocean wave.

Shoe was impressed, but a Christmas tree—inside or outside—could be seen anywhere this time of year. No, he was studying Fannie's face, which was wrapped in childlike awe. Nothing could compete with the sparkle in her eyes. "Lovely," he said.

"Now, aren't you glad we got to do this?" Fannie asked.

"Absolutely, Better than I ever anticipated. I guess we could do this again next year. If you want."

"Oh, definitely," Fannie said, twining her arm through his as they drifted away from the crowd. "Unless you don't want to." She stopped walking. "What's wrong, Shoe?"

"I, uh, I've been thinking. Maybe Washington isn't the best place for me . . . for us."

"I see."

Her head was down, and she seemed to be pondering her shoes as she slowly tilted a dainty foot from one side to the other. Shoe couldn't see her eyes. Please don't let them be cold or blazing, he thought as he waited for her to engage him.

"No more fancy shoes I suppose," she said with a sigh.

"Nevis isn't exactly a backwater anymore, Fannie. You can order anything you want."

"I suppose," she said, with a sigh even more glum than the first. "And then there's the F Street Dance Emporium. I shall miss that too."

"The Bayside dance room is packing them in with some swell singers. I can take you there if you'd like."

"Promise?" she asked, side-eying him.

"Pinky swear and however else you want me to say it, Fannie. Everything we need or want can be found right in Nevis."

"And a few things you don't want. The people you've crossed haven't forgotten."

"Well, when they remember, I'll deal with it. Until then, I'm not going to live in fear, and neither should you. I do think they will find bigger fish to gut than Tatum Shoemaker."

She looked at him and the eyes were shining. "Why, then I'd say it sounds perfect."

Somehow, he felt the decision had been made before they ever started the conversation. "You weren't as excited about going back as you professed, were you, even if we moved to someplace a little more respectable?"

The head went down again. "Don't get me wrong. I loved being in Washington, but if truth be told, I will always a be a small-town girl. Nevis is plenty big enough for me. I kind of got swept away by all the glitz and glamor of downtown. If you can imagine it, you can have it—"

"If your pockets are flush—"

"Exactly," she said.

"Which they are now."

"Walk a few blocks and buy your dreams, but that kind of happiness doesn't last long. Those shoes I bought from Hahn's just to stick it to you? I could have done with much cheaper and not felt half so guilty. After watching what Rudy's been through, I've decided to appreciate what I already have." Fannie leaned over and pecked him on the cheek.

Shoe pulled his fedora off his head and feigned surprise. "Just what

I was thinking!" He hesitated, then dropped to one knee, and taking her hand he said, "Marry me, Fannie Byrne. Marry me and I'll make sure that you never have cause to stick it to me again. I'll take you dancing—"

His heart sank as a look of shock and embarrassment colored her face. He released her hand and got up. "It's okay, I, um—"

"Yes!" she said, launching herself at him. "Yes! Yes! Yes!"

"Right answer," he said, staggering backwards under the momentum. He wrapped his arms around her, and with the National Christmas Tree as a backdrop, he kissed her right.

A flash of bright light suddenly illuminated them.

"*Washington Post*. Tomorrow's front page," someone shouted.

"I think we just saved money on an engagement picture," he whispered in her ear, and then, just to make sure, he gave it another go.

Thank you for reading The Dame on the Dock. I hope you enjoyed the story. If you have a moment, please consider leaving a quick review on the book's Amazon page.

If you would like to read more about Tatum Shoemaker and Fannie Byrne, check out The Church at Parkers Wharf.

Would you like to know when I release new books?
Here are three ways:

Join my mailing list at:
https://www.louisegordaybooks.com/contact

Like me on Facebook:
https://www.facebook.com/louisegordayauthor

Follow me on Twitter:
https://twitter.com/LouiseGorday